TWISTED JUSTICE

DI KAREN HEATH CRIME SERIES

JAY NADAL

JOIN MY VIP GROUP

If you haven't already joined, then to say thank you for buying or downloading this book, I'd like to invite you to join my exclusive VIP group where new subscribers get some of my books for FREE. So, if you want to be notified of future releases and special offers ahead of the pack, sign up using the link below:

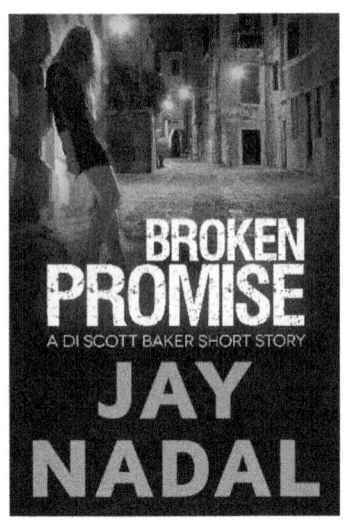

Type this link into your browser:
https://dl.bookfunnel.com/sjhhjs7ty4

Published by 282publishing.com

Copyright @ Jay Nadal 2020

All rights reserved.

Jay Nadal has asserted his right to be identified as the author of this work.

No part of this book may be reproduced, stored in any retrieval system, or transmitted in any form or by any means, electronic, mechanical, photocopying, recording or otherwise, without the prior written permission of the author.

This book is a work of fiction, names, characters, businesses, organizations, places and events other than those clearly in the public domain, are either the product of the author's imagination or used fictitiously. Any resemblance to actual persons, living or dead, events or locales is entirely coincidental.

1

"Cold takes on a whole new meaning in this country," Danilo uttered, as he tugged up the collar on his coat and pulled his hat down to cover his ears. He stepped off the bus, and with hands buried deep in his pockets, and a woolly hat warming his ears, continued the last part of his journey on foot after another tiring shift. The biting chill was a far cry from what he was used to.

January was the coldest month in his native Philippines. When Danilo had lived on the outskirts of Manila, average daily temperatures often hit twenty-eight degrees centigrade, and would rarely fall below twenty-two. He was more likely to die of heat exhaustion and heat cramps than of hypothermia. On finishing his shift back home, he'd be stepping into a hot, humid and sticky environment, and taking one of the many colourful buses adorned in vibrant colours of the rainbow. With their big, chunky off-road wheels and bull bars, the buses looked more suited to the treacherous mountain trails of Peru than the busy, hectic and crowded streets of downtown Manila.

Danilo had been in the UK three years now and still struggled with the big swings in temperatures.

Life was so different now. Chaotic, exciting, challenging, and dynamic. His role in the accident and emergency unit meant no two days were the same. That kept him busy. It stopped him thinking about home, his friends, and family. In Manila, he'd worked in one of the biggest hospitals in the country as an emergency department nurse. But with wages being so low, and the promises from NHS recruiters of a varied career, and a salary far beyond his existing one, the draw of moving to the UK had been a no-brainer.

With a heavy heart, he'd made the transition in the UK. The processes and protocols in the Philippines were mostly based on the American healthcare system, so he was more than surprised with how different practices were with his new employers. It was a struggle at first, but colleagues had rallied around him. There was a kindred spirit amongst them, as several others had also made the move from the Philippines.

A shiver snaked down his spine as his shoulders trembled. It was the kind of coldness that reached into his bones. The only thing that kept him moving and heading towards home was the promise of a warm shower, hot meal and his bed. A rolling blanket of cloud, the colour of wet ash hung above, as he tipped his chin down and pushed through the cold. Each step became a prayer for home as he walked.

His shift officially ended at eight p.m., but he could never foresee who would walk through the doors of the hospital. Today he'd dealt with a man fighting for his life after being struck by a van whilst cycling. A boy with cracked ribs after a nasty tackle in rugby, his mother not leaving his side. Then the homeless drunk, a frequent visitor to their department, who'd thrown up over Danilo's shoes, taking a swing at him before security had stepped in.

It was close on ten p.m. as he made his way along Water End, having crossed the River Ouse as he left the city centre. A few cars passed; their warm inviting interiors shrouded in the darkness, the beams from headlights forcing a squint from him. Danilo had never enjoyed this part of his journey. It was dark, desolate, and unnerving. A few minutes more and he'd be home.

HE'D WATCHED Danilo take this route home several times. Keeping his distance, following in the shadows, and using the darkness as camouflage, he'd trailed Danilo to build a picture of his routine. This night had been no different from the others. A creature of habit. A mistake.

Adrenaline coursed through his veins as his breath quickened. His skin tingled, and his fingers twitched with excitement as he quickened his pace along the grassy path that ran parallel to the road. He could make out Danilo's shadow walking hurriedly along the pavement, every so often his figure illuminated under each street light.

He crossed through the overgrowth and stepped out onto the pavement a few feet behind Danilo.

The man tightened his grip around one end of the crowbar and lifted it across his shoulder as he took a few light steps to close the gap. He swung with all his might, bringing his hands down across his chest to his waist. The crowbar followed in a sweep a second later and struck Danilo across the back of the head. Danilo stumbled, his hands being torn from the pockets of his coat as they reached for his head. A second strike of the crowbar sent Danilo flying onto the grass verge, collapsing to his knees. A third strike across his back flattened him. Danilo did nothing more than groan, as his body relented to the iron bar. A savage rain of blows shattered bones, tore through his coat, and left the back of his skull gaping open.

Grabbing his victim by the wrists, he hauled the lifeless body into the undergrowth like a predator dragging its prey away from unwelcome attention. With only illumination from a nearby street light for company, he eyed the battered and misshapen outline of Danilo's body.

The man took a few deep breaths, keen to control his racing heart. It echoed so loud in his head, that he thought that anyone passing within a hundred metres of him could hear it. Seeing Danilo's battered body wasn't enough. That was only the beginning. He knelt down and undid the last few remaining buttons that held Danilo's coat in place. After reaching into his own pocket, he extracted a scalpel, its small blade deceptive of its true power. He used it to cut through several layers of clothing before exposing Danilo's chest. The man stared down, a delicious thrill overtaking his senses. This was what it was all about, a final act to desecrate Danilo's body beyond comprehension. With studied precision, he delivered his first incision, slicing through a thin layer of flesh. He continued carving up Danilo, sliver by sliver, exposing his victim's chest cavity.

Content with his work, he let out a breath of satisfaction, sitting back on his heels and admiring his handiwork before rolling up his sleeves. He plunged a hand in and reached up under the ribcage. The warmth and stickiness soothed his cold skin. It felt like a warm bucket of jelly as organs swallowed his hand, enveloping it like human quicksand.

A few minutes later he was done. The bushes were deep and tall. Danilo's body wouldn't be seen or found for some time and that suited his purposes. He took a few steps back and stared at the mangled body before turning and disappearing into the shadows.

2

E*ight weeks later…*

The car hire firm was nothing more than a Portakabin in a car park, but he'd chosen it for a reason. It was hidden away from the glare and busy streets of the city centre. The woman handed back his forged driving licence and shoved a car hire agreement across the counter to him. Not wishing to make too much eye contact, he grabbed a pen, and scribbled an erratic signature on the form and then handed over the fee in cash.

When he'd wanted to pay in cash, the assistant had narrowed her eyes and despite her insistence on needing a card to complete the transaction, a menacing, cold glare from him was enough for her to back down, sliding the card machine back under the counter.

The assistant led him out onto the forecourt and towards a row of cars. The hire car was a white Ford Focus. Plain, unassuming, and easy to lose in heavy traffic. He slipped in behind her, watching her arse move smoothly from side to side in her tight trousers. Dark hair pulled up high in a tight ponytail accentuated her youthful face, along with her flawless skin, luscious full lips, and a plentiful chest hidden beneath the polo neck jumper. He licked his lips, wishing he could get a bit of action with her. For a moment he thought she could read his thoughts as her hips swayed even more.

He contemplated turning on the charm, as a vision of her bent over the counter back in the Portakabin flooded his mind and twitched his cock. But that could wait. He had more pressing needs. As she handed him the keys with a self-assured smile, the woman turned on her heels and strutted away.

He spent the next few hours travelling down the motorway, only coming off for a service break and something to eat before continuing to London. It felt like he'd been on the go for months, constantly looking over his shoulder whilst putting his plans into place. He felt shattered, desperate for sleep. Though it was cold outside, he kept the window half open for most of his journey. The cold fresh air whipped in through the window, slapping his face.

Though he hated London, it was a good place for him to be. It came with risks. More CCTV cameras and police required more vigilance as he picked his way through the maze of streets. He finally arrived on a quiet residential street, with few cars parked on the road, many of the house owners opting to convert their front gardens into off-street parking. This alone made it harder for him to blend into the background. Lifting the hood up on his ski jacket, he hunkered down in his seat and watched.

Not being familiar with the area, he'd relied on his phone to guide him. *Gone were the days of pulling out an A-Z map of London like in the old days*, he thought, as the corner of his mouth lifted in a wry smile. Thirty minutes passed with no movement. Concerned that a nosy neighbour would notice his car being parked there too long, he turned the key and pulled off, deciding to drive around the block a few times. Each time he passed the house, he would glance across to study it, think through his approach when the time came and check to see if there were any signs of movement.

He pulled up fifty yards from the target's house beneath a tree with spindly branches that crept out and hung in an arc over his side of the road. It afforded him cover whilst he ran through his plans again. A postman ambled up the pavement, disappearing every few seconds as he darted into front gardens, before reappearing and shuffling through the stack of letters in his hands. The man grabbed his phone from the passenger seat and pulled it to his ear, mouthing in silence. If the postman glanced over, it would appear as if the man in the car was in conversation, but he never looked up, oblivious to the car as he walked by, pulling a few letters from his pile and disappearing into another garden.

He'd seen enough. Few cars drove up the street, and even fewer pedestrians walked past. It was perfect. With deep-fronted gardens, many boxed in by tall hedges for privacy, it would make his entry and exit easier. He smiled to himself as he started the engine and pulled away from the kerb.

The stupid fucker won't know what's hit him.

3

A sense of reassurance and calm greeted Karen as she walked through the doors of Broomfield Residential care home. It was the same every time. It didn't matter what was going on in her life, how busy she was at work, or what was happening in the world. The soft swishing noise of the main doors as they glided across the carpeted floor always centred and calmed her.

It set the tone for her visits, as the calming vibes continued throughout the building with warm soft colours, comfortable furniture, and brilliant splashes of artwork that infused the environment with a positive energy. Though it was a place where her sister had been cared for so thoughtfully, it gave Karen an opportunity to quieten her mind and connect to normal life.

She made her way towards Jane's room, passing tables displaying fresh blooms, their floral tones tickling her nostrils. Karen was sure that it was a deliberate ploy on the part of the care home to create a sense of stillness and serenity amongst the staff, residents, and their families.

A familiar face appeared at the end of the corridor, close to Jane's room. The kind soft face of Nurse Robyn Allen hovered, her arms outstretched in readiness as Karen walked towards her. Everything about Robyn exuded sensitivity and professionalism. There was a warmth and compassion in her smile. Her hair, brown and glossy, was always tied up in a ponytail, and her blue tunic and dark navy trousers were always pristine.

"Karen."

Karen got swallowed up in Robyn's embrace. After a few moments, the women pulled apart and studied each other's features. Karen had never known someone to offer so much love and affection for the people she met. It was like an overflowing fountain of goodness that bathed everyone who was fortunate enough to be in receipt of it. All the strains of daily life melted away as Karen's tense muscles loosened and she became aware of a tiredness that washed over her.

Sensing the exhaustion in Karen's features, Robyn dropped her head to one shoulder. "You look tired. Are you not sleeping? I'm worried about you." Robyn rubbed her hand up and down Karen's arm reassuringly.

"I think that's putting it mildly. I'm always knackered."

"You probably need a good holiday. Think of it. Time on a hot sunny beach, with waves lapping on the shore, and hunky men in tight red swim shorts stepping out of the ocean, their drenched bodies glistening in the sun…"

Karen's eyes widened as she listened to Robyn's voice trail off, lost in her own fantasies. Karen burst out laughing, shattering the silence in the corridor. She threw a hand over her mouth to muffle the sound.

Robyn's face blushed in embarrassment.

"You need to get a room with your own thoughts," Karen teased. "I think it's you who needs the holiday. It sounds like you're ready for some hot-blooded Spaniard, and I feel sorry for the poor sod if you get your hands on him."

Robyn shook her head, and fanned a hand in front of her face, mockingly trying to cool herself down. "Ooh, I don't know what came over me," she replied, attempting to regain her composure.

"I do." Karen rolled her eyes and laughed. "It sounds like you're not getting enough."

Robyn shook her head. "Don't even go there, besides you're good at twisting things around," she continued, wagging an accusatory finger in Karen's direction. "How did it go from me asking about you, to the spotlight being on me?"

"That's why I'm a copper and you're not."

Though it was harmless banter, Karen enjoyed these light-hearted moments with Robyn. In recent times Karen had regarded her as a friend as much as Jane's nurse.

Flicking a nod in the direction of Jane's room, Karen asked how her sister was doing.

The seriousness returned to Robyn's face. "Generally, she's been okay. The physio sessions have been going well, and she's feeding okay. But we are beginning to notice longer periods of sleep and unresponsiveness."

Karen furrowed her brow. "Is that bad?"

Robyn pursed her lips and studied Karen for a moment.

The extended silence only confirmed the concern in Karen's mind.

"It's common for residents to experience periods where their bodies have to work a bit harder, especially those with long-term conditions."

"What does that mean for Jane?" Karen asked, as a dark cloud of confusion dulled her senses.

"Why don't we go along and see the doctor in his office? He examined Jane this evening, and he's better placed to describe what Jane is experiencing," Robyn added.

She led Karen to Doctor Keighley's office on the first floor. As they followed the stairs up, Robyn continued to offer words of encouragement to plug the empty silence that filled the open stairwell.

Karen had met Doctor Jeffrey Keighley occasionally and trusted his warm and reassuring manner on each of their meetings. He was a short man, with an extended waistline, and floppy brown hair which hung down over his forehead and brushed against the top of his glasses. He greeted Karen, extending a warm hand, before showing her to a chair opposite his desk. Robyn took the seat alongside Karen and offered her another reassuring smile.

"Doctor, I understand from Robyn that my sister Jane is having a few problems at the moment?"

Keighley interlocked his fingers and rested his hands on his desk, before nodding. "She is, Karen. We've been monitoring her for a few days now, and I decided to run a few tests on her this morning. We've always known that she has many underlying conditions, and Jane is now facing extreme pressure on her body from an enlarged heart. It's something that we call idiopathic cardiomegaly." Keighley paused for a moment in case Karen needed a further explanation. "In Jane's case, we believe that her enlarged heart is as a result of the weakening of the heart muscle, and possibly heart valve problems."

Karen's mind swirled as it struggled to take in the news. "How did you know that this was happening?"

Keighley cleared his throat. "The nurses, Nurse Allen in particular," Keighley cast an eye in Robyn's direction, "noticed that Jane was beginning to experience shortness of breath, and an abnormal heart rhythm."

Karen wiped her sweaty hands on her trousers. "Is this something more recent? I thought she was doing okay?" Karen knew that her tone had come out harder than intended, and bordered on accusatory, but didn't try to correct herself.

"It's hard to say. I know that sounds a weak and pathetic excuse, but with Jane unable to communicate with us, and often in deep periods of rest, these things can often appear with little or no notice. We noticed that her blood pressure was increasing to begin with, so we started to watch her more closely."

"Right. Right." Karen blinked furiously as she cast her eyes around the room, her mind struggling to make sense of the situation. "I know it sounds like a stupid question, but it's serious, isn't it? What happens now?"

Keighley nodded, the seriousness in his face confirming the gravity of Jane's condition. "It is. We noticed that her blood pressure readings this morning were elevated, and higher than yesterday. If that trend continues over the next few hours, then we believe it could be a sensible precaution to admit her to hospital, where they are better equipped to stabilise her and manage her condition."

Enlarged heart. Abnormal heart rhythm. Cardio something or other. Hospital. Shit.

A feeling of dread gripped Karen and tightened her chest. Jane had been such a constant in her life that she'd pushed all thoughts of losing her to the back of her mind, unwilling to accept that one day Jane could be taken away from her and she would be powerless to do anything about it.

"I need regular updates from you. I know I can be hard to get hold of sometimes, and if my phone is on silent, I may not hear the incoming call. If you don't get through, please send an urgent text. Would you be able to do that for me?" Karen looked at Keighley and then towards Robyn, before returning to the doctor again.

They both nodded in agreement, Keighley reassuring her that Jane was being well looked after.

"I DON'T GET IT. I really don't get it," Karen repeated softly as she cupped a mug of tea in her hands. Together with Robyn, she sat in the family lounge, going over what Doctor Keighley had discussed.

"I know it's hard to take in, Karen. But I promise you, she's in good hands. Jane has been doing really well despite all of her adversities. She's a lovely human being, as are you," Robyn said softly, rubbing Karen's knee.

Karen tightened her lips and felt the first signs of moisture filling her eyes. As she struggled to be strong for both herself and Jane, an overwhelming wave of emotion was fast swallowing her, one she was unable to fight off.

"I can't lose her. I can't lose my sister." Karen's voice cracked as she placed the mug on the coffee table and reached for a tissue from the box beside them. She dabbed the corner of her eyes, soaking up the tears, powerless to stop them.

Robyn had been in this situation countless times with the families of the residents she had cared for. There was an inevitability in the journey for most of the residents who came to their care home. The loss of a loved one was something that Robyn had become used to. Karen's pain still upset her, but she had a duty professionally and personally to support Karen through the highs and lows.

Robyn leant forward and rested her elbows on her thighs. "We are doing everything we can to look after Jane. You also need to prepare yourself for the fact that Jane has a battle on her hands. She has a weakened immune system, a damaged heart, as well as reduced brain activity." Robyn sighed. "Any one of those conditions would be challenging for most people to cope with. The fact that Jane has all of them and has remained strong and stable for so long is a testament to how much of a fighter your sister is. Don't ever forget that."

Karen nodded, her chin quivering. She puckered her lips and blew out her breath, trying to control the avalanche of thoughts and emotions tumbling through her. There was so much uncertainty, and Karen hated that. "Listen, I can't thank you enough for everything you've done for both Jane and me. I just hope she has the strength to beat this." Karen looked towards the ceiling, staring at the speckled tiles, before returning her gaze towards Robyn and offering her a half-smile.

"Karen, Jane's a fighter. Tomorrow is another day, so let's see how she gets on. It's late now, so I suggest you go home, have a warm bath and get some sleep. We'll catch up tomorrow, hey?"

Karen nodded, dragging her weary body out of the chair with a hefty sigh and slinging her handbag over her shoulder. She hugged Robyn, savouring the moment, and the physical connection, before leaving.

4

He'd been sitting in his car for fifteen minutes, waiting. The rush of the morning had calmed, people had gone to work, morning deliveries had been made, and many elderly residents had headed off to their morning clubs.

His eyes scanned up and down the road. He wanted to give his target enough time to be far enough away from the house before he made his next move. He knew the man's routine off by heart, having trailed him several times. At nine thirty every morning, the old man would set off for his morning walk. Thirty minutes to himself, where he would make his way to a local park, complete one circuit of the path, before making his way back. On the return leg he would pop into one of the local shops and pick up a few essentials before scurrying home.

His target followed the well-trodden path every day, sticking to familiar streets, visiting the same places, and talking to the same people. His pace would be brisk and energetic to begin with, but would slow to an amble as he returned home. Whether it was tiredness and old age that caused him to fizzle or knowing what waited for him each time he returned, who knew? His target led a mundane life, which made the planning even easier.

With the target out of the way, and the road clear, the man stepped from his car. Though he had driven up and down the street several times, his hope was that a nosy old neighbour hadn't been perched by the window, peeking through the curtains for anything unusual. He glanced up and down the street once more before crossing the road and making his way towards the house. One last look, and confident that the coast was clear, he hurriedly moved towards the side of the house, releasing the latch on the garden gate.

As he made his way onto the patio, he took a moment to glance at his surroundings. It was a small, functional garden with larch lap fencing on either side, and a row of conifers lining the rear. He'd scouted the area on an earlier visit, and knew that beyond the wall of conifers, a small rusty gate would give him an emergency escape route to an alleyway that ran along the back of the houses and onto an adjoining street.

From inside his jacket, he retrieved his crowbar. His trusted companion, his enforcer, and his weapon of choice. He paused for a moment and listened for any activity or voices in the adjoining gardens. When nothing came back, he wedged one end of the crowbar between the door frame and forced the lock.

The door relented easily. UPVC patio doors offered little protection, despite what their owners were led to believe. He edged the door open and poked his head into the kitchen before pausing. His eyes scanned the kitchen worktops as he tuned into any sounds or footsteps approaching. The sound of the TV blared from a room. He waited. Confident there was no threat, he placed one foot in front of the other, moving with stealth, his approach silent.

The sound of a female voice mumbling to herself attracted his attention, as he made his way towards the lounge. An elderly Asian woman was walking around in circles, and clumsily stumbling up and down the lounge, talking to herself incoherently. He couldn't make out her words, the foreign dialect unknown to him. The sound of a cat meowing caught his attention. He glanced down as the feline padded towards him and rubbed its body around his ankles. He smiled to himself before reaching down to pick up the cat. A deep purring reverberated through his arm as the cat contentedly lapped up the attention.

He placed the cat down, stepped into the lounge and ducked in behind the woman. She was so lost in her own world, and ramblings, she didn't notice or hear him enter. He watched as her confusion intensified. She wasn't making sense, but he couldn't care a shit. He wasn't here for her. Even though he wanted to kill her out of boredom, she was not his target.

"Who are you?" the woman muttered as she spun on her heels, catching the man by surprise. There was no malice or fear in her voice, just curiosity. "Have you come to do shopping?" she asked in broken English.

The man shrugged. "No, I'm here for another reason."

"Well, it's nice to see you again. You never come and visit any more. Why not?" she demanded.

The man hissed, "What's it to you anyway, you old bag?"

"Rajesh, you must come and visit your parents more. Your father waits all the time."

The man furrowed his brow and tutted. *The old woman has lost her marbles.* "Yeah, yeah, if you say so. Who the fuck is Rajesh anyway?" he questioned, as he stepped away from the woman, and began to scope the rest of the lounge.

The woman continued to rant in his ear. As he looked over his shoulder, the woman shuffled just a few inches behind him, following him around the room. He tutted and sneered again, before returning to the mantelpiece and shelves, looking for anything of value that he could take. One shelf in the alcove was crammed with framed photographs. He paused for a moment, scanning each one. The woman and her husband were stood either side of a younger man dressed in a black gown over his suit, with a mortar board, and a paper scroll in his hands.

His son. The man shook his head. *Rajesh is their son.*

"Rajesh, why you not listening to me?" the woman continued, jabbing the man in the back with her finger. "Why? Listen to me. Why? Have you come to repair the car? Are you the mechanic?"

The man wanted to turn around and rip her throat out. *That would silence her*, he thought. "I'm not your son. I'm the wrong stupid fucking colour," he grunted as he spun around to face her, his face beginning to redden as anger swelled in him. He shook his head in bewilderment as she smiled back.

"I will make you dinner, wait for Dad," she said before shuffling off towards the kitchen.

This is going to be a long wait, he thought.

5

The bag feels heavier, he thought as he turned into his street. Maybe he'd bought more than normal, or perhaps it was another sign that age was catching up with him. It was harder waking in the mornings, and he would barely make it through a whole day without having a nap in the afternoon. As a full-time carer, it was taking a toll on his mind and body.

He exhaled heavily, a plume of vapour escaping with his breath. His usual walk around the park had been uneventful. He saw the same familiar faces, struck up the same conversations, and promised to see them again the following morning. After a particularly restless night, and lots of cleaning up in the bedroom, they had run low on kitchen towel, so he dipped into the local Co-op and picked up fresh supplies. His friends had been on at him for months to organise a weekly home delivery with Tesco, but it had never sat comfortably with him. The thought of a stranger entering his home didn't appeal.

As the situation got tiresome, he'd thought of asking for

more home help. He did everything. The cooking, cleaning, washing, and shopping were all down to him now, and at his age, proved a challenge at the best of times. But there was no choice. He didn't like leaving his wife alone. On the odd occasion where he would be out longer, others would pop in and check up on her. This morning he'd left her asleep on the sofa with the TV on in the background. She had been awake most of the night, moaning, pacing around the bedroom, and wetting herself. With her asleep, through exhaustion more than anything else, it had been an ideal opportunity to go and get his paper, supplies, and her medication from the pharmacy.

At his front door, he placed his bag of shopping on the floor, and pulled out the keys from his pocket. The TV still blared in the background, but his wife was awake, her voice creeping into the hallway. He pulled off his coat and hung it up. Rolling his eyes, he listened to his wife talking about a holiday they had taken to Goa. He wondered if she ever tired of talking to herself and having imaginary conversations.

"I'm back," he shouted from the hallway.

Normally when he said that his wife would shuffle out into the hallway and continue her nonsensical conversation with him. He furrowed his brow in confusion. On this occasion she continued talking to herself from the other room. He picked up his carrier bag and wandered into the lounge. He'd only taken two steps when he froze on the spot.

His wife was sitting alongside another man. She didn't stop to acknowledge her husband, but continued her conversation, waving her hands in front of her as she recalled more eventful tales from their holiday.

The old man asked, "Who are you? What are you doing in my house?" Panic swelled inside him as he fought to contain it.

"Your dear wife invited me in."

The old man glared at his wife. He doubted she would have done that, but anything was possible with her these days. Just a month ago, she had discovered the keys to the front door and let herself out. After a desperate search by friends, neighbours and the police, she had been found a mile away, lost in confusion. Ever since that day, he had double locked the front door to keep her safe. He recalled the door still being locked when he had arrived moments ago, which sent an icy chill through his bones.

"She didn't let you in. The door was locked. You've broken in. Get out. I'm calling the police." The old man turned, mustering all his strength to charge back into the hallway to retrieve his phone from his coat pocket.

"You're very perceptive, old man," the intruder replied, as he leapt from the sofa and chased after him.

The old man fumbled for his jacket, his body trembling as much as his lips, panic gripping him, paralysing him, as his eyes widened in fear. A pain of which the likes he had never experienced tore through his body, a searing, sharp pain that spread across his back and down his arms. He yelled in agony as he collapsed to his knees, his hands clawing at the walls.

With the crowbar in both hands, the intruder ferociously launched it, bringing it down on the old man's head. The crack of bone amplified in the hallway as the noise bounced off the walls. As the blows continued, the old man's skeleton crumpled like delicate eggshells crushed underfoot. Each time the crowbar descended, it became embedded deeper into the old man's skull, until there was nothing left of the back of his head than shredded, mushed up brain matter. Splatters of blood spread across the walls like some abstract painting by an unknown artist in a top London gallery.

As the old man's body slumped to the floor, the deformed shape of his head pressed up against one wall, his arms tucked beneath his chest, and his legs splayed out.

The intruder gasped for breath as adrenaline tensed his body. His eyes were wide with rage, fiery red spheres that glared at the battered remains of his victim. The intensity was powerful, one he'd experienced before. It was raw and savage and, even now, his body shook at the power he had wielded over the man. His nostrils flared as he stared at the broken form.

He placed the crowbar to one side and reached inside his jacket to retrieve a scalpel. From experience, he knew that the quickest way was to make a deep incision in the abdomen just below the ribcage, and about ten centimetres across. From there, he would reach inside and up with his hand, grab the heart and pull it out with such force, that it would come out in one piece. It would take less than a minute.

Moments later, he sat back on his heels, the warmth of the organ seeping into his fingers. He smiled to himself as he rose to his feet and walked into the kitchen.

6

Karen shifted in her chair as her mind wandered everywhere but on the boring course material. Dull didn't begin to describe it. Worse yet, she'd done it to herself, signing up for one on digital intelligence and investigation, always keen to increase her depth of understanding in different facets of policing. Whether it was the material, or the instructor, Dan Kennedy, was debatable, but she kinda swung towards the latter as she listened to him drone on all morning.

Karen thought it was a good move with the powers that be, and a way to get into their good books. Her goal now was to get her DCI job back, and with Skelton gone, it left a vacancy open for her that was currently under review with a decision imminent. She'd had a chequered past with her bosses. Though they loved her results, they were less enthusiastic about her approach. Maverick, selfish, insubordinate, were a few of the words thrown in her direction. She was perhaps her worst own enemy. Striving to always improve and push herself, she expected the same from her team. And though most investigations could often be long and protracted, part of her always looked for a shortcut to getting a result, and if that meant bending rules, she was first in line.

The majority of the other eight officers attending with her looked just as bored. Karen lost count of the number of times she had stifled a yawn, and the other officers weren't faring any better. From the corner of her eye, she glanced across to the officer sitting next to her and noticed him doodling on paper. He'd drawn boxes, arrows, and circles all over his notepad. They had been drawn with such intensity, probably out of frustration and boredom, that the tip of his pen carved deep grooves into the pad.

Get on with it! You must be the life and soul of every party you turn up at, you prat.

The force had picked the wrong trainer, probably down to cost more than anything else. And with all the will in the world, staying focused was going to prove hard for the whole day. Seven hours of listening to a man who bore a striking resemblance to Mr Bean. Karen noticed how Kennedy's eyebrows had a mind of their own each time he spoke. They would creep halfway up his forehead, and do rolling waves, but everything below his nose hardly moved. Karen thought Botox had fixed half of his face in a permanent and awkward grin.

The officer next to her scribbled something down on his notepad and twisted it in Karen's direction.

Karen craned her head ever so slightly and narrowed her eyes to read his cryptic message.

He has the personality of a wet cardboard box!!!

At this, Karen's eyes, projecting biblical levels of boredom a moment earlier, flashed wide. Unconsciously, Karen let out a laugh which she quickly disguised behind a cough, as the other attendees and the trainer looked in her direction.

Karen held out her hand, apologetically. "Sorry, I choked on my own saliva." A sense of awkwardness crept over Karen when she realised how daft it sounded.

The officer next to her scribbled something else before turning his pad once again in Karen's direction.

Better than choking on something else!!

Karen's eyes widened as she valiantly held back a shriek of laughter. She turned and glared at the officer in a manner that suggested, "you're going to get me in trouble."

Her colleague smirked in reply.

A few moments later, Karen refocused her attention on key points Kennedy had put up on a slide. He had gone to great lengths to emphasise how policing had to adapt and respond to the digital environment, to make sure that it could relentlessly pursue criminals, protect the vulnerable, and reduce crime wherever that occurred. Though Karen agreed one hundred per cent with Kennedy's thoughts, the man had such an uninspiring way that it took the shine off the whole experience.

The whole purpose behind this course was to support the Policing Vision 2025, which aimed to make it easier for the police and public to communicate with each other, to improve digital investigations and intelligence, and to transfer all information within the criminal justice system digitally. Karen was particularly interested in the second stream of work around digital intelligence and investigation, informally known as DII. This set out to improve the knowledge and skills of frontline officers and their supporting staff to address digital crime. The emphasis was to ensure specialist capabilities were in place to respond to cybercrime which was becoming a real thorn in their side when dealing with serious and organised crime groups.

As Kennedy's voice started to grind on Karen, she glanced at the time on her phone and groaned inwardly when she realised it was a further two hours until they had a break for lunch. The more Kennedy spoke, the more strained he sounded, like his vocal cords were being squeezed together. His S's sounded like high-pitched whistles, and Karen expected a bunch of dogs to come storming through the door at any moment.

Karen's eyelids grew heavier with Kennedy's every word. The room was stuffy, and no one had had the bottle yet to open a window to let cold air in. A nudge in her side brought her back into the room. She glanced across at her colleague, who motioned with his eyes towards the door. Perplexed, she mouthed "what?" Her colleague pointed with his eyes again towards the door. Karen looked in the same direction to see Jade's face peeking in through the glass.

Jade pulled a face and crossed her eyes, as she teased Karen. Karen shook her head and rolled her eyes in reply, before tapping her wrist and holding up five fingers to let her know that they might get a break shortly.

Jade shook her head, now beckoning her with her hand. Karen mouthed "no" creating an O shape with her mouth. An unrelenting Jade pointed at her phone, before pointing at Karen. The penny dropped, and Karen reached for her phone. She scanned the content quickly before looking up at Jade, who now nodded furiously. Karen cleared her throat before gathering her stuff up.

"I'm really sorry, Dan, something urgent has come up, and I'm needed. I should be back in five minutes."

Dan looked perplexed and annoyed at the interruption. As Karen pushed her chair back, the male colleague next to Karen muttered under his breath, "That old chestnut."

"As I said, Dan, I shouldn't be too long, and besides, Alex my colleague here," Karen began, staring at the officer sitting next to her, "said that this stuff is *really* interesting, and wants to chat to you about it over lunch." Karen threw the officer a smile as she stepped away, momentarily glancing over a shoulder as she opened the door. Alex was staring up at the ceiling shaking his head.

"Oh my God, Jade, you… are… a… life… saver. I would have been pulling out my hair by lunchtime. In fact, I would much rather be sitting on the toilet, shitting through the eye of a needle, then going back into that room."

Jade laughed. "Okay, that's a bit extreme," she added, scoffing the last bit of Danish pastry in her hand.

"Anyway, what's up? Please tell me we've got something important to do?"

"We have, Karen. We've got a body."

7

Jade and Karen raced from the office, and with Jade driving they tore through the traffic, the wail of the siren, and the blue flashing grill lights forcing drivers to swerve as she raced past them.

Karen tried to ignore the squirming anxiety twisting her insides into knots. Nerves and uncertainty knotted her stomach each time she attended a crime scene. Not knowing what they were walking into always took officers by surprise.

The call had come in that morning when neighbours noticed the front door of the property wide open, and what appeared to be the lower half of a person lying in the hallway, the rest of their body hidden behind the front door.

"Who put in the call?" Karen asked as she stepped from Jade's vehicle and watched the hive of police activity around the property.

"A neighbour. A Mrs Jean Bartlett was waiting on a pint of milk and popped next door to pick it up."

"I think she got more than her pint of milk, Jade," Karen replied, imagining what the woman had witnessed.

"You're telling me. I think she practically passed out on the spot. You should listen to the 999 call that the controller took. It was so garbled, it sounded like a message beamed from outer space by an unknown civilisation."

Officers had sealed off the street fifty yards in each direction, and she was thankful for that. It kept prying eyes at a distance, and it allowed her officers and the forensic team to work uninterrupted. A blue forensic tent had been positioned across the front door, shielding onlookers from the worst of it. The front garden became a staging post for officers coming and going, as boxes of protective clothing sat alongside metallic silver cases that the forensic team had brought with them. A single uniformed officer positioned on the boundary of the front garden acknowledged Karen and Jade as they approached.

Karen offered the young officer a nod asking, "How bad is it?"

The officer sucked in air through his teeth and shook his head as if he was a builder overwhelmed with the size of the estimate he was about to deliver. "It's an absolute mess behind that door, guv. The location of the body is making it hard for SOCO to work in such a confined space," he replied, passing the scene log to Karen, who signed in, before handing it over to Jade to do the same.

Karen and Jade grabbed protective overalls, booties and gloves, keen to preserve the crime scene as best as possible, before they slipped in through the flap in the blue tent.

Karen wasn't one of those officers who barged into an active crime scene, throwing around her weight and asking dozens of questions. She preferred to observe, form a picture in her mind first, and allow her thoughts to form naturally.

She swatted away a few flies that buzzed around her head. In front of them was a narrow hallway. To aid the investigation, SOCO had removed the front door from its hinges, and it sat propped up against the front wall of the house. Karen saw Mason Brophy, the crime scene manager, further down the hallway instructing his team, guiding his resources to where they were needed. Beyond him and towards the rear of the property, the white silhouetted figure of a crime scene investigator worked diligently on the rear patio doors, leaning in and taking close-up photographs of evidence.

From her vantage point, Karen could see that the front door hadn't been inspected yet. Mason would already have decided the sequence in which the scene would be examined, and having worked with Mason, she knew that her colleague placed his focus on the body first, before extending his search outwards in concentric circles.

The aroma of death surrounded them. A sickly sweet-sour essence, blended with an overwhelming deeper and vile smell of blood, rotting flesh and body matter from the decomposition process.

The scene took Karen's breath away, with Jade expressing her disgust and horror as she gasped from behind Karen's shoulder. Blood splatter trails snaked across the walls, and the mangled remains of an elderly man lay face down. A halo of blood spread out from his body. SOCO had placed stepping plates around the corpse to avoid disturbing or contaminating the scene.

"It's a bloody massacre," whispered Jade, her breath short and sharp.

The grisly scene was already etched deep in their minds, their eyes unable to track the horrors, nor comprehend the ferocity with which the attack had taken place. Karen had attended many suspected homicides and brutal slayings. She hoped to have been hardened to it over the years, but human emotions still crept into her thoughts and feelings. Though she wanted to stay neutral and objective, a life had still been extinguished prematurely. Someone's mother, father, brother, sister, uncle or aunt. And the day that she felt no emotion would be the day that she quit the force.

Karen swallowed hard, taking in the scene in front of her. She could hardly describe the man as having a head, because there was practically nothing left of the back of it. Congealed blood sat with sticky brain matter in large clumps around the scene. She looked up to see splatters across the ceiling, and on the wall behind her. Each direction she looked in was a mini crime scene within the context of the overall crime scene. Each wall, ceiling, and floor carried its own story.

"I'd like to say, in fact I hope, that the victim was already unconscious before most of this took place, but I doubt it. I can't begin to imagine how he felt," Jade said, talking aloud to no one in particular.

Karen couldn't be certain, not until the post-mortem had been conducted, but from the extent of the injuries, blunt force trauma would be up there as to the cause of death.

Flashes of brilliant light shook her from her thoughts. A crime scene investigator was kneeling beside her, taking detailed close-ups of the victim's remains. Another investigator was perched on the steps placing swab samples into small glass bottles, whilst a third investigator was carefully dusting down the door frame to the lounge.

"We are going to be here a while." Mason sighed as he navigated the stepping plates in the hallway towards Karen. "It's such a big crime scene, that we've got our work cut out for us," he added, craning his head towards the ceiling, his eyes scanning the patchwork of blood splatters.

"Rather you than me. Anything you can tell me so far?" Karen asked.

Mason tipped his head towards the kitchen. "It looks like there was forced entry from the rear of the property. The back patio door has been prised apart."

"With what?"

"The gouge marks are more significant and deeper than what you could achieve with a screwdriver."

Karen returned her gaze to the battered body just a few feet away from her. "Okay. Cheers, Mason. From the looks of it, something bigger than a screwdriver did that as well."

8

Wainwright pulled the hood back from his protective suit and tugged his mask beneath his chin. He'd arrived a few minutes after Karen and following his assessment had joined Karen in the front garden.

"It's a pleasure as always to see you lovely ladies," Wainwright offered, smiling towards Karen, and nodding in Jade's direction.

"Likewise, Wainwright. Have you done what you needed to do in there?"

"Indeed, I have, Karen. I guess you'll be wanting my informed opinion?" he continued, raising a brow as he sought confirmation.

Karen shrugged. "It doesn't take a pathologist to tell me that the poor bloke has had his head caved in."

Wainwright smirked. "True. I'm a little redundant here. But you're right. As you so eloquently put it, I'd say that severe blunt force trauma injury to his head, was indeed the likely cause of death. However, until I have the opportunity to examine him in close detail, I can't be certain. We can't rule out the possibility that there may also be knife wounds, or any other injuries that may have contributed to his death first."

Jade interjected. "The neighbour found him in the last few hours, so it's still a new crime scene. That works in our favour. The evidence is fresh, the scene is undisturbed, and the body wouldn't have suffered too much decomposition."

Karen agreed with Jade's assessment.

Wainwright packed his bag, and stepped out of the Tyvek white overalls, before bagging them up. "I've signed all the necessary forms, so you're good to go."

"Brilliant. Jade and I will head back in so that we can start looking around the place, and I'll catch up with you a little later?"

"Of course," Wainwright replied as he dashed off.

THOUGH KAREN HAD BEEN at the scene for a few hours, it remained busy, but calm and organised. Mason's team moved in and out of rooms, completing their analysis and evidence retrieval. Another SOCO stayed positioned by the front door, a female officer perched on a silver box, with a pad in hand. She compiled and documented each evidence bag that her colleagues brought out to her. This was a crucial stage in any investigation, the collecting and preservation of all evidence which would then be logged back on the HOLMES database by an exhibits officer.

Karen moved through the ground floor, navigating each stepping plate as she moved through the hallway and into the lounge. There was no sign of a disturbance here, which suggested that the attack had been confined to the entrance. The TV was still on in the background, and Karen took a moment to become familiar with the environment. Two worn sofas lined one wall, and a low, oblong coffee table sat squarely in the middle of the lounge, with a small stack of newspapers and magazines neatly piled to one end. As she slowly stepped around the room, she paused by the shelves and examined the photos. Many of them contained pictures of an elderly Asian couple, and she assumed that the man in the picture was the man who lay battered, cold and dead in the hallway. A few pictures had the man beaming proudly as he stood beside a younger man, dressed in university garb. A jubilant and celebratory moment in the young man's life, and Karen wondered if he, who she assumed was the deceased's son, had been informed yet.

Karen stepped into the hallway and noticed the presence of bloody footprints leading away from the scene into the kitchen. They stopped midway before returning to the hall which suggested that the assailant may have entered through the back before the attack but left through the front door. *He's got a lot of balls to step out into broad daylight, no doubt probably covered in blood.*

The kitchen was larger than expected. The kitchen worktops were clean, plates had been neatly stacked in a rack, and pots had been tucked out of sight. A few letters sat beside a kettle, the first of which was addressed to Anil Kumar. She decided not to touch them until SOCO had completed their sweep of all surfaces. A small kitchen table sat to one side, with two chairs tucked beneath it. More photographs were pinned to the wall, this time not of people, but of places. She recognised the Taj Mahal and the Eiffel Tower. It looked sunny, warm, and inviting. *Just what I need now*, she thought.

Karen left the kitchen before heading upstairs. It was a regular three-bedroomed semi, with one small box room, and two large double bedrooms. The box room had been converted into a small office come prayer room, with a filing cabinet tucked into one corner, statues of gods draped in floral garlands propped up on the windowsill and a computer desk. The rear bedroom had a double bed and appeared to be used, with a few items of clothing folded neatly on the bed, and a pair of black Nike Air Max sitting in one corner. Karen wondered if their son came to stay occasionally.

Moving into the front bedroom, Karen began to build a true sense of its occupants. A sickening smell turned her stomach. On the dressing table were several packets of pills. The bedroom hadn't been checked by SOCO yet, but with her blue nitrile gloves on, she picked up a few of the packets to see that they were made out in the name of Aruna Kumar. She wasn't familiar with the labels, and Aricept, Amlodipine, and Prednisolone, meant nothing to her. One or both of the occupants clearly needed added medical support. When she noticed a commode in one corner of the room and the source of a foul smell, Karen turned up her nose and grimaced, unwilling to lift the lid to see what horrors lay beneath it.

As she made her way back onto the landing towards the stairs, she peeked into the bathroom, which also displayed evidence of assisted medical support, with support rails by the toilet and the bath.

She walked the length of the hall, pausing momentarily to

look at the body, before stepping out into the front garden. Jade was talking to another officer, making notes, when Karen joined her.

"Anil and Aruna Kumar?" she asked.

Jade nodded. "Yep, that's the names we've got."

Karen's gaze travelled across the road, to where a middle-aged couple stood in their front garden in deep discussion, a worried look on both of their faces.

"His wife was in the house…" Jade offered.

Karen's head snapped up. "What?"

"Yep. She was there. We've now got her in an ambulance down the road being treated."

"What have we been able to get from her?" Karen asked.

Jade shook her head. "Absolutely diddly-squat. She's in a state of confusion."

Karen left Jade checking in with the uniformed officers, whilst she made her way over to the ambulance. A male paramedic stepped out of the rear doors as Karen approached.

"How is she?"

The man grimaced. "Not great. She's not making any sense at all. We can't be certain whether it's shock, or an underlying neurological condition. She doesn't appear to be carrying any signs of injury."

"Does Aricept, Amlodipine, or Prednisolone, mean anything to you?" Karen asked.

"Yep, they're used to treat a wide range of conditions.

Aricept is often used to treat symptoms associated with dementia. Amlodipine is to treat blood pressure. And Prednisolone is a powerful steroid used as an anti-inflammatory in conjunction with meds like antibiotics," the paramedic replied.

"Well, they're all made out in her name."

The paramedic rolled his eyes and nodded. "That makes sense, and why she's *not* making sense."

Karen returned to catch up with Jade. "We need to track down the next of kin, which I imagine is their son, going by the pictures in there. I think it would also be useful to find out who their GP is. It seems as if the victim's wife had a lot of underlying medical conditions, so let's find out what we can about the family and her care."

Jade scribbled down the instructions and nodded in confirmation. She was about to ask a question when a crime scene officer beckoned them back into the property and through to the kitchen.

"What's up?" Karen asked, looking around the kitchen bemused.

The officer pointed down towards something beneath the small kitchen table Karen had seen earlier.

Karen bent over to see a cat bowl that had been pushed under the table, and what appeared to be the remains of a partially eaten heart.

9

A buzz of energy crackled around the incident room as Karen made her way towards the front. An undercurrent of murmured conversations echoed around her as details from the scene filtered through. On her way back, many of her officers had taken the opportunity to review the body cam footage captured from the scene. The horror and shock were palpable with the team.

On Karen's instructions, Steve had started to muster the troops, and arrange for more support staff to be drafted into the team in anticipation of what lay ahead. Desk space had been cleared, a bank of computers installed, and additional whiteboards added.

Jade grabbed a spare seat towards the front of the crowd, and squeezed herself in between two other officers, whispering for them to budge over.

Karen placed her folder and phone on a desk beside her and turned to face the assembled crowd. Many of the faces she recognised, officers who were part of her permanent team, as well as those who were drafted in when a major crime landed on her desk. They were well versed in handling a major investigation, knew their position and their role, which in Karen's mind made the transition into a full-scale investigation seamless. It also meant that they could throw all of their available resources into the investigation from the outset, especially during the first twenty-four hours. With the crime being committed several hours ago, they had missed the golden hour, and were playing a game of catch-up.

Though the forensic evidence had been uninterrupted on the whole, they had potentially lost witnesses who may have still been in the proximity at the time of the crime, as well as any CCTV footage. That was a pressing need in Karen's mind, and why they needed to act quickly because if any footage was recorded on a loop, her team needed to seize it before it was automatically erased. In her mind, the more time that passed following an offence, the more likely it was that evidence was going to be lost, compromised, or destroyed.

"Okay, team, settle down. Thank you for getting everything organised so quickly, Steve," Karen began, offering an appreciative nod in his direction. Returning her gaze to the sea of eyes that hung on her every word, Karen addressed them. "If you haven't seen the body cam footage so far, make sure you do so straight after this briefing. To say it was a bloodbath is an understatement. Though the victim hasn't been formally identified, we are assuming that he is Anil Kumar, the occupant and owner of the house."

A voice towards the middle of the crowd piped up, "Are we

running with the assumption the victim was bludgeoned to death?"

Karen nodded. "At the moment, yes. Blunt force trauma was the likely COD according to Wainwright. The victim was lying face down when I was there, and there were no other injuries that I could see that may have contributed to his death. We will know more shortly once forensics are done. They anticipate being there for most of the day."

"What's this about the heart?" asked another.

Karen suppressed a shudder. "The remains of a large heart were found in a food bowl. It looked like the cat had had a go at it."

Several of the officers squirmed and narrowed their eyes at the ghoulish images forming in their minds, as Karen pinned pictures to the whiteboard.

"Human?" an officer asked.

"Quite possibly, based on the size and shape. Forensics assumed that it was a human organ."

"That's bloody gross," Brad interjected as he blew out his cheeks. "Do you think it belonged to the victim?"

Karen nodded. "More than likely. Let's see what forensics and the PM throw up. Can you give Mason a quick shout for an update?"

Brad nodded in confirmation, jotting it down on his notepad.

"Jade, can you give feedback to the team on what you've found from your initial enquiries?"

Jade stood and moved alongside Karen before turning

towards the team. Jade hadn't done this often and found the mass of faces staring back intimidating. Though she knew most, and had worked with them on many occasions, standing up in front of them and addressing the briefing still jangled her nerves. "Officers on the ground began to do door-to-door enquiries. Early indications suggest that they were a retired couple, Anil Kumar was a retired doctor. We haven't found out what his wife did."

"Doctor of what?" Karen asked.

Jade shook her head. "That's the bit we're not certain of. When we spoke to the neighbours, a few thought he was a doctor in the medical field, whilst others thought he was involved with something to do with psychiatry or psychology."

Jade continued, "From what we can gather, Mr Kumar's wife had been unwell for a few years with dementia, so he had become her full-time carer."

"Not much of a retirement? Poor sod," DC Craig Martin piped up, an officer drafted into Karen's team on a few occasions, and whom she highly regarded as an up-and-coming talent in the force.

Karen agreed.

After Jade had updated the team, Karen glanced over her shoulder at the crime scene photographs.

"We need to put in as much effort as possible to find out where the assailant went next. From what we can gather, he most likely left through the front door, and with the savagery of the attack, there's no doubt in my mind that he'd be covered in blood. Someone must've seen him."

"Can we be certain that it's a male?" asked Jeff, another seconded to her team from earlier cases.

Karen considered the question for a moment. "We are going on the assumption that it's male. The bloodied footprints were large. I'd say at least a size eight or nine, and as I mentioned earlier, the intensity of the attack would need a lot of effort, as well as a bit of muscle to break through the patio door at the back."

"It could have been a large woman?" Brad speculated.

His suggestion was met with a ripple of laughter amongst those gathered, as one officer ribbed him by suggesting that if the assailant was a large woman, she'd have no problems picking him up and swinging his skinny arse around the room. Brad offered nothing more than a one-finger salute and a smug smile in return, as Karen rolled her eyes.

Jeff waved his pen in the air to catch Karen's attention. "Boss, have we got a motive yet? Was it a random killing? A robbery gone wrong? Or was it targeted?"

"It could be all the above, to be honest, Jeff. We don't know at the moment. It could have been a random psycho, and if it's a stranger killing, that's the worst-case scenario for us."

Jeff raised a brow before he continued to hypothesise. "It could be a disgruntled patient from whenever he was a doctor. He may have given a patient a misdiagnosis or missed something altogether. Maybe he had an affair with one of his patients, and the husband found out after all this time, and tracked him down, before beating the crap out of him. Or he hit on an old dear at the pensioners club down the road, and the knitting club took their revenge on him. Or…"

Groans, heckles, and obscenities were thrown back in Jeff's direction.

Karen held up a hand to stop him in mid-sentence before his imagination got out of hand. "Yeah, Jeff. I think we get the idea, mate. My advice would be that you need to get out a bit more!"

"Are we going to the press with this?" a young DC asked, attempting to restore sensibility back to the conversation.

Karen turned and noticed that the young man asking was DC Amari Adebayo, a tall slender black officer, with a goatee beard and a strong jaw. He had been involved in a number of her cases and she'd found him an excellent officer. Though he was much younger than her, she considered him good-looking, with a charismatic smile and pearly white teeth that stood out from his dark skin. He had a self-assured confidence about him, which she no doubt thought women would find attractive. If she was honest, she certainly fell into that category, as did many of the female officers who appeared to be taken in by his charms.

"I think to begin with, we'll release a basic press statement. The hope is that it might stir the memories of those who live nearby. Don't forget, we've also got postmen, delivery drivers, and dog walkers who may have been in the vicinity at the time and noticed something unusual. It might prick someone's memory."

"Our focus now is to find any CCTV footage from neighbouring residents and start trawling through those. Jade, can you also double our efforts with the door-to-door enquiries?"

Turning towards Steve, Karen glanced down at her notes before continuing. "Can you run PNC checks, and a

HOLMES database search for anything like this. And gather a few people together to start digging into Anil Kumar's family connections."

Karen spent the next few minutes fielding a few questions before dismissing the team. The time on her phone told her it was late; the day had disappeared in the blink of an eye. She glanced out of the window in her office. Darkness veiled her view, and Karen wondered when she'd get her next break. With so much on her plate already, it was hard to know where to start. In the absence of a DCI, she would need to update Hinchcliff first thing tomorrow. In the meantime, Karen had an urgent call to make.

10

Tiredness crept over Karen as she dropped into her chair and leant back with her arms up in the air to relieve an achy back. It was the first time she'd been in her office all day and an almighty groan escaped as she wheeled her mouse to wake up the PC screen. Her inbox of emails seemed to be growing by the day, and no sooner had she worked through the most recent ones, then new ones replaced them.

Karen picked up her phone and pulled up the number for Broomfield, before resting the phone between her ear and left shoulder, whilst scrolling through the emails for anything of importance that needed her immediate attention. One in particular piqued her interest. The psychiatric evaluation team wanted a follow-up meeting with her after the events involving Skelton. She tutted, and though she wanted to press the delete button, Karen knew they'd keep chasing her.

The switchboard at the care home finally answered, and Karen asked to be put through to Nurse Allen. Whilst they located her, she was put on hold and left listening to melodic windpipe music which she found strangely relaxing. Karen closed her eyes, and pictured herself standing on Machu Picchu, high in the Andes mountains in Peru, listening to pan flute music and hearing about the Inca civilisation. *Fuck, it seems like a distant dream*, she thought as her chest sank.

"Karen."

Karen was shaken from her reverie as Jade sauntered into her office and planted herself in the chair opposite.

Karen let out a long sigh. "I'm just waiting for an update on my sister, so I won't be long."

It didn't appear to bother Jade, as she slouched in the chair and stared at the ceiling, yawning at the same time. The long day, and stress of a new case had taken its toll on the whole team, and Jade was ready for bed.

"Hi, Karen," Nurse Allen said as the music cut out and she hopped on the line.

"Hi, Robyn. I thought I'd put in a quick call before heading home to check on Jane. I thought if there were any problems, I'd come to the care home first?"

"Aw, that's good of you. There is no change in your sister's condition. We are still monitoring her very closely. The doctor popped in and checked on her during his evening round, and was pleased that she was stable."

Karen let out another sigh in relief, not realising she'd been holding her breath for what seemed like the last few minutes.

"Listen, I accept you're concerned, Karen. We all are.

We're checking on her regularly, and we are doing everything we can to make her comfortable. If there was any change in her condition, we'd call you straight away."

"Well, you know how it is. Everyone is doing a fantastic job over there, but I worry. And I feel guilty that I can't be there often. We've taken on a hefty case this morning, and my time is gonna be limited, so at least it feels as if I'm doing something when I call you. I hope you don't think I'm being a pain in your backside?"

Karen could hear the smile in Robyn's tone when she replied.

"Karen, you could never be a pain in our backsides. I only wish you could come here more often. We all look forward to seeing you. Every time Kevin pops in, he always sticks his nose into my office to find out if you have been in, or are planning to. He knows the difficulties that you are going through, and I think he's found a kindred spirit in you as someone he can turn to for support."

Karen felt a stab in her heart, and a twist in her stomach, as a wave of guilt flashed through her. "Bless him. It's quite nice to have a bit of downtime, and a catch-up with him. It's awful he's going through a terrible time as well. But with my schedule being so erratic, it is so hard to predict when I can steal a couple of hours to get over there. But the next time you see him, please say hi from me. He's got my number anyway, so tell him to call me?"

"I will. Now you get yourself off for the evening, and if there's any change in your sister's condition, I promise we will call you immediately. Deal?"

Karen nodded to herself. "Deal."

Karen hung up and dropped her phone into her handbag on the floor before dragging her fingers down her face. "God, give me strength. I would do anything at this moment to sit on my fat backside, with a box of Maltesers, and watch that sexy arse of John Travolta in *Grease*, before imagining that I'm Sandy, and he's wanting to play tonsil tennis with me."

Jade scrunched up her eyes, desperate to wipe the image from her mind. Placing two fingers in her mouth, she pretended to gag. "Does this happen to all women in their forties? Suddenly on heat all the time. I think you need a man in your life before you wear out your batteries."

Karen widened her eyes and shook her head in mock offence. "I don't think you know me very well. I'm a lady," she replied, her words sharpening in pronunciation, and her voice rising in pitch with each word that passed the lips. "Not a loose floozy on a grab a granny night at the local disco."

They both burst into laughter, the sound causing a few heads to turn from the incident floor.

A few moments of silence settled between them as they enjoyed the brief light-hearted interlude in what had been a crazy day already.

"How's your sister?" Jade asked, dropping her head to one side, a look of concern chiselled in her features.

Karen went on to tell Jade about the latest turn in her sister's condition and what Doctor Keighley had said. Jade didn't confess to knowing much about an enlarged heart, but could tell from the way Karen was describing it, that it could potentially be a serious condition.

"You must be worried about her…? Sorry, stupid question

really. Of course, you'd be worried about her," Jade added, annoyed with herself.

"I am. I've always known that she is very ill. Her life expectancy was always going to be short, and she's far outlived the doctor's expectations. My parents even agreed to a DNR order in case she ever fell seriously ill one day. Sometimes I don't know if she's got months, or even years, to live. The way I see it, every day that she's still with us is a blessing."

Jade offered a sympathetic smile, knowing how much Karen was hurting.

Karen pushed back her chair and logged off her PC, before tidying up files and gathering her things to leave. "Jade, you get yourself off, and I'm about to head out too. At the moment a long hot shower, a hot meal, and a bit of TV is about as fun as my evening will be."

"Don't knock it," Jade replied, following Karen out into the corridor. "I think that's all I'll be fit for as well."

THE APARTMENT FELT cold as she dropped her handbag in the hallway and flicked on the hall light. "Bollocks, I must have pressed the wrong button on the timer this morning," she cursed, as her shoulders shuddered from the icy chill that clung in the air. "Manky. Where are you?" Karen asked as she kicked off her shoes and flicked on the light in the kitchen. With no sign of her cat, Karen moved into the lounge, to find Manky curled up in his cat bed, oblivious to her calls, and reluctant to move from the warmth of the blankets that surrounded him.

"That's no way to greet your mummy. You pissed off with me? That's it, isn't it? You're pissed off with me because I didn't have your dinner ready for you this evening. Well, I'm sorry," she said, kneeling down to stroke his warm fur. "I got stuck at work, so how about I fix us dinner? For a treat, I've got you chopped liver in the fridge. Peace offering?" Manky opened one eye and purred as Karen smiled and got back to her feet before heading into the kitchen.

After dinner, a long hot soak in the shower, and swaddled in a thick dressing gown, Karen dropped into her sofa and flicked through her list of recorded TV programmes. There were so many she wondered if she'd ever have time to go through them all. Not even a week of sitting there for ten hours a day, every day, would be enough to get through the long list that appeared to be growing by the day. She sipped on a cold glass of white wine. Her body relaxed, the wine doing its job of hitting every tight spot, ache, and sore muscle.

With her body loosening, Karen sunk even deeper into the sofa as she put her head on one cushion before stretching out along the full length. With the TV on in the background, and an old episode of *Marcella* to catch up on, her eyelids began to feel like heavy lead weights. She never got to the end of the episode before sleep took her.

11

Karen stretched her neck from ear-to-ear, feeling the bones crack. She had slept like a log last night but falling asleep on the sofa had done little for her posture this morning, as her neck and shoulders ached.

Wainwright had already begun the post-mortem on Anil Kumar by the time she had arrived. As much as she had wanted to arrive on time, Karen had found it hard to get herself going this morning. Standing in the sterile and cold environment of the examination room, staring at the battered remains of the victim, her head thumped, and her stomach protested as she listened to Wainwright recap for her benefit.

The chest cavity had been opened up, and the skin reflected back. Each organ had been removed, measured and weighed, before its details were noted on a large whiteboard to one side of the room.

"It's not a pretty sight, is it?" Wainwright remarked.

"I've seen worse. At least he's got most of his organs intact. What are your thoughts on the heart?" Karen asked when she noticed the remains of an organ they had discovered yesterday in the kitchen now sitting in a metal tray.

"I'm confident that the heart recovered from the kitchen did belong to Mr Kumar. There's evidence of an extrapleural injury which was caused by damage to the chest wall tissues on the outside of the pleural space. There's also evidence of an intrapleural injury due to damage to the inside of the pleural cavity."

Karen shook her head. "Plain English, please, for those who are not gifted mortals like yourself."

Wainwright lifted an eyebrow as he studied Karen. "There was significant blood loss following a traumatic injury which led to blood being collected in a space between the chest wall and the lungs. There is enough structural damage to the blood vessels supplying the heart to suggest that force was used."

Karen furrowed her brow. "So the heart wasn't cut out?"

"No, Karen. Significant strength was used to *yank* the heart from its chest cavity. It was then left in the food bowl, and the cat had a special treat."

"That's bloody gross," Karen said, pulling a face and baring her teeth.

"Indeed it is, my dear."

"And the cause of death? Was it blood loss? I guess what I'm saying is was the victim alive when his heart was removed?"

"He was already unconscious by the time his heart was

removed. He wouldn't have suffered any further. If you come around to the side, I'll talk you through the damage he sustained towards the back of the head."

Karen joined Wainwright at the top of the table. The skin around the upper part of the cadaver's head had been pulled back over his face, revealing the tangled mess of bone and brain tissue that remained. Karen could hardly call it a head with so much missing. The front of his face had remained intact, but everything from his forehead backwards to the back of his neck had caved in. A metal dish lay on a trolley beside them, and various bloodied bone fragments had been extracted and laid out.

"It doesn't take a genius to see that the victim suffered significant trauma to the back of his head. We extracted many bone fragments from within the brain matter that remained." Wainwright tapped his metal probe on the dish beside them as he moved between the head section and the upper torso, covering his findings to date.

"Did the victim put up much of a fight? Or was he taken by surprise?"

"He certainly tried to defend himself. But the attack was so savage, that the poor old boy had little chance of surviving or defending himself." Wainwright picked up the wrist on one arm of the cadaver and with his metal probe pointed out the defence marks on both the victim's arm and hand. There were similar injuries on the other limb.

The extent of the injuries and the savagery horrified Karen. She listened as Wainwright pointed out further damage and tears in the skin structure around the neck and shoulders. The skin had been separated across the front and top of the shoulder to show more broken bones.

"Could you make out much from these injuries?" Karen asked.

"There were deep wounds inflicted with what appeared to be a heavy object. It resulted in damage to the clavicle and scapula. With the age of the victim, and the fragility of the skeletal system at that age, bone density is lighter and more porous. It's like using the back of a spoon on an eggshell. It just shattered. There is extensive bruising to the skin and subcutaneous layers."

Karen made notes as Wainwright gave her a running commentary. She paused, pen in hand as a thought crossed her mind. "Any ideas on the kind of weapon used?"

"Good point, Karen. Closer examination of the bone surfaces proved inconclusive. We couldn't find any wooden fragments, so my guess is that the instrument was more solid. To cause this kind of damage, probably metal. We examined a lot of the breaks closely, and it suggested small, concentrated areas of impact. We'll need to undertake further detailed analysis of the bone and tissue to see if we can narrow down the weapon for you."

"That would be helpful if you could, Wainwright. A metal object could be anything. A hammer, scaffold bar, or a tyre lever. Anything like that."

Wainwright agreed with her assessment as he continued with the examination for another hour.

THE HOT COFFEE tasted like a golden elixir as it trickled down her throat and warmed her stomach. Wainwright had laid out a plate of Rich Tea biscuits, and the thought of dipping a Rich Tea in coffee had crossed her mind, but it didn't feel right. Instead, she nibbled the biscuit dry, and when her mouth ran out of moisture, she washed down the biscuit remnants with a slurp of coffee.

Wainwright pushed back and forth in his chair as they caught up. It had been a couple of weeks since she had last seen him, and even though they had agreed to catch up for lunch, their schedules had never coincided well enough for them to do that.

Wainwright furrowed his brow. "I notice you're not having many of them," he asked, looking towards the plate of biscuits. "Are you not a fan of Rich Tea?"

"I am, but they don't really go well with coffee, I don't think. Besides, I'm getting fat, and you spoil me every time I come around here."

"Karen, you and fat don't really go in the same sentence. You're perhaps a little softer around the edges..." he teased.

"It's not too late for me to throw my coffee over your lap, you cheeky git. You could give a girl a complex."

"Karen, Il n'y a qu'un bonheur dans la vie, c'est d'aimer et d'être aimé."

Karen sat open-mouthed, unsure of what she'd heard. "Excuse me?"

Wainwright repeated the statement and folded his arms before leaning back in his chair again, with a smug smile on his face.

"Wainwright, you have to understand that I'm thick in comparison to you. You've got a list of qualifications as long as my arm. I can write mine on the back of a postage stamp."

"Well, you'll have to find out what it means, my dear. It's a compliment."

"Yeah, yeah. Brilliant. A compliment. A compliment I don't even bloody understand. I won't even know how to write it out for Google."

Wainwright shrugged. "I'll tell you another time. I don't want you getting big-headed."

Karen fired back a sarcastic smile. She hated it when Wainwright got one over on her, but he had a way with words that often left her tongue-tied.

Wainwright changed the subject. "How's your sister? I know you said yesterday that her condition had worsened a bit?"

Karen tipped her head for a moment, playing with an imaginary thread on her trousers as a vision of Jane flashed through her mind. "She's not good. Jane's stable, and that's the main thing. She's got over worse in the past, and Jane's a battler. I'm hoping that the meds they give her will help to stabilise this enlargement of the heart. To be honest, I'm not a hundred per cent sure of what it really means, nor the long-term implications. I'm grateful that she is being looked after properly."

"I know it must be hard. I see pain, misery and broken bodies every day. I sometimes feel emotionally detached. I guess I have to, as you do to a certain extent in your job. But we're only human. When something happens to a loved one, it can make it so real and raw. It gets you here," Wainwright said, jabbing his chest. "It's only natural to feel concern and confusion."

Karen nodded. "I should be used to it by now. Jane's been in the care home for a long time. And unwell since she was born. She is my sister. And part of me avoided going there for so long, because I didn't know how to handle how I felt. And now I'm just riddled with guilt. I feel like I let my sister down — like I abandoned her because I couldn't deal with how I felt."

Wainwright paused for a moment before continuing. "You didn't let anyone down. You went through a period of chaos and confusion in your mind. You're very good at your job, and that's where you excel. As I said, when there's something closer to our hearts, we feel more vulnerable. There was no right or wrong way of handling how you felt. You did the best you could. More importantly, you are there for her now."

Karen huffed. "Yeah, at a time when her health is deteriorating. What bloody good am I now?"

"You'd be surprised. I've spent all of my working life in the medical field. Just being there with her, holding her hand, or even talking to her makes a difference. Somewhere within her mind she can feel you and hear you. Don't ever forget that. Be there for her."

"You do have a way with your words. You could charm the pants off a corpse. Oops... sorry, bad taste," she said, throwing a hand over her mouth. "Listen, I've got to get back. Thanks for the tea and biscuits."

"My pleasure. Any time. We must do that lunch soon."

Karen threw her handbag over her shoulder and checked

her phone before stuffing it back in her pocket. "We will. Wainwright… thank you," she said, letting her eyes settle in his direction.

"For what?"

Karen smiled. "You know why."

12

A wall of suffocating heat hit Karen the moment she walked into the incident room. Ties were undone, and sleeves were rolled up, whilst a few officers fanned their faces with spare notepads. The thermostat must have been pushed up a few notches by an overzealous member of the maintenance team during the recent cold snap.

"Tell me it's not gonna be like this all morning?" Karen asked, dropping her bags by Jade's desk. "It's like an oven in here. I know it's cold out there, but this is taking the bloody piss," Karen said, blowing out her cheeks as her face reddened.

"It's unbearable. I've already moaned to maintenance. They reckon it's a faulty thermostat on our floor that is causing a problem because they've had no complaints from any other teams."

"Typical. We've kicked off a major investigation, and we're melting. Any idea as to how long it'll be until they fix it?"

Jade shook her head. "The bloke I spoke to on the phone didn't really give much away. I'm not even sure he knew what I was saying. But he said he'd speak to his manager, and hopefully they'd get it fixed in the next couple of hours."

"Terrific."

The team were hitting the phones and sharing information across the desks as Karen settled in. Civilian support officers had begun the task of compiling and recording paperwork, uploading witness statements, and doing background searches on behalf of the detectives. A good team surrounded Karen, and several of the officers drafted in for this investigation were retired detectives who had rejoined the force as civilians in a support capacity. Their knowledge and experience were invaluable to her as the SIO. It meant that they could dig deeper and draw upon years of knowledge and past cases.

"Okay, team, let's have a quick catch-up. For those not on the phone, pull up a chair and let's see how far we've got."

With some of her team out on active enquiries, and others following up leads on the phone, about a dozen officers gathered around Karen, notepads in hand.

"What have we managed to find out so far about Anil Kumar and his wife?" Karen asked, glancing over her shoulder at the whiteboard. More notes had been added as new information came in. The board was filling up fast, which was good in her eyes.

Amari chipped in first, glancing down at his notes. "Anil Kumar, aged sixty-three, came from the York area, and spent most of his life there. He was a retired consultant psychiatrist. He has family in York, an older brother Suresh, aged sixty-eight."

"Any other family?" Karen asked.

"The couple have a son, Rajesh," Amari continued. "He's a surveyor based in Manchester. We are in the process of contacting him. It turns out that Anil retired early to care for his wife and decided to move to London to get support from his family. His wife has a sister down here in Wembley. The sister's name is Leela Panchal."

"Okay, good work. Any joy in contacting the sister?"

Amari shook his head. "Not yet. We are in touch with the social services, as I'm sure they would have had more regular contact with Mr Kumar's family over the care of his wife."

Karen agreed. Building a full victimology was crucial at the start of an investigation to piece together the victim's background as well as key influences, and those who may have wished to harm him. In compiling information on Anil Kumar, Karen's team would build a profile of his work, hobbies, clubs, where he went grocery shopping, his spending habits, medical history, past relationships… everything.

"Anything else?" Karen asked, looking around the room.

Jeff continued from where Amari had finished. "I've been doing a bit of research into any similar cases, especially ones where the victim was bludgeoned in much the same way."

"Anything of interest?" Jade asked, swivelling in her seat to face Jeff.

"I did as a matter of fact, sarge."

"There was a fifty-nine-year-old male victim in Kent who died as a result of severe head injuries seven months ago. The post-mortem discovered that he had at least twenty injuries to his head, including stab and puncture wounds. One stab wound penetrated the brain."

Jade folded her arms. "Yes, but that seems to imply a sharp instrument if you're saying stab and puncture wounds?"

"It does, sarge," Jeff agreed. "But… a specialist forensic pathologist was brought in to conduct a second post-mortem on the victim. They concluded that the injuries were entirely consistent with the use of a crowbar. The injuries were caused by deliberate, thrusting actions with the sharp end of the crowbar in contact with the victim."

"That's good, Jeff," Karen replied. "Our victim didn't appear to have been jabbed with thrusting actions of a crowbar. Having returned from the post-mortem, I couldn't see any stab wounds consistent with using a crowbar. Unless of course the tip was used on the head. Wainwright will be sending the bone fragments away for further analysis. I don't know whether that will give us any clarity, but it's worth a try."

"That's a fair point, boss. The pathologist did say that two of the injuries were possibly caused by the crowbar being used to bludgeon the victim. What if a crowbar was used on our victim?" Jeff asked.

"Then that would work. Let's see what Wainwright comes back with first. Hopefully detailed analysis will help us to narrow down the type of weapon used."

As door-to-door enquiries continued good news flowed in.

Neighbours had said the couple were quiet, friendly and helpful. Officers on the ground had managed to recover CCTV footage from a few surrounding houses, the nearest one being about a hundred yards away. Karen assigned several officers to camp out in the video room and trawl through the footage for anything of interest.

"I want Anil Kumar's life turned inside out. I want to know why someone would not just kill him but do it in the most savage and barbaric way. Being bludgeoned to death is bad enough, but then being sliced open, and his heart ripped out, well… That takes this to a whole new level."

Several nodding heads met her thoughts, as officers took in the information, including photographs from the post-mortem that were being handed out by a civilian member of staff. A few tuts and expletives echoed around the room as the full magnitude of the attack came to life in the pictures. Karen took a set and pinned them to the incident board.

"What do you think the motive was, boss?" Craig asked.

Karen paced up and down in front of them, her head bowed as she rummaged through her thoughts. Her team watched her every step, ready to hang on the next few words that tripped from her lips.

"We've got so many potential motives. It could be revenge, but as yet we don't know why. It could also be a disgruntled former patient, especially if he'd been working with lots of unstable patients, or even a member of his family."

"He could have been the victim of a random psycho…" Jade speculated.

Karen rolled her eyes. "That's the last kind of perp we need. A random psycho, a stranger, they're all the same thing. That could make it almost impossible for us to find him. And then we have to consider if there have been other victims? Or is this the beginning?"

The team was working hard. She needed to prove a point with a good result, and this was her opportunity to get her DCI job back. Many of the things that were holding her back seemed inconsequential now. The Connells as a major crime group were depleted. Steve Connell, one of the brothers, had died in a firefight with police. His brother, Terry, had been seriously injured in the same altercation after being shot in the chest when charging at officers with a club hammer. Thankfully, he was on remand awaiting trial.

Karen knew and accepted that there would be repercussions, but a large part of her felt relieved. She'd finally got to the bottom of the hijacking, and in the process uncovered a corrupt senior officer, providing the breakthrough that resulted in the collapse of the Connells. Her nemesis, Sally Connell, was still at large. Intelligence suggested she had slipped out of the country and was being protected by associates in the Sierra Nevada hills of the Andalusia region.

That wasn't her problem now. The NCA were leading the investigation into tracking down Sally Connell, but Karen hoped that Sally would be brought to justice one way or another, dead or alive.

13

The smell of a warm jacket potato with chilli con carne stirred her senses, and teased her stomach as it grumbled in protest. Like so many officers in the job, sticking to regular mealtimes was only something she managed to do on her days off. In Karen's experience, it wasn't uncommon to go for most of the day without even thinking about food, or having the free time to grab anything.

"This smells so good," Karen cooed, her eyes widening in delight at the prospect of a proper meal.

Jade had opted for the same as they settled into a quiet corner of the office canteen. With lunchtime having come and gone, there were a few officers mingling around, taking the opportunity for a quick cuppa and a biscuit away from the hubbub of a noisy office. The place was never fully empty, and there would always be a slow trickle of people coming and going.

Karen savoured the first few mouthfuls, the warmth of the

potato, and the spice of the chilli teasing her to eat faster. Having only had a slice of toast and coffee this morning before the post-mortem, and just a few biscuits with Wainwright, Karen's body flagged. Karen had promised dozens of times to take better care of herself, but something always got in the way. One of the promises had been to drink more water because she had read somewhere that consuming two litres of water a day was great for her digestion, skin, fatigue, and overall fitness. Great in principle, but the reality was she'd probably end up going to the loo every thirty minutes, and in her job there was really no guarantee of where she would be hour to hour.

"Definitely," Jade agreed, as hot steam rose from her plate. "I can't remember the last time I had a jacket potato."

"Are you serious? I thought that was a staple in everyone's grocery cupboard?"

"Not in mine," Jade protested with a shake of the head.

Karen laughed. "Oh, I forgot. You're a posh family. You probably grew up being told that jacket potatoes were for the working class!"

Jade rolled her eyes. "As if. My parents are successful, but we're not that stuck-up, or at least I'm not. Mum always made sure we had home-cooked meals and we'd prefer them to grabbing a takeaway. It was only when I was at uni that the great British jacket potato figured prominently in my diet."

Karen noticed Jade shoving in large mouthfuls as if she hadn't eaten for a month. Karen had only finished half of hers, but Jade was almost finishing the last few scraps on her plate. "You seem to be eating more than normal recently? Are you exercising more? Or trying to put on weight?"

"No, nothing like that. Like you, I didn't have much in the way of breakfast. I'm famished."

"Yeah, pull the other leg. Don't think I've not noticed the biscuits on your desk, and the triple pack of sandwiches that you often buy, with a yoghurt, a piece of fruit, a bag of crisps, and a bar of chocolate. And then you're bloody hungry again three hours later. You're not…"

Jade paused, her fork heavily laden with potato and chilli hovering in the air. "What?"

Karen leant in and whispered. "You're not pregnant, are you?"

Jade recoiled, as if Karen had hit her squarely in the face with a sucker punch. Her mouth hung open in a mixture of surprise and consternation before she narrowed her eyes. "Oh my God, Karen, are you for real? No. I'm not pregnant. How on earth does your mind work?"

Karen's shoulders shook as she contained a laugh. "You never know. It sounds plausible, doesn't it?"

"Karen, you have such a warped mind! I'd have to be *doing it* for starters, and secondly, I'd need a boyfriend to help me out with his part."

"You're so easy to wind up, Jade." Karen smiled before returning to her food.

Jade had long finished by the time Karen scraped the last remains of her plate. "Have we had any further updates on Kumar's wife?"

"We've spoken to her sister, Leela. Aruna is under the care

of the local social services team. They did an occupational therapy visit some time ago, and as a result of their visit, things like the commode, stair rails, handles around the bath and toilet were installed. She was also getting one visit a week, but that was being reviewed on a monthly basis."

Karen toyed with her napkin. "That goes a long way to confirming the presence of the medication, and assistance aids. I feel sorry for the woman. She really wasn't making much sense in the back of the ambulance."

Jade nodded, sharing the same degree of sympathy for her. "She is being cared for by Leela's family since being released from hospital."

"I think we should go and see her. Even just a few words from her might help us to build a better picture of what happened. At the moment we don't even know what IC code of perp we're dealing with. Even a steer in that direction would help."

14

After their late lunch, Jade drove them towards Wembley, passing the impressive Wembley Stadium, the largest sports venue in the UK, and the second largest in Europe. As Jade weaved in and out of traffic, Karen glanced out of her passenger window to admire the magnificent structure, and the hugely recognisable steel arch that rose more than a hundred metres above its roof. Though she hadn't tested the suggestion, it was believed that you could see the arch from every elevated position in London.

The backstreets were busy and narrow. Many roads were double-parked, with random spaces to pull in to allow for oncoming traffic. Houses were densely packed, many built before and after the Second World War when London went through a period of extensive reconstruction.

Once they had found the location, Jade pulled up further down the road, and they walked back towards the address.

Karen knocked on the door and waited a few moments.

Through the frosted glass panels in the door, she saw the silhouette of a figure make their way up the hallway. Soon after a woman pressed herself against the glass door, her eyes darting left and right, viewing the visitors with a hint of suspicion.

"Are you sure you told her that we were coming?" Karen whispered from the corner of her mouth.

"Yep," Jade replied in an equally hushed tone.

The door opened ever so slightly, and the face of a middle-aged Asian woman filled the gap.

"Leela Panchal?"

The woman nodded. "Yes, that's me. Are you the police?" she asked softly.

Karen held up her warrant card. "I'm Detective Inspector Karen Heath, and this is Detective Sergeant Jade Whiting. May we come in?"

Leela nodded. She opened the door and guided them through to the lounge.

Karen saw Aruna sat in an armchair, her hands trembling and eyes wide open in fear.

"Please, take a seat," Leela offered, before settling herself on a dining room chair beside Aruna, and taking her hand.

"Thank you for seeing us," Karen began. "We are so sorry for the loss that your family has experienced. We've arranged for a family liaison officer to be with you in the next few hours. They'll be able to answer any questions about our investigation, as well as give you any support or advice that you need."

Leela nodded and pursed her lips into a smile.

Karen took a quick moment to glance around the room. It was a small lounge with oversized furniture, which made the room appear compact. The sofas were grey velour, deep and soft, which had both Karen and Jade sinking so deep into them that Karen wondered how they could gracefully pull themselves out when the time came to leave. Family photographs lined the narrow shelf above an empty fireplace, and an excessively large television was positioned in one corner of the room. On the coffee table Karen noticed that the remote controls were still wrapped in their protective plastic bags from new. The theme continued with a clear plastic sheet draped across the coffee table, to no doubt catch spillages.

Strangely, it wasn't until Karen was sitting in the lounge that she realised there had been a plastic hallway runner to protect the carpet from wear and tear. Come to think of it, she'd often noticed the same feature in many Asian homes she had visited over her time in the East End of London. The need to keep everything protected and pristine. On the wall behind Leela hung a large, framed photograph with religious connotations. Again, she had seen this in many Asian households, and had since learnt they were images of the gods they worshipped.

"How is Aruna?" Karen asked.

Leela glanced across at her sister and rubbed the back of the woman's hand. "In a way, she is no different. The dementia has robbed my sister of her awareness. Most of the time she doesn't know what's going on around her. Maybe she can make sense of things, but can't say them."

Karen watched as Aruna glanced around the room. Her lips

mumbled incoherently, words so soft they were barely audible. Karen wasn't sure Aruna had noticed them enter, because she'd glance in Karen's direction, and then look straight through her.

"Has Aruna said anything about what happened?"

Leela shook her head. "I've asked her, but she's not making sense."

"Do you mind if I ask her a few questions?" Karen asked.

"Sure."

Karen nudged her backside towards the front of the sofa, looking uncomfortably in Jade's direction, before pushing herself off the edge. Karen moved across the lounge and settled on her knees in front of Aruna. This was the closest she had been to the woman and could see the delicate crow lines around her eyes. For a woman of her age, her skin was still relatively flawless, and she had aged well.

"Aruna, I'm Karen. Can you remember anything about what happened in the last few days?"

Karen waited for a few moments, Aruna's eyes still darting around the lounge. Leela tapped her sister's shoulder and pointed in Karen's direction. Aruna first looked at her sister, before turning to stare in Karen's direction. Aruna studied Karen intently, as if trying to recall where she'd seen that face.

Karen continued, "Aruna, do you remember someone coming into your house?"

There was a lengthy pause, and then nothing. Karen repeated the question. Still nothing. Aruna continued to examine the person kneeling, her lips shaping some words in silence.

Even one word or observation from Aruna could help their investigation. As Karen was about to give up, Aruna muttered a few words.

"Rajesh. My Rajesh came."

Karen glanced across at Leela, who shook her head. She was certain that Aruna hadn't seen Rajesh, after initial investigations confirmed he was in Manchester at the time of his father's death.

Karen continued to play with that theme. "I know Rajesh came. Did he say anything to you?"

"Rajesh came. He was going to stay for dinner. He is my son."

Karen turned towards Jade and pointed at a framed photograph above the fireplace of Rajesh standing with his extended family. Jade energetically thrust herself forward from the sofa and grabbed the photograph.

"Aruna, it's really important. Did he look the same?" Karen asked, pointing towards Rajesh. "Is this Rajesh who came?"

Aruna's face lit up as she pointed at the picture. "This is Rajesh. He's my friend. Are you Rajesh?"

Karen let out a deep sigh as she dropped back on her heels. Any hopes of getting the smallest of leads faded in front of her eyes. This was her first experience of dealing with someone with dementia and realised how hard it must be for family and care staff to get through to sufferers of this disease. She turned towards Leela. "Do you have any ideas as to who might have wanted to hurt Anil? We are really keen to build a detailed picture of his life, his connections, and whether he had been in any sort of trouble."

Leela shook her head. "Anil is... was always a very hard-working man. Very professional, and helpful. He didn't have a bad bone in his body. He never hurt anyone. He never said anything bad. We don't understand."

"Is Aruna always like this?"

Leela shook her head. "Not always. She does have moments of remembering things clearly. But those moments are becoming fewer as the months pass."

Jade's phone blipped, and she excused herself from the room as Karen continued.

Karen nodded. She reached out and rubbed her hand reassuringly over Aruna's knee. "Has she said anything at all about the event? Who she saw? What happened? Anything?"

"Not really. All she keeps saying is that Rajesh came, and when is he coming back again?"

Karen hoped that *Rajesh* wouldn't be returning, for Aruna's sake.

Jade stood in the doorway waving her phone to catch Karen's attention.

"Leela, we have to go now. If Aruna says anything that may be of interest, can you make sure that you let the family liaison officer know? Even the smallest of details could prove significant. We'll see ourselves out. Thank you for your time."

15

"There's a lot of history here," Jade said as she stared down the tree-lined street that snaked off into the distance.

They stopped to admire one of the most famous streets in London, Harley Street. The north end of the street remained almost entirely Georgian in character, its narrow, elegant town houses blessed with beautiful detailing: cast-iron balconies, arched doorways, vast first-floor windows. More flamboyant Victorian and Edwardian styles dotted the southern half, with each of the town houses spread across five floors. With the buildings reaching towards the sky, the road had an effect of cocooning you.

"It's certainly impressive. Can you imagine the amount of money being made behind these doors?" Karen wondered.

Shortly before leaving Leela's house, Jade had received an update from the office to confirm that Anil Kumar last worked in partnership as a private consultant psychiatrist, and Karen felt it was necessary to visit his ex-partner as they continued to build a picture of their victim.

Jade seemed in her element soaking up the splendour and grandeur of the architecture and its history. With more than five thousand specialists working in the area, Harley Street was the Mecca for private medical practice.

"Do you know that Florence Nightingale once lived here, as did Sir Joseph Lister, the pioneer of antiseptic medicine?" Jade recalled. "I can't remember his name, but there was also a renowned doctor here who treated Joseph Merrick, the elephant man. Can you believe how much history is here? We are walking in the footsteps of great people."

"I can. But seriously, are you a walking encyclopaedia?"

"I love this stuff, Karen. My parents paid a lot of money to get me educated, with private tutors and all sorts. This place has history." Jade smiled, pointing down the street.

"When I think of Harley Street, dodgy boob jobs, gastric band surgery, and nose jobs spring to mind, costing a fortune."

Jade shook her head. "Do you have to be so negative?"

"No, I'm being a realist."

"Karen, I'm sure that those things do take place here, and that a few unethical medical professionals take the piss, but just as many well-qualified, and experienced specialists treat thousands of people for every condition under the sun."

They both argued their side as they stepped through the

door, the sheer opulence of the interior stopped them in mid-flow.

"Jesus, this is bloody posh," Karen said, as her feet sunk into the rich, deep pile carpet that lined the hallway. "I haven't even got carpet like this in my bedroom."

Jade followed Karen into the first reception area and confirmed they were here to meet Doctor Laurence Humphreys. The receptionist behind the large oak desk topped in deep, rich red leather smiled politely, and guided them towards the first floor, before pausing at a door to their immediate right. A brass nameplate carried the inscription "Doctor Laurence Humphreys, Consultant Psychiatrist". The receptionist knocked and waited a few moments before Humphreys invited them to enter.

Humphreys was a short man, slightly rotund, with short brown receding hair. His half-rimmed glasses sat low on his nose in a way that reminded Karen of an academic professor, with a well-trimmed, silver goatee beard, and a warm smile.

"Doctor Humphreys, I'm Detective Inspector Karen Heath, and this is my colleague Detective Sergeant Jade Whiting. Thank you so much for taking the time to see us."

He gestured towards the empty chairs. "It's my pleasure, please take a seat."

Karen was surprised at his soft and gentle tone which was almost lost in his cavernous room. His desk sat in the middle, with two chairs opposite. More books than Karen had ever seen lined one wall, and she wondered if he'd ever read all of them. Another wall held an impressive display of framed certificates. The room was modestly decorated, but she admired the deep, red velvet curtains that hung from floor to ceiling either side of the window.

"How can I help you?" Humphreys asked, settling back in his chair. "Can I get you refreshments?"

Karen declined the offer as Jade got out her pad and pen.

"I understand my officers contacted you about Doctor Anil Kumar, an ex-partner of yours?"

Humphreys momentarily stared at his desk, before interlocking his fingers and resting them on his belly. His warm smile melted, replaced with a look of sorrow. "Yes. I was devastated when your officer broke the news. Utterly devastated. I can't believe anyone would do such a thing. He was a good man."

"Can you tell me a bit about what you do?"

"Where do I start?" he began, his smile returning. "I have over thirty years of medical experience and have practised general adult psychiatry at consultant level within the NHS and privately for the last twenty years."

"And what type of cases would both Doctor Kumar and you have worked on?"

"We never got involved in couples or family work, since we preferred to work with individuals. But we generally worked around personality disorders. Things like schizophrenia, bipolar, OCD, and so on."

Karen's mind was working faster than her words would form. "Would any of those kinds of individuals have been dangerous enough to have attacked him? Especially if they weren't in complete control of their thoughts?"

Humphreys grimaced. "It's possible. Generally, we work

within the remit of Section 12 of the Mental Health Act 1983. And everyone we work with has a care plan in place already, and if necessary, an appropriate level of medication to control their behaviour."

"So, it's within the realm of possibility that someone who had either forgotten to take their medication, or had even stopped taking it all together, could become unstable?" Karen questioned.

"Absolutely. Although, that would be rare. The care plans in place are tightly monitored, because individuals can pose a threat to themselves as well as society."

"That sounds like dangerous work at times, doctor?"

"It can be. Sometimes we are dealing with highly unstable people."

"Can you think of anyone that Doctor Kumar may have worked with who could have posed a threat to him?"

Humphreys stared up towards the ceiling, his mind sifting through the hundreds of cases that they'd dealt with. "Nothing springs to mind at the moment. We are often called to be expert witnesses in criminal law cases, and we've had the odd threat from those who haven't welcomed our assessment of them. But that goes with the territory."

"Can you think of any particularly contentious court cases?"

Humphreys shook his head. "I can certainly get my secretary to have a look over cases that Doctor Kumar was involved with? If that's of any help to you?"

Karen thought that would be a good idea and agreed.

Karen asked a few more questions before thanking Doctor Humphreys for his time.

KAREN WAS BACK in the office by early evening and reviewing notes made during their meetings. The motive for Anil Kumar's death was still unknown, and visits to his family and work yielded little. No one had a bad thing to say about the victim, and yet he'd suffered a demented and savage attack with little chance of defending himself. The post-mortem of Kumar's battered remains haunted Karen.

Her body slumped as sorrow washed over her. The poor man had been doing right by his family and cared for his wife despite his esteemed professional career being cut short by his wife's illness, and yet his life had been snuffed out in minutes. The real prospect of it being a stranger played heavily on Karen's mind. But the question still remained, *why him?*

Nothing made sense, and though in many cases, it never did to begin with. Karen desperately wanted to push the case forward.

One lingering thought did remain, and it was something that Humphreys mentioned during their meeting earlier. What if the perpetrator was someone who Doctor Kumar conducted a psychiatric evaluation on, and due to their instability, tracked down Kumar and attacked him? But she was back at square one again. Why?

"Karen."

Karen jumped in her seat, so engrossed in her thoughts that

she hadn't noticed Mason stick his head around the door. "Fuck, you gave me a fright."

Mason laughed. "I have that effect on women. If you think I'm ugly now, you wait until after midnight. Give me a full moon and I prowl the streets like a hairy werewolf, looking for my next victim."

"Funny you should say that because that's exactly what I heard from your last girlfriend."

Mason splayed out a hand on his chest. "Ouch, that hurt." He dropped into a chair opposite her. "You doing a late one?"

"Not intentionally. I'm desperate to get traction on this case, and I hate it when I don't know the motive. The forensic team are a pile of shite here…" Karen fumed in mock disgust.

"Double ouch. You've really got it in for me today. That tongue of yours is sharp."

"Exactly, don't mess with Boss Bitch." Karen laughed as she threw her pen at him.

"Well, hopefully I can get back on your Christmas card list. We managed to recover one full and one partial footprint from the scene. Find us the trainer, we'll match up the print."

"What size?"

"We are looking at approximately a size nine, Karen."

"Great."

"Not so great, Karen. Size nine is a very common size in

the UK. Forty per cent of men's shoe sizes in the UK are either size eight, eight and a half, or nine."

Karen rolled her eyes. "What about the method of entry? Anything there?"

"A blunt instrument for sure. The gouge marks are about an inch wide. They're too big for a screwdriver, so it has to be something like a tyre lever, or a crowbar. But we are still running tests." Mason stood up and yawned. "Right, I'm off. I suggest you get home soon, because you look like you need some beauty sleep. Mind you, I'm not sure that would help."

"Oi, you cheeky fucker," Karen shouted as she grabbed another pen from her desk and threw it, hitting Mason in the back as he legged it from her office.

She smiled to herself after Mason left. He was a good bloke in her eyes, and it was nice that they could wind each other up. Karen was excited by the footprint recovered and the ongoing investigation into the tool that was used. She knew all tools carried imperfections, patterns and marks, often left during the manufacturing process and unseen by the naked eye. Each embedded mark or pattern was unique, and forensic teams were able to investigate the "story" that lay behind the simple act of forcing the door through unique markings. These marks acted as individual and original signatures at all crime scenes.

The footprint analysis would be just as enlightening. She already knew that they were looking for someone who wore a size nine trainer, and that was a good start. She now needed to find the man wearing them.

16

"Due to a passenger being taken ill at Bethnal Green, control has asked all trains to stay in stations."

Karen rolled her eyes as she sat listening to this announcement. It was a Saturday morning, and passenger traffic on the Tube was light. The Central line train that she was on was being held at Leytonstone Tube station. It didn't happen often, but when it did, it was frustrating. Sometimes it could be over in a few minutes, and the service would resume, other times, when a passenger had been taken under a train, the service would be out of action for hours. Karen had been stuck in a situation once before when her train was held at Chancery Lane, and with no other connecting services, she had been stuck there for over two hours.

Karen prayed that this wouldn't be the case today, especially after receiving a text from Brad who was on the early shift. He said there had been developments, and with excitement, Karen had scrambled to get dressed and into work.

"Come on. I haven't got all day," she whispered under her breath, tapping her foot furiously on the floor. Her impatience grew, and the longer they were held, the harder she tapped.

A middle-aged woman sitting opposite glanced over her magazine, and raised a brow, clearly showing her displeasure at the noise.

Karen returned a steely glare and began to tap both feet to annoy the woman further. *If you think staring at me is going to stop me, you're sadly mistaken. Perhaps you should focus more on that big, fat hairy mole on your chin.*

Following the tense stand-off, Karen sighed when the driver came back over the PA system.

"We've been given permission to proceed. The journey may be slow, so bear with me."

Karen offered the woman a patronising smile before she looked away and plugged her earbuds in to listen to music.

"Brad, what have we got?" Karen shouted from across the incident floor, as she barged through the double doors and made a beeline for his desk. Throwing her bag on the floor, she unbuttoned her coat.

Brad spun in his chair taken by surprise at the speed with which Karen closed the gap between them. He swallowed hard as he grabbed his notepad. "Boss, the team have been going through CCTV footage of the local area and they picked up a white Ford Focus that cruised by in both directions on the victim's road."

"And why is it suspicious?" Karen asked as she pulled up a spare chair and sat herself next to Brad.

"It appears the same vehicle had been up and down that road on eleven separate occasions in the seven days before the murder. And on the day in question, that same car was seen on footage three times in the two hours prior to the call being made."

Brad pulled up the CCTV footage on his computer and replayed it for Karen's benefit. Karen rested her elbows on Brad's desk and leant in to get a better look.

"It looks newish, but I can't see the plates. Have you got any better angles?"

"I'm afraid not, boss. We've still more footage to go through. We may get lucky with another angle."

Karen chewed on her bottom lip as she reran the footage and watched it again. "I can't even tell if it's a male or female driving. There's too much glare."

"I know, boss. I zoomed in to see if I could get a better look. I even played around with the colour, brightness and contrast, but none of that helped."

"Good idea, Brad. I think we need to extend our search for CCTV footage to nearby streets. The car would have had to have entered from an adjoining road. I know it's more work, but can you oversee that?"

"Sure, no problems, boss."

"Also, can you run these current images through the high-tech team, and see if they can enhance them?"

"I will do, any particular ones that you want…" Brad was interrupted by another officer who pushed back his chair and made his way towards them.

"Guv, we've been doing searches in the London area for similar crimes. We found one about six months ago. It was dealt with by another MIT in south London."

Karen sat bolt upright, all ears now.

The officer placed down an image of a man. "Darren Crabtree, aged fifty-three. He was arrested and charged with the murder of a woman, his ex-partner Silvana Bordon. She was an Italian national who started a new relationship with someone else after they split up. It was a frenzied attack on her, where she was stabbed over thirty-five times and then Crabtree cut her and pulled her innards out."

"How long did he get put away for?" Karen asked.

"Twenty-one years, boss, but there's an interesting twist in this. Apparently, he was assisted by someone else, and that person was never found."

"Okay, good work. Pull up the case file and check it out."

"There's something else. I decided to extend the search to beyond five years in London, but I didn't find anything. However, I did put in a request for a nationwide search and found a recent case of a victim being attacked. They were bludgeoned to death with a blunt instrument and had their heart cut out."

That piece of information piqued Karen's interest. "Go on. I'm all ears."

"Eight weeks ago in York, a male nurse returning home from his shift was attacked in an isolated spot. His body was found in overgrown bushes and trees beside the road. From what I've read so far, it was pretty savage. He was attacked from behind with a blunt instrument and suffered significant head trauma, before being dragged into bushes, and mutilated. His heart was cut out. Sound familiar?"

"Get me the SIO from the York case on the phone, I'll be in my office," Karen said with a sense of urgency, as she grabbed her bag and coat, and raced back.

17

Karen had settled into her chair when Jade came through the door and sat down opposite her. "No joy with the SIO in York, Karen. He's in a meeting at the moment, so we've left him a message to call you directly, if that's okay?"

"Yep, the sooner the better. It will be great if I could have a chat with him before lunchtime today."

"Do you think it's a coincidence?"

"I'm not sure to be honest. The M.O. is too similar for us to ignore. I know it's over two hundred miles away, but two cases in two different parts of the country a few months apart makes me think it's worth following up on, don't you think?"

Jade nodded in agreement as she rolled her tongue. "It's not often that you hear about such a brutal killing. Yes, we get people being sliced up, attacked with machetes, and large kitchen knives, but the exacting nature of these cases, and the fact that in both instances the heart has been removed, makes you wonder."

"Exactly," Karen replied. "Do you remember that case that Hertfordshire officers dealt with in Waltham Cross, where a person was attacked by a man wielding a samurai sword, and had disembowelled his victim?"

Jade's eyes widened as she jabbed a finger in Karen's direction. "I do. I do remember that. I'm sure it was racially motivated or something. But the bloke only got nine years, didn't he? Nine years for taking a life," Jade said, shaking her head in disgust.

Karen was about to speak when the screen on her phone flashed. Her breath caught in her throat, and her heart thumped in her chest.

The Broomfield Residential Care Home. Shit.

Karen grabbed the phone and hit the green button. "Karen here."

"Karen, it's Robyn. Your sister, Jane has taken a bit of a turn for the worst, and she's not responding well to the medication. We could do with you being here so that we can discuss the next course of action with Doctor Keighley. I know you're busy, but could you get over here?"

"I'm on my way," Karen replied hesitantly, before pushing back her chair and grabbing her handbag. "Jade, I'm really sorry, but I'll have to dash off. My sister isn't well."

"Oh my God, Karen. What's happened?" Jade asked, concern etched on her face as her eyes widened.

Karen threw on her coat before turning to Jade. "Jane's been suffering with an enlarged heart for a few days. The doctor at the care home has been treating her, but it looks like she's not responding as well as they'd hoped. And they need me there now to talk about the options available to them."

Jade threw a hand over her mouth, understanding what Karen had said. She wanted to offer words of support and sympathy but didn't know what to say. "Listen, you get off there. Leave everything to me. If the SIO from York calls, I'll speak to him and feedback to you later. Just get yourself off there now." Jade ushered Karen out of the door, and walked with her to the lift before saying goodbye with a hug.

KAREN'S MIND was in turmoil as she made the journey over to the care home. A dozen "what if's" rolled through her mind. *What if she won't get better? What if the doctors can't help? What if I can't help?* Though the journey wouldn't take long, it felt like an eternity, and every minute that she was away from the care home added another minute of anxiety.

When she finally arrived, she pushed through the doors in a hurry. The familiar swoosh as the doors glided across the carpet were lost on her, as her eyes scanned the corridor for Nurse Robyn Allen. With no sign of Robyn in her office, Karen made her way towards Jane's room. As she neared, she caught a glimpse of Kevin Fenn towards the far end of the corridor. His familiar smile faded as he walked towards her, noticing the look of concern in her eyes.

"Karen. It seems like ages since I last saw you. Are you okay?" he asked, placing a supporting hand on her arm.

"Yes. Yes, I'm fine."

"Karen, come on. What's the matter?"

Karen sighed as her shoulders sagged. With reluctance, she opened up. "It's Jane. She's taken a turn and has an underlying health issue that's of concern to the doctors. I wish I could stop and talk, but my mind is all over the place, and I need to see Jane."

"Of course, of course," Kevin reassured her, taking a step back to give her space.

Karen dropped her head to one side. "I really appreciate it. It feels like ages since I last saw you, too. We could do with a catch-up over a coffee, but today is not the right time, sadly. I'm really sorry."

Kevin waved his hand in front of him. "Don't be silly. You can be with your sister. We can catch up later."

With that, Karen offered a small smile before dashing off. She pushed through the doors of Jane's bedroom, to find Doctor Keighley, Nurse Allen, and another nurse that she hadn't met, standing around Jane's bed in deep discussion. They paused when Karen entered, and her face reddened with heat as she felt a little embarrassed at interrupting them.

"Karen, thank you for getting here so quickly," Robyn said, walking towards her and offering a welcoming hug.

Karen put her bag down on the chair and joined them beside Jane. She reached out and placed her hand on Jane's. Her sister's fingers felt bony and cold, which saddened her. "How is she?" she asked, looking towards the doctor.

"She's struggling a little, Karen. She responded well to the medication we put her on to begin with. But its effects seem to be wearing off quicker than we anticipated, and we've noticed the slight worsening in her condition. Even though we are capable of treating her, I do believe it would be in her best interests if she was admitted into hospital for further assessments."

Karen remained paralysed to the spot. "Is it that bad?"

"At the moment, it's not bad. But we do need a more detailed assessment by those who are specialised. I'm not a cardiologist, so my knowledge of her condition is limited. It would be best for her, and that's our main priority."

Karen's eyes widened. One minute Jane had been fine and stable, the next they were talking about admitting her to hospital.

"I am... um... fine with that. If you think that's the right thing for her?"

"I do, Karen," Doctor Keighley replied.

"When do you think you'll be admitting her?" Karen asked, a part of her not wanting to know the answer.

"At once. We wanted to wait until you arrived before we arranged for an ambulance."

"Can I go with her?"

Doctor Keighley moved around to join Karen by her side. There was care and warmth in his eyes as he looked at Karen. "Of course, you can. I think Jane would like that."

HAVING GONE with Jane in the ambulance, Karen sat in the

waiting area, whilst doctors began their examination. It was a tense and nervous wait, the not knowing getting to her. As much as she wanted to be in there, holding Jane's hand, offering her words of support, she felt powerless sitting in an uncomfortable plastic chair that had seen better days. Though she wanted to stand in the cubicle, she knew she would get in the way of the doctors whilst they conducted their tests. Bloods had been taken, and results were due back soon. Her sister had been wired up to an ECG, and an ultrasound scan conducted on her heart.

Karen tapped her feet furiously as her fingers drummed out a random noise on the armrest. She glanced at her watch. It had been an hour since they'd arrived, though in her mind it had felt more like three. The second half-finished cup of coffee sat beside her. If the coffee machines in the office were bad, the ones at the hospital should have come with a government health warning. The coffee was thick, the taste acrid, and the residue at the bottom unpleasant to look at. Often when she was nervous, she would eat to occupy herself. The empty wrappers by her side confirmed that.

A further hour passed before doctors came to find her and take her to Jane's bedside. A young doctor in scrubs, who Karen thought didn't look a day over twenty-five, flicked through notes before greeting Karen.

"I'm Doctor Appleby, and we've completed the first round of tests on your sister."

Karen remained silent, desperate for news whilst Appleby glanced at the test results.

Karen wanted to reach over and grab him by his top and shake him for answers.

"Following the first round of tests, we believe that your

sister has polycythaemia, also known as erythrocytosis, which means that your sister has a high concentration of red blood cells in her blood. This makes the blood thicker and less able to travel through blood vessels and organs, and as a result your sister's heart has had to work harder. We believe that has contributed to the enlargement of her heart."

Karen processed every single word that Appleby spoke. In part, it made sense, but it left her more confused. She shook her head. "How? I mean these things don't just happen, do they?"

"Unfortunately, not everyone with this condition has symptoms, but many do. Because of your sister's underlying condition, the symptoms may have gone unnoticed."

"Such as?" Karen asked.

"Headaches, blurred vision, tiredness, dizziness, itchy skin, digestive problems. It's quite an extensive list. But one of the symptoms the care home picked up on and wanted examined closer was the high blood pressure, a symptom present with this condition."

Worry overwhelmed Karen as her stomach turned. Her sister lay there, and she felt helpless to do anything about it. She wanted to wrap her sister in her arms, and take away her pain, but she knew that wasn't possible. Karen turned towards Appleby again. "Are there serious risks?"

Appleby nodded. "It can cause blood clots, which can lead to other complications, like pulmonary embolisms or DVT. Both of those would be incredibly difficult for your sister. An embolism would involve a blockage in the blood vessel that carries blood from her heart to her lungs. Because your sister is bedridden, there's a greater risk of DVT, and a blockage forming in the blood vessels in her leg. If such a blockage became dislodged and worked its way to her heart…" Appleby trailed off.

Karen didn't need him to spell it out as she bowed her head. "What happens next?"

"We'll be admitting her and beginning her treatment straightaway. The easiest and quickest way is to remove some of her blood, so that it reduces the overall number of red cells in her system. As a secondary measure, we'll be placing her on medication that will slow down the production of red blood cells, as well as administering a low dose of aspirin to prevent blood clots."

"And then what?" Karen said hesitantly.

Appleby smiled. "Let's take it one step at a time. Even though her condition changed at the care home, she's stable. Other than a few bedsores, Jane's comfortable, and we expect her to stay that way."

"Do you mind if I wait around until she's admitted to a ward?"

Appleby nodded. "Of course, no problem. But with most hospitals, there's a shortage of beds. We might have a little bit of a wait until a bed becomes available."

Karen returned to the waiting area and pulled out her phone. Jade had sent a text telling her that she was holding the fort, and everything was fine, whilst also asking how Jane was.

Karen pressed the redial button, and as Jade answered at the other end, a wave of emotion washed over Karen as she began to cry.

18

From somewhere to Karen's left, loud snaps ring out, which sound like firecrackers. Her heart races in her chest, pounding, banging, trying to escape. She pushes away from Skelton as he staggers and screams. His eyes twist with rage and surprise. His hands, curled like claws, reach out for her. Her limbs move on their own, but she fumbles and tries to steady herself. Everything is disconnected.

Karen falls to her knees, all the whilst gasping and trying to force air back into her winded lungs.

No, it can't be true. Skelton is still coming towards her. He's about to take her down into his dark world, never to return.

Karen woke with a jump as her body twitched in the chair. For a moment she couldn't move, her body paralysed. Her breath came hard and fast, and a fine mist of perspiration coated her face. She squinted as bright lights in the ceiling drilled into her eyeballs. As everything came back into view, her eyes darted from left to right. For a moment she wondered where she was. Karen craned her head around before realising she was in hospital and had fallen asleep in the chair.

Every muscle in her body ached. She felt sore and stiff, with a gnawing pain that chewed into her shoulders and neck. Karen let out a breath in relief, realising it had been a dream. Her pulse raced in her neck as she took a few more deep breaths to calm herself. Blinking hard, she cleared her throat before groaning. Karen glanced at her watch and realised she had been asleep for three hours already.

Thankfully, the visitors' lounge was empty, so she hadn't looked like a tit when she'd jumped in her chair. Karen stretched and released the tension in her locked spine. Somewhere within her back, bones cracked. The long table beside her and two handwritten notes drew her attention. One was from the nurses who'd left details of where her sister had been moved to, including the ward. The second note surprised her even further. She read it twice, before glancing around, and then back at the table where a packet of biscuits and a bottle of water had been left for her.

Karen read the note again. It was from Kevin Fenn.

Hi Karen,

I was worried about you, and your sister, so I popped in to see you. You looked tired. I didn't want to wake you. I didn't know what else to get you, and to be honest the vending machines looked crap, but the biscuits and water are for you when you wake up. Hope you're okay.

Kevin

Karen smiled and then felt a flush of embarrassment at the thought Kevin had seen her slumped like a drunk in the chair with drool probably running from the side of her mouth.

A chill rushed through her as she stood. Karen waited for the light-headedness to subside before she went in search of the nurses for an update. In the middle of the night, the unit was quiet, nurses were checking on patients and the lights were low, which only added to Karen's tiredness.

A lone nurse sat at the nurses' station, completing paperwork on the computer. She looked up as Karen approached, surprise and confusion on her face at the late-night visitor.

"Hi, can I help?" the nurse asked, a welcoming smile on her face.

"Yes, if you could. Sorry I fell asleep downstairs after they brought my sister in," Karen replied.

The nurse smiled knowingly and nodded. "Don't worry, it happens a lot."

"I understand my sister, Jane Heath, was brought to this ward. I wanted to find out how she's doing?"

"Of course, let me find out for you." The nurse stepped away from the station and disappeared further down the corridor before returning a few minutes later. "I've spoken to the doctor briefly because she's dealing with another patient. Your sister is asleep. She's comfortable and stable, having had her first round of meds. So that's good news?"

Karen breathed a sigh of relief and nodded.

"They'll review her again later this morning when the

doctors do their rounds. If there're any changes, I'll get someone to call you?"

"Yes, that would be great, thanks."

The nurse smiled. "Why don't you get yourself home and to bed? You look shattered. There's a cab company outside the front door if you haven't come by car."

Karen lingered, unsure what to do.

"Seriously, your sister is being well cared for. Go home and get some rest."

"Yeah, you're right. Promise you'll call if there are any changes?"

"I promise," the nurse replied with a reassuring smile as she watched Karen slope off, weary and half asleep.

19

Whilst most people would be safely tucked up in bed, enjoying a Sunday morning lie in, Karen was already in the office. With less than three hours sleep, she felt drained and shattered. She thought about the thousands of people having a lazy breakfast in bed, or going for a morning walk, dressed up against the brisk, chilly wind, and wished she had more time to enjoy those things. A thought crossed her mind about how wonderful it would be to wake up in the arms of a man and enjoy sleepy sex. Her thoughts raced away with her as she absent-mindedly stirred her coffee, lost in an imaginary world of love, lust and happiness.

She sighed to herself and rolled her eyes. *If only.*

"Karen!"

Karen jumped, almost knocking the spoon out of her cup, and sending her mug flying. "Christ, you scared the shit out of me!"

Jade laughed before placing a hand on Karen's back and

reaching across to grab a mug from the shelf. "What are you doing in? You should be at home getting some sleep, before heading back into the hospital."

"Too much on my mind, I can't sleep."

Jade shook her head and tutted. "Seriously, you should be at home. No one would think badly of you."

Karen didn't reply as she gazed at her mug and the swirls of steam pirouetting as they rose.

Jade nudged Karen in the side. "Oi."

Karen tutted and shook her head. "Welcome! Today's specials are: lack of sleep, up too early, and low on patience. Thank you, please come again."

Jade's brow furrowed as she took a step back, surprised at Karen's comeback.

Karen clamped her eyes shut and gritted her teeth as her body tensed. A few seconds later she opened them again and turned towards Jade as her face softened. "I'm so sorry, Jade. I didn't mean to snap at you. That was out of order. I think it's a lack of sleep and stress that's getting to me."

Jade softened her tone. "That's why I said that you need to get yourself home. You need rest."

"No. I don't want to feel like a spare part sitting around. I know what you're suggesting seems right, but you know me. I can't sit around on my fat arse doing nothing. Besides, we have too much going on here. Keeping busy is a good thing. It will stop me worrying about Jane."

"How is she?"

Karen shrugged. "As far as I know, she's stable. They

started on a round of meds during the night, and they were going to remove some of her blood."

"Stable. That's the main thing," Jade said, rubbing Karen's arm for support.

"Hey listen, Jade. I'm sorry for calling you in the middle of the night, and then blabbing. I was a snotty mess at the end of that. I spoiled your sleep as well."

"It's fine. I would have been pissed off if you hadn't called me."

Karen reached out and gave Jade a hug, as her eyes welled up, and threatened to overwhelm her again. "I'm not usually a soppy cow like this. I don't know what's wrong with me."

Jade followed Karen back to her office and grabbed a seat opposite her. With most of the team not in yet, an eerie silence surrounded them.

They spent the next few minutes catching up on what Karen had missed last night, and from the sounds of it the team had made little in the way of progress. Door-to-door enquiries were still ongoing, and the team were actively working through every piece of information that neighbours had passed onto them. Many leads would be inconsequential, but they couldn't afford to ignore them.

Just as Jade was about to leave, Karen's internal phone rang. "Karen Heath here."

"Karen, this is DCI Zachary Walker from York. I understand that you are trying to get hold of me."

Karen's eyes lit up as she bolted upright and pressed the

speakerphone button before placing the handset on her desk.

"Yes. Thanks, sir, for calling me back."

"Absolutely fine. Don't worry about the sir stuff." He laughed. "I'm not into titles. It's Zac."

Karen shot Jade a glance who raised a suitably impressed brow in response, before adding a nod.

"Great. Thanks, Zac. I wanted to pick your brain. We've taken on quite a horrific murder. It carried similar parallels to a case that your team were dealing with about eight weeks ago."

"Go on, I'm all ears."

"Four days ago, we found an elderly gentleman in his sixties bludgeoned to death in his home. We've not been able to confirm the murder weapon yet, but not content with beating the living daylights out of the poor fella, our killer then proceeded to rip out the man's heart and leave it for the owner's cat to have first dibs on. I understand you had a similar case, involving a male nurse?"

"Yes, we did. It's still an active investigation, and we haven't had a lucky break to be honest. The scene of the attack is very remote. Other than a few passing cars, and the odd pedestrian, it's not a place where we would have many witnesses. Forensics haven't come up with much, other than a few clothing fibres."

"But your victim had his heart removed as well, which is why we felt it had crossover. I've certainly not come across a case like this before," Karen commented.

Jade listened as the conversation ebbed and flowed between

the two senior officers. Several theories were suggested, but both Karen and Zac had drawn a blank on likely suspects.

"Was there anything in the nurse's background that would have pointed to anyone having targeted him for a reason?" Karen asked.

"Not that we could see. He'd only been in the country for a few years. Hard-working, incredibly well liked by both his colleagues and patients. He lived on his own in a small, rented apartment, and wasn't in arrears, or owed any money."

"Nothing homophobic or racial?" Karen suggested.

"Nope, we looked at both of those avenues as well, and drew a blank."

Karen let out a yawn, and though she tried to stifle it, it came out loud enough for Jade to throw a hand over her mouth to stop herself from laughing.

"Hey, am I keeping you up? Luckily, I'm at the end of the phone, so I won't take offence, but I promise you, I haven't got the personality of a shiny turd."

Karen sat open-mouthed, as Jade's shoulders shook with laughter.

"Sorry, sorry. I had a really late night and only grabbed three hours sleep. I'm shattered." Karen's tone was deeply apologetic and remorseful.

Zac's laughter echoed around the room. "Don't worry, I'm playing with you," Zac paused for a moment, "but seriously, am I that boring?"

Karen stared at her phone before glancing in Jade's direction. She couldn't tell if Zac was being serious or not. Jade shrugged her shoulders, confused too.

Karen's voice started. "Um… Um. No. But…"

"I'm kidding. It should be me who is apologising. Me and my team are known for taking the piss out of each other, and I sometimes forget that I need to be more professional on the phone. Well, that's what my mother always told me!" He laughed.

Karen struggled to make out what she thought of Zac. He sounded nice on the phone, cheeky, with a hint of dry humour. Without seeing him face to face, it was hard to know how seriously to take anything he said. As Karen looked across at Jade. She could tell that Jade was thinking the same too, as she made a soft cooing noise.

"So where is your investigation now?" Karen asked.

"We're still searching for new information. We've had two press appeals go out, and received a barrow load of information, most of which we've disregarded. But we're still following up lines of enquiry."

"Have you considered the possibility that it could be a stranger killing?"

Zac sighed at the other end of the phone. "We have. That would be the worst to be honest. If there is a connection between our case and yours, then it brings a whole new angle to the investigation. If it's the same perp, he could be anywhere…"

That possibility sat uncomfortably with Karen. It would be hard to map out the profile of the perpetrator. Worse still, the motive may never be known, and the real prospect dawned on her that further random killings could take place.

As if reading her mind, Zac continued, "What I'll do is send over what we have so far. If they are random, then we may need to liaise with other forces. We can't afford to have someone moving across the country killing at will."

Karen agreed, and before hanging up, confirmed that once in receipt of the information, she would get back to him with her own thoughts.

20

Karen spent the next few hours reviewing the notes sent through from Zac. The details of the investigation were meticulous.

She followed through with Zac's case note reviews, and despite every angle, his team had come up with little evidence, or suspects. Karen read several witness statements, many locals unaware of what had taken place. She read the account given by the witness who discovered Danilo Reyes's body. For a moment, her heart went out to the female dog walker. According to her statement she'd chased after her dog, a brown Labrador called Rollo, who tended to rush off and rummage around in bushes. Karen shook her head. *No wonder the woman got the shock of her life.*

Karen examined the background to the Filipino nurse. He'd been in the country for three years and brutally slain one evening on his way home from a shift. Karen tutted in sympathy. Zac's team had done a full and detailed investigation into Danilo's background, and discovered nothing more than a person who was well liked and loved by everyone he came in contact with. A reference was made to Danilo being verbally and physically abused in the course of his work, and as Karen knew, it came with the territory of being a member of the nursing staff.

Just studying the location map of where the body was discovered, Karen appreciated how difficult it would have been for anyone to witness the attack. The killer had chosen his spot well. It was isolated, dark, not overlooked, and on the outskirts of the city. *If it was a stranger, then he knows the area well.*

As much as she didn't want to, Karen studied the photographs taken from the post-mortem. The beatings in both cases looked similar. The slash marks across Danilo's chest suggested a more violent and disturbing attack. Perhaps it was the same killer perfecting his technique as he moved from one victim to another.

Karen felt like she was spinning in circles as her eyes scanned the multiple reports within the file. Nothing jumped out at her, not one nugget of information that she could take away from it that would help her own investigation. Karen wasn't sure what she'd hoped to gain from reviewing the case notes. An insight? A clue to a motive? A small piece of evidence linking back to the perpetrator. There was nothing. No wonder Zac had sounded frustrated during the conversation.

The only thing certain in Karen's mind was the strong possibility that both cases were linked. The one answer she still needed eluded her. Why were they linked?

Karen had updated Detective Superintendent Hinchcliff on how her case was progressing. With no DCI as the SIO,

Karen groaned at the idea of reporting in to Hinchcliff. He wasn't a man who tolerated loose ends, and he'd made it clear that her every move would be watched after recent events. One of her last conversations with him was etched uncomfortably in her mind. "Karen, if the events involving DCI Skelton have affected you psychologically, I would have no choice other than to insist that you take time out and use the professional services offered to you to sort out that mess in your head."

At the time, Karen insisted that she was fine, especially after so many unknowns had been resolved. With a clear head, she'd convinced Hinchcliff that her mind was fully focused on the job. In reality, that wasn't the case. She still carried a deep hatred for the man who'd died. Skelton. He'd done everything possible to make her out as an officer on the edge of losing it. He'd questioned her authority, her ability, and state of mind. With him out of the way, she should have felt better, but didn't. Karen was still angry. Angry at Skelton, and angry with the institution.

"Anything new to report, Craig?" she asked, perching on the corner of his desk.

"Yes, boss. We've managed to recover more CCTV footage from further down the street, and from surrounding areas. We've only started going through it, so don't hold your breath."

"Do we need extra bodies thrown at that?"

He raised his eyebrows. "It would help to speed things up, boss."

Karen grimaced. Resources were tight in every department, but when there was a major investigation, it was accepted that other teams would give up their staff. "Leave it with me, Craig. I'll make some calls in a minute."

"Cheers, boss." Craig turned towards his PC to carry on with his task.

"Boss," Jade hollered across the desks. She waved a few sheets of paper in Karen's direction.

"Yes, Jade?" Karen replied as she shuffled alongside and leant over her shoulder.

"The high-tech team has enhanced the digital CCTV images. We've got one occupant in the car, and it's a white male. That's it. Unfortunately, the more they attempted to enhance it, the grainier the image became. We still can't get a plate, but hopefully other CCTV footage might give us a clearer look."

"We really need a plate. That would help us to narrow down the registered keeper and location. It would certainly give us the break that we need. Nothing is ever easy is it, eh?"

"If it was that easy, Karen, we'd have a hundred per cent detection and clear-up rate," Jade said, chuckling. "And then we could stick to doing a nine-to-five shift and have lots of time off to go on holidays and live a normal life… Oh, the joys of dreaming," Jade added, staring towards the ceiling, and entertaining the vivid images in her imagination.

Karen agreed with the sentiment. "We'd be supercops, and have capes, and criminals would crumble the minute they saw us. And then there's reality!"

"Spoilsport," Jade mumbled in mock protest. "Mason came back to us on prints taken from the back doors. Unfortunately, they only matched the Kumars', so whoever gained entry was gloved up and forensically aware."

Karen dragged herself away from Jade's desk, frustrated. Evidence was thin on the ground, and her only hope at the moment was getting a clear image of the number plate on the Ford Focus. She hoped that it wasn't running on false plates.

21

Sunday nights were always quiet on this road. He had parked up here on a number of occasions, checking the ebb and flow of traffic, whilst watching and waiting for her. It wasn't the most ideal of locations, but it was on her route home with a petrol station a few hundred yards away, and an army barracks an equal distance in the opposite direction. He knew he needed to be careful.

The odd set of headlights blinded his vision momentarily, before he watched the red tail lights disappear into the darkness. The pure black of the night was his comfort, a blanket of camouflage that kept him safe, and allowed him to move freely.

He had seen a cold and chilling darkness before each time he had closed his eyes, the kind that made the images in his mind feel like an old-fashioned photograph, everything a shade of grey. Rather than fight it, he had embraced it. A side to his life that had finally made him take this journey. The lack of light that had bothered him so much at first became normal as the months and years passed. When he had been ill, and secured to a hospital bed, day and night blended into one another and all the time he'd shivered. He'd coughed and spat up black phlegm, a sign that his lungs were deeply infected. At one point he'd thought death was near.

He blinked hard before checking the time on his phone. If she stuck to her schedule, she'd be passing in the next ten minutes. That was his cue to move off and drive a short distance down the road before pulling over to the side, his hazards ticking away rhythmically.

There were no cars in either direction as he stepped from the car and cast his eye up and down the road. He looked down at his clothes, and in the darkness of the night it was hard to make out his silhouette against the black canvas that surrounded him.

One set of headlights approached; the vehicle passed. It wasn't hers.

A second vehicle approached moments later. He checked his phone; she was bang on time.

With the screen from his phone illuminated, he moved out into the middle of the road, and waved his phone to the approaching car. The car continued at speed, and for a brief moment he wondered if it would slow before the car came to a halt in front of him. He walked around to the driver's side.

Bending over and smiling, in an altered accent he said, "Hey, I'm really sorry. I've broken down, can you help?"

The woman pursed her lips and glanced at the shadowy face through the closed window, unsure what to do, before lowering it a few inches. "I'm in a hurry to get home. I can call you a recovery service when I get back. I'm only two minutes away. I won't be long."

The man stomped his feet on the spot and flapped his arms across his chest, pretending to be cold. "I could really do with help now. There's a petrol station a couple of hundred yards down the road, I don't suppose you could drop me off there? At least it's warmer, and I can call for help."

The woman hesitated, her mind tossing between being cautious and being the Good Samaritan. She turned away and glanced through her windscreen at the darkened road ahead, no doubt weighing up her options. "I'm not going that far. To be honest I'm going to be pulling off on the next left, so it would be much easier for me to call for help when I get home."

"But you will be going past the petrol station, you always do." His voice was cold and menacing.

Her eyes narrowed in confusion, wondering if she had heard him correctly. "Excuse me?"

"I know where you live. You're right. You're only two minutes away, but it's such a shame you won't get there," he shouted, as he smashed his crowbar into the window, shattering it. Tiny jewels of glass littered the ground and the inside of the car.

The woman screamed, as the man's features hit her like a lightning bolt. She froze, paralysed in fear and shock as he reached in and grabbed her keys from the ignition. "What the fuck do you think you're doing?" she screamed again, grabbing his wrist, desperate to hold on to her property. She tried to strengthen her grip around his wrist but felt a jolting pain as his elbow crashed into her jaw. He leant across and undid the seatbelt before reaching in to pull her from the car.

He came around behind and grabbed her by the shoulders, pulling the woman back towards the pavement. She screamed, but he met each wail with a crunching punch to the side of the face. Her eyes struggled to focus in the darkness as her head spun, waves of pain spreading down her face and into her neck. Her stomach began to turn as bile raced up her throat and scorched the back of her mouth.

"Please, let me go. Take anything you want. Take my car," she pleaded with all her life, as her heeled shoes fell from her feet. Her one hope was her phone in her handbag, but that was in the car. Every part of her hurt as he manhandled her from the pavement, across the grass and into the field beyond.

He lost his footing for a brief moment, releasing the grip. *This is my only opportunity to make a run for it*, she thought. She spun over and scrambled to her feet, disorientated, but a burning fear pushed her on to get as far away as possible from this maniac. Pitch black met her terrorised gaze in every direction, so she ran, her feet catching on the cold muddy soil. Tears streamed from her eyes. She screamed. "Help! Please help!" Terror gripped her further. Her feet sunk into the muddy ground, slowing her progress.

"You stupid, fucking bitch!" he snarled as he took a swipe at her.

Pain tore through her body, leaving her paralysed, unable to move. She fell to the ground, her breath coming in gasps, acrid vomit spewing from her mouth. "Please… please stop!" the woman begged, as she rolled onto her back to face the darkened shape of her attacker. He raised his arms above his head but she didn't recognise his weapon. Not that it mattered. When it descended with brutal force, it left her with the most intense pain. Her instincts kicked in, and with the heel of her foot she rammed it into his legs, sending him flying forward.

The woman rolled away, and scrambled to her feet again, her left arm hanging loosely by her side. The broken limb swayed as she continued to run. Up ahead of her, a clearing in the trees, a crossing or bridge, and the sound of running water. She regained her footing on something cold and solid, *concrete or metal*, she thought. Perhaps there was a house nearby — hope blossomed inside her for a blissful moment. She had made it halfway across when a pummelling pain erupted across the back of her head. A scream trapped in her throat. Reaching up with a hand, she felt the first signs of wetness. Panic spread, stealing the breath from her lungs, and the harder she gasped, the more difficult it became to inhale. Another crunching pain erupted from the side of her face, a blinding shard of agony that sent her reeling. The clang of metal on a hard surface sounded nearby as she dragged herself along the floor. Then he leapt on top of her, punching her and wrapping his fingers around her throat.

The pressure grew as her cheeks reddened. She clawed and raked at his face before her thumbs found his eyes.

He yelled in agony, which only fuelled his anger further. The blows rained down hard on the woman, vicious and unrelenting.

Her screams died down with each impact as her body loosened and fought less. After a few minutes, he noticed her limp form just lying underneath him motionless. He sat back on his heels, waiting to launch at her again, but the life had already slowly seeped from her mangled body.

He wiped the sweat from his forehead with the back of his hand before reaching into his pocket and pulling out his knife. He undid her coat, and then ripped at her blouse, before making an incision below her ribcage. He plunged his hand into the warm cavity, before tearing it away. His breath was hard and laboured as he stood in the darkness. Throwing the organ with all his might, he screamed and raised his fists in the air. His body tensed.

Hatred and anger coursed through every sinew of his being.

22

The phone shrilled for thirty seconds before ringing off, followed by the buzz of an incoming message. Karen had slept through that. A few minutes later the phone rang again, and somewhere within her deep subconscious, alarm bells began to sound. She opened one eye, unsure if it was a dream before her mind clicked into gear with the realisation that it was the phone ringing after all.

She reached out an arm from underneath the warm duvet and felt the chill of the morning tickle her skin. Fine arm hairs stood up in protest. She made a clumsy lunge for her phone and blinked hard to focus on Jade's name.

Karen licked her dry lips and felt the taste of stale breath in her mouth. She cleared her throat and answered the phone. "Jade…" she croaked.

"Sorry, Karen, did I wake you? Or do you always sound this sexy in the mornings?"

Karen groaned. "I always sound this hot in the morning. That's why I struggle to kick a man out of my bed."

"I know you weren't due in for a few hours, but we've had a call from DCI Walker in York. He wants to talk to you. They've got another body."

"Shit. Okay, I'll call him. I'll be there within the hour," Karen replied, as she hung up and tossed the phone on her bed.

Karen raced around her room, grabbing any clothes that were at hand. A creased blouse lay on the floor, and a pair of trousers were draped over the back of a chair. *They'll do*, she thought, as she snatched them and raced into the bathroom to brush her teeth and grab a quick shower. Within fifteen minutes she was out of the door, walking at a furious pace towards Epping Tube station. With phone in hand, she called DCI Walker.

KAREN WAS out of breath by the time she reached work. She charged through the incident floor and straight to her office. Jade, seeing Karen arrive, grabbed her notepad and pen and followed into her office.

Karen fired up her PC, and whilst it warmed up, whipped off her coat and hung it on the back of her door, before settling into her chair with a heavy sigh. "I couldn't get through to him, so I left a message. Did he give any details?"

Jade shook her head. "He was rushed off his feet with an active crime scene. It was literally a thirty-second call out of courtesy, and then he hung up."

Karen punched the number into her desk phone and put it on speakerphone. It rung for a while and Karen was about to hang up, when Zac finally answered.

"Zac, it's Karen. What have you got?"

Zac's voice faded in and out, sounding like he was outdoors somewhere. She could hear the sound of others talking and caught the occasional noise of what sounded like running water each time the wind direction changed.

"We've got another body. A female. We found a handbag nearby and believe it belongs to the victim. We don't believe it was a botched robbery."

"Do you think it's our man?"

Zac paused on the other end for a moment. Karen could hear his heavy breathing.

"I think so. I'm ruling out robbery because the handbag contained her purse and cash. We've found a driving licence in the name of Donna Anderson, solicitor, aged thirty-six. We believe the estimated time of death was last night between six p.m. and midnight. Details are sketchy at the moment, and we are on the scene. But it's definitely a similar M.O. The pathologist has confirmed that based on the deep incision across her abdomen, that her heart has been removed. But there are deep wounds across her arms, face and neck."

"Defensive marks. She put up a fight?"

"It looks that way, Karen."

Karen's mind swirled as she glanced across at Jade, who looked equally dumbstruck. Karen scribbled three words on a notepad. York London York.

"If it's the same perp, that's two on my patch, and one on yours. You have a Ford Focus as a suspect vehicle. A cashier at a petrol station down the road was tidying up the forecourt when he saw a white car pass at speed. We can't be certain that it's the same vehicle, and this stretch of road attracts a lot of joyriders racing at speed, but I've dispatched officers to secure any CCTV footage from last night."

Karen added the words "white car" to her notepad and underlined them several times. "That would be a lucky break, but most cameras are trained on the forecourt. You never know, but you might have picked up the odd second or two in the peripheral field of one of the cameras."

"Yeah, that's what I'm thinking."

"Okay, Zac. Thanks for the update. Let me know how you get on, but my gut tells me we are looking for the same person. If that's the case, then he's probably still in the York area."

Karen put the phone down and leant back in her chair. "I was not expecting that," she said wide-eyed, her mind processing the new information.

"Me neither," Jade replied with a shake of her head. "If it's the same person, and the M.O. is too similar to ignore, then we're looking in the wrong place? He's not even on our patch."

Karen rapped her fingers on the desk as she formulated a plan. "I'm going to see the super. I'll be back in a jiffy." Karen jumped out of her seat, leaving a perplexed Jade rooted to her chair.

Karen dashed up the stairs and down the corridor towards

Hinchcliff's office. His door was wide open, and peering around the corner, she noticed him engrossed in paperwork, his pen furiously scribbling additions to the documents he was scanning. Karen knocked on the door. "Sir, have you got a moment?"

Hinchcliff said nothing other than offering her a nod, as he eyed her coming into his office, and taking a seat opposite him.

"Sir, I've been on a call with the SIO in York, a DCI Zac Walker. My team has been looking for similar cases to the one we've been dealing with and identified a very similar case in York eight weeks ago. A nurse walking home from his shift was brutally attacked and suffered significant trauma to the back of his head. He also had his heart removed. Both of which are identical to our case of the retired doctor."

Hinchcliff folded his arms across his chest and pursed his lips as he listened in silence. He offered the smallest of nods in agreement.

"DCI Walker contacted us this morning. They had another case last night. A solicitor was attacked and murdered. The same M.O. again. Severe trauma to the back of the head with a blunt instrument, and although the post-mortem is yet to be conducted, the pathologist is certain that her heart has been removed due to the large incision across her abdomen."

"Same assailant?"

"Quite possibly, sir. Three victims in eight weeks, similar injuries to the back of their heads, and all had their hearts removed."

"So he's moving around the country?"

Karen shrugged. "I'm not sure, sir. But we've got two incidences in York, and one in London. A white car was seen in the vicinity of both of the last two attacks. If it is our man, he's in York."

"Fine. Let York deal with it. We'll deal with our case."

"Sir, I'd like to go to York. It would help our investigation, and I would like to see the crime scene. It's all well and good relying on the information that DCI Walker provides us, but we really need a set of eyes on the ground to review the actual crime scene and understand the victim's background."

"Waste of time, Karen. We can't afford to keep spending money on jollies. That's why we have technology now so that we can share information."

Karen understood Hinchcliff's argument, and it was valid. Nevertheless, she was still dealing with a murder on her patch, and an insight into how the killer was operating would be invaluable for her. She wanted to get a feel on the ground for where the other victims had been attacked, why the killer had chosen those locations, and how the crimes were connected.

"Sir, I appreciate that. But our victim, Doctor Kumar, was from York. Whilst we are still in the process of building a victimology, it would be helpful for me to meet his family as well as see the site of the recent murders. We are dealing with a serial killer here now, and my worst fear is that he could just disappear into the shadows and pop up in a different part of the country There is a risk he could be heading back here or move to a different area altogether. I'm happy to work with the York team. We can pool our intelligence and resources together and stop this person before another force has a victim on their hands."

Karen rested her hands on her lap, hoping she had made a strong enough case to convince Hinchcliff to let her go. An uncomfortable pause settled between them whilst Hinchcliff thought it through. They exchanged the odd glance. She could see the cogs turning.

"I want regular updates, Karen. And I want our team still tracking down every available lead. Do I make myself clear?"

Karen jumped up from her chair. "Absolutely. I'll get up there as soon as I can and report back." She waited a few moments in case Hinchcliff had anything further to add, but he dismissed her with another nod.

Karen raced back down to her office to find Jade still there, playing with her nails, searching for any evidence of dirt beneath them. She greeted Karen with a confused look. "Well? What did you go and speak to the super about?"

"I asked the super if I could go to York. We've got two cases in York, and one in London. Doctor Kumar's family came from York, so it makes sense to speak to his family to look for any connections. And I also want to see the latest crime scene."

"And?"

"He said I can go. Are you able to oversee things at this end?"

Jade laughed. "Other than having to handle a bunch of officers who act like they're still in kindergarten, I'll manage, though I'd much rather be going with you."

"If only it was that easy. I thought the super was going to say no. I would have been chancing my luck if I'd asked for both of us to go," Karen replied, logging off her PC, and gathering her notebook and anything else that she needed to take with her.

Karen made a quick call to DCI Walker informing him of her decision to make her way up to York and gave Jade a few instructions before dashing from the office.

On her way home, she called the hospital for an update on Jane. Her sister's health troubled her, and if the nurses had said anything about Jane's condition deteriorating, she would have sent Jade to York instead. The feedback, however, was that her sister was stable, and responding well to the medication, which Karen found reassuring. With York being a few hours away, if there was any change in her sister's condition, she could return and be back by her sister's side in double time.

23

After grabbing the train back to Epping, Karen made up a travel bag with all her essentials. She threw in her underwear, a few tops and bottoms before gathering up all her toiletries into a wash bag and squeezing them into any available space. Having checked with her neighbour and given her a spare set of keys, Karen knew Manky would be fed and cared for. Though she hated the thought of leaving him, it would only be for a day or two, and he'd hardly notice her absence.

Just as Karen was about to dash out, she paused and rushed back in, unplugging appliances. Kettle, toaster, hairdryer, even the television. For some strange reason, the thought of leaving appliances plugged in always worried her. She had seen first-hand how things like kettles had exploded and torched a property, or an overheated TV plug that had set fire to a lounge. Maybe it was paranoia, but it was a ritual most days out of habit more than anything else.

She made her way across the city towards London's King's Cross. Jade had organised a ticket for the eleven forty-five to York. London was a busy hub, and all the mainline stations had tens of thousands of passengers come through their doors as they made their way to and from London and further afield. A sea of bodies met Karen as she squeezed through them towards the announcement board. She had arrived with fifteen minutes to spare, only to find that the train's departure had been delayed by ten minutes. Karen made her way to the platform before boarding the train and finding her seat.

Since it wasn't something she did often, it was both strange and relaxing to settle in her seat and experience a gentle rocking and swaying. She'd travelled to many parts of the country, mainly for her job, Leeds, Bristol, and Exeter to name but a few. Travelling to York was no different. Karen watched as passengers entered through one of the carriage doors, and shuffled along the narrow aisles, staring at the different seats, and available spaces before deciding where to sit. Others moved through the carriage, and on to the next one, sighing in annoyance each time they got stuck behind someone navigating the aisles, and trying to manoeuvre their bags into the overhead storage areas.

A whistle from somewhere on the platform signalled the train's imminent departure. The on-board manager came over the tannoy system to welcome his passengers, before delivering a well-rehearsed speech on their journey today and their estimated arrival time of thirteen fifty-five, calling at Peterborough, Newark North Gate, and Doncaster. He continued to drone on about the in-service menu, and the availability of hot and cold food from the buffet car.

No mention of the extortionate prices, Karen mused.

The train pulled off, and slowly edged its way along the tracks and out of the station, its wheels screeching as it rocked from side to side. The further it moved away from central London, the speedier it became until they were charging through the British countryside. Though they were in the midst of winter, the countryside still offered a patchwork quilt of green fields, raised hedgerows, and ploughed land. She reflected on the tranquil and serene view, such a contrast to the cityscape that surrounded her in London. Tower blocks that reached towards the sky, narrow streets double-parked with cars, the sound of wailing sirens in all directions, and housing, both modern and historic, that sat shoulder to shoulder. It really was a melting pot of cultures, eras, and history.

That seemed so far away now as she gazed off into the distance, the green landscape a blurred haze as the train continued at speed. Its gentle rocking relaxed Karen to the point that her eyes began to droop, and her body sunk deeper into the chair. She rested her head to one side and fell asleep.

She wearily opened her eyes when the on-board service manager came over the tannoy to announce that they would shortly be arriving at York station. The journey had flown by, and after the train came to a standstill, she gathered her belongings, and stepped from the train to be hit by a cold chill that hung in the January air. She felt a shiver race down her spine. It certainly felt colder than London, or perhaps it was the cold wind as it swept through the arc of the station.

Karen stared up at its magnificent architecture, and the glass roof that snaked along the length of the platform. She had once heard the roof being described as a "cast-iron cathedral", and she could see why. It reminded her of a bygone era when steam power had revolutionised travel.

Everywhere she looked from down the tracks to the roof, every inch of its design was ingrained with signs, symbols and meanings integral to York and its rich past, most of which would be entirely unknown to the everyday commuter who travelled through it. It really was an architectural marvel in her eyes.

She followed the flow of passengers along the platform and through the station concourse towards the entrance. The temperature dial above her said it was only six degrees, but Karen could have sworn it was even lower when she blew out her cheeks, and a vapour cloud erupted from her mouth.

Karen glanced around, looking for her lift. Zac had told her he would be sending one of his team to pick her up, but he'd failed to mention who.

She dropped her bag on the floor, and waited by the entrance, scanning every person who walked towards her.

A few minutes later, a woman approached, a warm smile on her face. She leant her head forward a bit in a questioning manner. "DI Karen Heath?"

Karen returned the smile and extended a hand. "Yep, that's me."

"Good to meet you, guv. I'm DC Belinda Webb, Zac sent me to pick you up."

First impressions were positive, as Karen made small talk in the car. Belinda had long flowing blonde hair that cascaded over her shoulders and down her chest. She had a warm smile, with chipmunk cheeks, and a slightly pointy chin, which made her look impish. Karen thought she reminded her of the actress Amy Schumer, who she'd watched recently in *Trainwreck*, a movie on Netflix.

"How was your journey?" Belinda asked.

"Oh, you know. Uneventful. To be honest, every time I get on a train I crash out. I don't know why, but I get so sleepy."

Belinda laughed. "To be honest, I haven't been on many trains, but I've ended up the same way. I sink deeper into the chair, and when I wake up, I look a total mess, with bloodshot eyes, and spit hanging from my chin. Not the best look!"

"It's a lovely city," Karen commented as she stared out of the window, and the ancient city walls that popped up along her route.

"It is, guv. As they say, 'there's no other city in northern England that says mediaeval quite like York'. You've got a medieval spider's web of narrow streets enclosed by 13th century walls. You've got the impressive York Minster, museums, restaurants, cafés, and pubs. You name it, we've got it. But it's all been tastefully done. Heritage is really important up here, and they've worked hard to keep it."

"I feel like I'm on an open-top bus tour!" Karen laughed.

Belinda blushed. She joined in the laughter. "Sorry, guv. I'm really passionate about this place, and I am known to go on a bit. When you get me started, I can't stop. Tell me to shut up if you want."

Karen waved it off dismissively. "Don't be daft. There's certainly a lot to take in."

24

Belinda parked her car outside the police station, which was situated on the outskirts of town. It consisted of a group of buildings in a small cluster, three stories high, and surrounded by large mature trees that hung over many of the paths that led away from a handful of car parks to the various buildings.

Karen reluctantly stepped from the warmth of the car and covered the short distance to the closest building, with Belinda leading the way. One thing she did notice, which took her by surprise, was how quiet it was. Other than the wind stirring the branches above her, there was little sound of traffic, or city life. Her first impressions were that it reminded her more of a university campus than a large police station.

The warmth returned to her bones as she was guided through the myriad of corridors into the bowels of the building. Belinda took her up a central staircase, and along a carpeted floor towards the DCI's office.

"Do you want to grab a seat, and I'll get you a hot drink? What would you like, tea, coffee or herbal?"

"A strong coffee with one sugar would be fantastic with just a splash of milk, please. Thanks, Belinda," Karen replied, settling herself into a leather seat.

Even the seats took her by surprise. They were more akin to a corporate environment than a police station. The frame was shiny metal with a leather seat slung between the arms. Karen glanced around Zac's office. He was surrounded on three sides by glass walls. The carpets were clean and new with what appeared to be a state-of-the-art computer nestled to one side. The rest of his desk appeared relatively clear except for a caddie to hold his pens, a landline, and one notepad.

"Here you go, guv," Belinda said as she came in and placed the cup on the table. "Zac won't be long. He's finishing up a meeting on another floor, but he knows you're here. Is there anything else I can get you?"

Karen shook her head. "No, that's fine. Thanks for your help."

"My pleasure. I've got to get back to work, but I'll hopefully see you later," Belinda replied before leaving the office and disappearing down the corridor.

Karen raised a brow approvingly. Her experience of York so far had been encouraging, and as for these offices, though they looked like nothing special from the outside, had a contemporary, modern and clean styling inside. She was certain the fresh smell of carpet lingered everywhere.

There were a couple of framed photographs on Zac's desk, but theyfaced away from her. Though she wanted to have a peek, she dreaded Zac walking in to find her nosing around.

"Karen," a strong voice came from behind, which made her jump.

Karen swivelled in her chair, whilst also rising to meet the man who had entered. He was nothing like she had expected, but then again, she had only been going by his voice, and she'd added a few years and a few pounds to the vision in her mind. Zac was neither of those images, but a tall, slender man, with smouldering grey eyes, tight cheekbones, a full head of dark hair, and a few days' worth of stubble. He was wearing suit trousers, and an open-necked white shirt with his lanyard draped around his neck. *Italian, Greek, or Spanish heritage?* She couldn't be certain. *One thing was certain, he was bloody good-looking.*

"Nice to meet you, I'm Zac." He offered her a warm handshake, and an equally welcoming smile. His hand lingered on hers perhaps a second or two longer than Karen had expected and put it down to northern hospitality. "Did you have a good journey?" he asked, whilst stepping around to his side of the desk.

Karen returned to her seat and straightened her blouse. "I did, thanks. It was surprisingly quick."

Zac smiled. "I think people from London think York is bloody miles away, and would take the best part of half a day."

"Belinda was nice. Talkative. Gave me a whistle-stop recital of York."

"Bless her. I think most people in York are passionate about this place. It's a popular stop on the tourist route. They love the cobbled streets, the quaint tea rooms, the Gothic buildings and even its slightly murky past. If you fancy a ghost walk, we've even got one of those," he said with a laugh. "I must admit — I was a bit surprised when you contacted me to say you were heading up here."

Karen felt a bit awkward. Perhaps she had been too hasty but wasn't going to admit it. "I probably wouldn't have to be honest, but after the discovery of your second victim, I became quite concerned. I'm pretty certain that we are dealing with the same person, and now that he has committed three murders, we've got a serial killer on our hands." Karen took a sip of coffee before continuing. "If we don't find him, then we could lose him to a different part of the country. He could pop up anywhere, and then we'd have another force involved, and before long there'd be a national manhunt for this person."

Zac nodded. "Agreed. I don't think either you or I would welcome the extra attention from the media."

"How are you getting on with the latest crime scene?" Karen asked, getting straight down to business.

"It's early days yet. My team are still down there, and we've got forensics gathering evidence. As soon as they're finished, we can deploy a search team."

"Any more witnesses?" Karen asked.

"No. My team is trying to track down the vehicle seen speeding away. We've secured footage from the petrol station, and there's an army barracks further down the road, so we've spoken to them requesting any footage that they may have."

"Is it a built-up area?"

"No, Karen. It's a quiet road, other than the speeding idiots. Strensall Road is surrounded by fields, and a few isolated hubs of residential housing. The roadside is fringed with overgrown grass and bushes eight feet high."

"Not somewhere you want to be stopped, or be walking alone at night?"

Zac nodded. "It's not like we can even knock on a ton of doors and ask for doorbell footage either. We are liaising with the city's CCTV operators and plan to review the footage from any cameras towards the outskirts of town closest to our crime scene. It's a big job because they also cover the park-and-ride sites, and a number of schools. Even if I doubled the size of my team, I still think we'd have our work cut out."

"Well, there's a lot I want to cover with you, and time isn't on our side," Karen said, slapping her hands down on her thighs.

"I know. But you're going to be here for a while, so let me introduce you to the team," Zac said, as he rose from his seat.

25

Zac led Karen along the corridor to the major incident room where his team was based. The first thing Karen noticed was the continuing theme of a contemporary corporate environment. The floor itself was huge, with desks spaced so far apart that officers would have to shout to be heard. Sleek, streamlined desks, ergonomic chairs, and large computer screens that were mounted on flexible arms were available to all officers. Some desks had two or even three screens, which reminded Karen of a trading floor in an investment bank rather than the regular police set-up that she was accustomed to.

It was a real eye-opener for her as Zac walked her around the office, talking about how they ran investigations, and what resources they had available to them. The first desk they came to was Belinda's. She was busy on the phone as Zac moved on.

"Belinda is a solid part of the team. As you've gathered, she talks a lot, and that works in her favour. She could start up a conversation with a corpse. Everyone seems to like her. Be wary of first impressions, mind you. Get on the wrong side of Bel and she'll cut you down with her venomous tongue!" Zac smiled as he glanced in Bel's direction.

Belinda's jaw dropped, her eyes widened, and she shook her head. Belinda gave Karen a small wink as they passed.

"This is DC Tyler Owen," Zac continued, stopping at the young DC's desk.

Tyler pushed back in his chair and stood up, extending a handshake in Karen's direction.

"Tyler, this is DI Karen Heath from the Met." Zac went on to explain Karen's visit, and asked Tyler to make a desk available for her.

First impressions of Tyler were favourable in Karen's mind. He was tall at six-foot-two, but not well built. Slim and lanky were words that sprung to mind. He had a charismatic white smile that stood out against his dark African skin.

Zac moved on as he checked the time on his phone. "Mark, I'd like to introduce you to DI Karen Heath." DS Mark Burton looked up from his work, his round face deadpan, and offered nothing more than a slight smile and nod as he ran his fingers through his silvery goatee beard.

Karen extended a hand when Mark didn't move, and he returned the gesture with the loosest of handshakes. The man's eyes darted between herself and Zac, and she didn't know if it was paranoia or not, but his eyes, features and body language appeared more defensive and aloof than the others.

"Mark is often known as Ron, the management," Zac

commented.

Karen looked blankly at Zac, clueless as to what he meant.

"Hale and Pace? The Two Rons as the management? No…?" Zac questioned, before Karen cottoned on.

The last occupied desk was Zac's number two, DI Anita Mani. The Asian woman pressed the phone to her ear as her gorgeous dark brown hair cascaded in waves across her shoulders. Her dark brown eyes and light brown skin made her look like a Bollywood actress in Karen's opinion. Karen put her in her forties.

As she put down her phone, she stood to greet Karen with a warm and welcoming smile.

"Anita, I'd like to introduce DI Karen Heath. Karen's come up to find out more about the double murders that we're dealing with. They've had a similar case in London, and we now believe that the cases are linked."

"Hi, Karen, nice to meet you. These are particularly difficult cases, especially because of the randomness, and the locations of the crime scenes. The bastard has certainly made it difficult for us."

Karen appreciated her bluntness. There were no airs and graces with her, and Karen liked that.

"I can imagine. But I find it disturbing that the perpetrator committed the murder on our patch in a built-up residential area. He is certainly bold."

They hung around Anita's desk for a while, exchanging information and observations about the three cases. During the discussion, Tyler and Belinda joined them, and Karen noticed how cohesive the team was, but her eyes were drawn to the DS, and wondered why Mark kept his distance and showed no interest.

Karen followed Zac back to his office and reflected on the generous feedback about Zac from members of his team. Many were out on the investigation, but of those who remained in the office, they had nothing but good things to say about him.

"I couldn't help but notice how every single member of your team out on the floor call you Zac, even the civilian staff," Karen said as she sat back down in Zac's office.

"To be honest, I'm not really into titles. It's far more important to create harmonious working relationships, and I'm in no mood to have egos on my team, nor do I want any titles getting in the way of creating good relationships."

"Refreshing." Karen raised a brow, as her mind flipped back to DS Mark Burton. She wondered what the story was with him.

"It is. We all socialise together. We have barbecues around each other's houses in the summer, and I have an open door policy both in and out of the office."

"I'm impressed, and a little shocked by the openness of the approach fostered up here." She suddenly realised that she may have come across a little critical or patronising and quickly continued to explain her thinking. "It would be fantastic if anything like that could ever work in London, but I doubt it. Everyone seems to be looking after number one, and there are plenty of officers who'd be happy to stab you in the back if it meant they got the glory, the praise and reward." Karen thought back to several officers that she had come across during her career that fitted that description, including Skelton.

Zac sighed and interlocked his fingers behind his head as he leant back in his chair. "The Met is a bigger force, with huge responsibilities, and a much larger population to police. I also get the impression that they have a lot more political pressure, and so bureaucracy, targets, and stress, all have an effect on that."

Karen agreed. "I know it's getting dark, but I'd really like to go and see the latest crime scene if that's okay?"

"Yep, that seems like a good idea. You might not be able to see much by the time we get there, but I guess that's what you're here for…" he replied, rising from his chair, and retrieving his coat.

A SHORT DRIVE took them to the latest location. A hive of activity continued with the crime scene still taped off by blue police tape.

Zac and Karen signed into the scene log before Zac talked her through what they had discovered. The victim's car had been removed on a low-loader for forensic examination, allowing traffic to flow again. Crime scene tape mapped out a path that officers took through the hedgerow and into the field. It was four p.m., the natural light had all but faded, but the scene was still lit up with arc lights that had been set up at regular intervals leading off into the distance, and towards what Karen could see as a small bridge.

Karen followed Zac as he navigated the metal stepping plates positioned by the forensic team to preserve the scene. Yellow plastic markers had been placed on the ground close to the discovery of any evidence. Further into the field they stopped by the bridge, a small concrete structure with metal railings that spanned a stream which cut through and separated two fields. Much of the stream was concealed from the air by a line of trees on either bank.

Streams of light bobbed around in the darkness as officers with torches maintained the far end of the cordon.

"We've had officers wading through the small stream most of the day sifting for evidence. The problem is anything of importance could have been carried away."

"It's certainly a remote location. Anything could happen here, and anyone passing along the road would be oblivious." Karen glanced back towards the tall hedgerow and road. The victim had either been chased or dragged more than fifty yards through the field until she was savagely killed. *She had no chance.*

"The search team are ready, but it's too dark now, so they will begin at first light tomorrow. I suggest that we come back then. I think it's only in daylight that you begin to appreciate and understand the surroundings."

Karen and Zac made their way back towards the road and watched as cars slowed not because of the weight of traffic, but out of curiosity as they passed a long line of police vehicles parked up on the kerb.

"Have you got accommodation sorted out?" Zac asked.

"Yes, Jade, my DS organised a hotel in town."

"Let me drive you there, but I need to pop home first to check on a few things. Is it okay if we go via my house?"

Karen shrugged and threw her hands in the air. "Yeah, it's fine by me."

26

Zac pulled off the road and into his driveway. It was a semi-detached house in a quiet residential street. All around them, lights glowed through lounge and bedroom windows, evidence of family life carrying on as normal. She had spent most of her adult life coming home to an empty apartment and wondered what it would feel like to come home to her family. But then again, she enjoyed being responsible for herself, free to do what she wanted to do, go wherever she chose to go. The thought of coming home to a house of screaming kids, dirty dishes piling up in the sink, and a pile of washing to do didn't feature highly in her bucket list.

"Come in," he said. "I'll introduce you to Summer."

"Ah, that's nice. Is that your dog?"

Zac spun on his heels by the front door, as he was about to put his key in the lock. "No, Summer's my twelve-year-old daughter."

Karen felt the colour drain from her face. Every sinew of

her body wanted to turn around and run in the opposite direction. She was mortified. Anything she said now would sound pathetic and lame. The uncomfortable silence between them only added to the awkwardness.

"Oh, I'm so, so sorry. Look, listen, take me back to the hotel. I feel awful."

Zac smiled before he let out a laugh. "Don't be silly. It's a simple mistake to make. Come in."

Zac opened the door, and led her through the hallway, yelling up the stairs as they passed on their way through to the lounge and on to the kitchen. "Sumbum, can you come down, sweetheart?"

Sumbum? Karen had already put her foot in it once and dared not ask.

"Her nickname. I needed to pop in and check up on the dog… I mean, daughter. Coffee?" Zac asked with a smile.

Karen's face flushed again. "Please, I'm so sorry. You're making it worse."

"I'm teasing. Coffee?" he asked again.

"Yes, please. Milk one sugar."

From somewhere above them, the floorboards creaked, followed by the thumping of heavy footsteps on the stairs as if a herd of elephants were charging through the Serengeti.

Karen turned towards Zac, who appeared unfazed by the noise, before she spun her head towards the doorway to see the petite figure of a young girl stomp through into the kitchen. She was dressed in leggings and a black Nike sweatshirt. Her hair was lighter than Zac's, light brown. In fact, that wasn't the only thing that was lighter. Whereas Zac had an olive complexion, his daughter was paler, with small blue eyes, fuller cheeks, and a more pronounced chin.

Zac placed two mugs on the table. "Sumbum, this is Karen. She's a colleague from London who's travelled up about a case that I'm working on at the moment."

Summer offered Karen a warm smile and tossed her hand up in the air and gave her a sheepish wave.

"Nice to meet you, Summer."

Summer joined them at the table, pulling out a seat, and dropping herself in with all the grace of a Hippo. "I'm hungry, Dad."

Zac rolled his eyes. "And how was school today, sweetheart?"

Summer imitated her dad with both the eye-roll and the nosy question.

Karen bit her bottom lip to hold back a laugh.

"Listen here, you cheeky madam. I've not seen you all day, so I'm showing an interest because I care. Just like when I come home, you should say, 'Hi, Dad, how was your day?' and show an interest."

Summer pulled a face. "Err, who wants to know about your boring day. All you deal with are dead bodies. That's grim, bruv!"

Zac tutted. He hated the urban lingo his daughter had picked up. "Bruv? Bruv? Really?"

"Oh, Dad, get with the programme. It's the vibe these days. Just chill. Do you deal with mashed up bodies as well?"

Summer asked, turning towards Karen, her eyes narrowed and probing.

The question took Karen by surprise. She glanced across at Zac, trying to figure out whether this was a discussion he was happy with. Karen decided to take the diplomatic approach. "I deal with lots of crimes. Our job is to keep people safe. It's a lot more interesting than you think."

"Boring… That's what it sounds like to me when I listen to Dad talk with all his workmates."

Karen laughed. "It can be boring at times, I agree."

"Have you got dinner planned, Karen?" Zac asked.

"Give me a chance. I haven't even got to my hotel yet."

"Well, why don't you stay for dinner, and then I'll take you back afterwards?"

Karen was taken aback by the suggestion, and caught on the back foot, but shrugged before accepting the offer.

"That okay with you, Summer?" Zac asked his daughter.

Summer was already out of her seat and heading back upstairs. "Yeah, Dad. But hurry up, because I'm starving."

Zac let out a long sigh. "She can be a bloody nightmare sometimes," he said as he whipped out a couple of pizzas from the freezer, and a bag of salad from the fridge.

"Aren't all kids like that?"

"I don't know. We've only got one, and that's enough for me," Zac laughed.

Karen suddenly felt awkward, feeling like she had imposed on family life. "What time is your wife due back?"

"She's not," he replied, without turning around as he continued to prepare dinner.

"Oh. I'm sorry." Karen felt like she had put her foot in it again, and that Zac had experienced a personal tragedy.

"Don't be. We are divorced," he said as his body stiffened.

Karen let out a breath. *At least she's not dead.*

"We share custody. Summer stays with me every other week. But I do feel sorry for her sometimes, because I'm not around much, so she has to keep herself entertained after school."

Zac didn't mention anything else about his wife or the relationship, and Karen didn't probe further. She got the impression it wasn't something he liked to talk about.

Summer joined them once dinner was ready. By now Zac's daughter had lightened up a bit and joked with her dad whilst they talked about school. It wasn't something that Karen had first-hand experience of, so in part, she remained a spectator for some of the evening as Zac and his daughter discussed homework, and the latest updates on Summer's friends.

Summer had already polished off four slices of pepperoni pizza, and Karen wondered where she had put it, especially when she asked what was for pudding.

Karen looked up at the clock. "I really should go. I've already taken up much of your evening, and I still need to check into the hotel."

"Yes, of course. Sorry. You probably wanna settle in for the evening. It's been a long day," Zac replied as he got up, and cleared the table. "Sumbum, I'm going to drop

Karen off, and then I'll be back. I shouldn't be gone long. Okay?"

"No problem, Dad. I've got homework to do that's due in tomorrow."

"Last-minute.com again?"

Summer looked at her dad, perplexed.

"Doesn't matter, sweetheart. Say goodbye to Karen, and head off upstairs."

Summer made her way towards the hall, stopping briefly in the doorway. "Nice to meet you, Karen. We don't get many visitors here. Dad doesn't bring a lot of people home."

"That's not true, sweetheart. We have a lot of my work friends come over for dinner and barbecues and things like that."

"I meant female friends. All your mates are boring!"

And with that parting comment, Summer thundered back up the stairs, leaving an uncomfortable and awkward silence between Karen and Zac. Keen to break that stalemate, Karen threw on her coat quickly. "Shall we go?"

KAREN THANKED Zac for dinner as they made their way through town towards the Park Inn by Radisson hotel in the city centre. Karen chose to stare out of the window and kept the conversation to a minimum more through tiredness than anything else, though Zac continued to give her a running commentary of the main features of the city, and how it was ringed by Roman era city walls. Zac dropped her off at the entrance, agreeing to pick her up in the morning before driving off.

Karen's hotel room was comfortable and warm. She welcomed the opportunity to soak in the bath, uninterrupted. The warm water soothed her aching muscles and relaxed her to the point where she could have fallen asleep. Swaddled in a comfy dressing gown and sipping on a cup of tea, Karen looked out of the window at the city beyond. From her elevated position, the bright lights of the city were warm and inviting. The River Ouse shimmered in the dark, as the lights from the hotel and the many pubs and restaurants across the way danced on its surface.

Her thoughts turned towards her case. She had so much to do, and so little time. There was a killer that needed catching, and somewhere out there he could be prowling the streets right now looking for his next victim. The thought didn't sit comfortably with her and she couldn't wait for tomorrow to arrive. Before turning in for the night, she called the hospital once again to check up on her sister. Happy that Jane was still stable, Karen switched off the light and climbed into bed.

27

There was something about sleeping in a comfy hotel bed that Karen found incredibly relaxing. Whether it was because of a change of location, or the mattresses were of better quality she wasn't sure, but she had the most amazing sleep. The bed was both soft and supportive, and utterly luxurious to sleep in.

She swung around and dropped her feet to the floor before standing and affording herself a long stretch. Karen pulled back the curtains and squinted hard as warm winter sunshine bathed her face. York looked fantastic. The sunlight glistened off the river beneath her, and the city was coming to life, as cars weaved their way through the narrow Gothic streets, pedestrians made their way to work, and early morning joggers took the opportunity to run alongside the river.

After showering and getting dressed, Karen called Jade.

"Morning, Karen. How's things going up there?"

Karen gave her an update on how she had met the team,

and had visited the crime scene yesterday evening, but due to the failing light, would be visiting again first thing this morning.

Jade listened with interest. "Does the DCI still believe that our killer remains in York?"

"He's not sure. And neither am I, to be honest. The fact that the killer has moved between London and York several times makes it harder for us to figure out his next move. For all we know, he could be long gone by now."

"And then what?" Jade asked.

"Then it becomes a national manhunt. And we really don't want that. Both forces have already put a lot of time and effort into tracking down this killer. I'm certainly not prepared to let another force get a lucky break and claim the glory."

Jade understood the ramifications of Karen's words, even though she didn't say it directly. With the manpower and resources of the Met Police, questions would be asked as to why they were unable to get any credible leads on the killer.

"I have a feeling that the answers lie in York, Jade. I'll know a lot more by the end of today," Karen added. "How are we getting on with the investigation in London?"

"We've got nothing that would suggest a motive. So our earlier discussions of revenge, or a disgruntled former patient still remain. As does the worrying possibility that it was a random psycho or stranger."

"How much closer are we to building a full victimology of Doctor Kumar?" Karen asked.

"Pretty good. Unfortunately, he didn't have any hobbies or interests in recent years as it became a full-time job to care for his wife. He did go out regularly for quick walks, and once a week for shopping. There are no recent flags on the system for the police being called, and his banking records are clean. There are no unusual or large transactions."

"Phone records?"

"Yep, we've checked them as well. He used a landline and rarely used his mobile."

Karen felt the first stabs of annoyance and frustration. There had to be something they were missing. "What about his work, and his past professional relationships?"

"That's what we're turning our attention to. Nothing new has come back from forensics or CCTV and doorbell footage. But we're still pushing on, Karen."

Karen thanked Jade for the update, before telling her she needed to shoot off soon, and promised to update her later. After hanging up, she called the hospital again for a further update on her sister. Jane had slept well and continued to respond to the treatment plan in place. Karen breathed a sigh of relief. She was finding it hard to keep her mind focused on the job, when so much of her wanted to be back in London by her sister's side.

KAREN CHECKED the time on her phone as she helped herself to breakfast. Though she wasn't a big breakfast person, and with her eating habits being so erratic, it was a treat to sit down and enjoy the full English breakfast on offer. With a croissant and jam to one side, and refillable coffee, she made the most of the opportunity, not knowing when she'd get a chance to eat again. As she savoured each mouthful, she took a moment to reflect on yesterday as her eyes scanned the other diners. It was a transient group of individuals scattered around the large dining room. A mixture of couples on mini breaks, businessmen passing through on their way to meetings in different parts of the country, and the odd person eating alone whilst reviewing the papers.

Karen found the team and the pace of life quite different to London. The DCI wasn't what she had expected, a complete contrast to Skelton and many of the DCIs she had met through the course of her career in London. She put it down to the sheer vastness of London and the fact that though the Met Police were one big family, it was the kind of family that was so spread out that you rarely formed deep friendships with many of them. Karen had made many friends as she'd moved around stations, but they'd often moved to different boroughs through the course of their careers, so it had become harder to keep in touch with them.

She raised a brow, questioning her internal dialogue. Maybe York was different because it was smaller, people knew each other, and so friendships were stronger. Other than the current cases that Zac was dealing with, she was led to believe that the rate of serious crime was relatively low. Having spoken to Zac and a few of the other officers, she had witnessed more in her career than all of those officers put together.

A psychiatrist, nurse, and solicitor. The fact they all had meaningful and important careers wasn't lost on Karen. That in itself formed a question of suspicion in her mind.

Some of the cases she had dealt with involved an organised criminal element, and it was easy to understand why those victims had been killed. Gangland feuds, drug deals gone wrong, turf wars, and domestic violence had often been the motives behind many of the homicides that she had dealt with. But this felt different. *Professional careers and York.* That's the connection that played heavily in Karen's mind. *If I need an answer, the answers will be here*, Karen thought.

"MORNING, DID YOU SLEEP WELL?" Zac asked, as Karen opened the door seconds after Zac pulled up outside the main entrance to the hotel.

Karen fastened her seatbelt and scrunched up her nose. "Like… a… baby. I swear, I never sleep that well at home," she replied, as an overwhelming wave of aftershave tickled her nostrils. She was too polite to say anything, but laughed inwardly.

Zac smiled. "What are your thoughts about yesterday?"

"Funny you should say that, but something tells me that the answer is up here, not London." Karen relayed snippets of the conversation with Jade, as well as her thoughts over breakfast. "I just hope to God he hasn't done a runner. I can't be arsed to chase his tail all over the country."

"Me neither. My arse was already on the line over the first murder. Eight weeks on and we're no further in the investigation. The second death has only placed the spotlight firmly on my shiny forehead!"

"Shiny bald head more like, if you don't get a result," Karen teased as they arrived at the station.

After signing in on her visitor's pass, she followed Zac through the building to meet his boss. They had both been so busy that Zac hadn't had the opportunity to do formal introductions.

"What's she like?" Karen asked as she glanced down to check her clothes, and then ran a hand through her hair to straighten it out.

"She's good. Tough, but good. Laura's been a copper for twenty-eight years, and done stints in London, Manchester, and more recently up here. She's also spent four years in the National Crime Squad. And she's already introducing a raft of changes to how we do our business here. Laura knows her stuff."

Zac poked his head around the open door. "Ma'am, are you free?"

"Of course, come in."

Karen followed Zac into a large and expansive room. A woman in a grey suit and white blouse stood up and came around her desk.

"Ma'am, this is Detective Inspector Karen Heath from the Met Police. She arrived yesterday to discuss our two murder cases, and how it may be linked to her case."

"Ma'am," Karen said, offering her hand.

Detective Chief Superintendent Laura Kelly stepped up to greet her, offering a firm handshake that went on for a few seconds longer than Karen had anticipated.

"Karen, good to meet you. I hope you've found your visit useful so far and that the team has made you welcome?"

Laura Kelly had a round face, a button nose, and cheeks with deep dimples that showed every time she smiled. Her smile looked sincere, and she portrayed professionalism in her smart business suit. Behind on a coat hanger hung her police uniform. Her dark brown hair was tied back in a low ponytail, and other than a bit of eyeliner, she adopted a natural look.

"Yes, ma'am. It's been refreshing, shall we say," Karen said with a wry smile.

Laura nodded knowingly. "Good. If there's anything you need, and Zac isn't around, give me a shout. My door is always open. An officer with your depth of experience in the Met will be a valuable asset to us in bringing a conclusion to both our cases. I won't keep you now, and besides, I have a meeting to attend to in five minutes. So, I'll let you both get on." Her eyes darted between Zac and Karen.

"Thank you, ma'am. We're heading down to the latest crime scene as Karen wants to see it in daylight," Zac said as they left.

"She seems nice," Karen commented as they made their way out of the building and towards Zac's car.

Zac paused by the driver's side. "Looks can be deceiving," he said, winking in her direction before unlocking the car and getting in.

28

Zac pulled up behind a long line of police vehicles parked up on the kerb. Karen noticed an increased police presence, much more than last night, with small huddles of officers in police overalls going through their plan of action to conduct a wider sweep of the area.

The local press teams were already there alongside film crews from all the major TV channels. She was glad that Zac's team had organised a strong enough police presence to prevent members of the public and press from getting too close and trampling over an active crime scene. Karen and Zac signed in with the scene guard before donning their protective overalls, booties, and gloves.

"They're watching our every bloody move," Karen tutted, when she noticed a long zoom lens pointed in her direction.

"They're desperate for a story. A press release isn't enough for them these days," Zac replied as they made their way through a clearing in the overgrown bushes, and into the field. The stepping plates from last night were still in place, but muddy and wet.

"Watch your footing," Zac warned Karen as he took the lead.

Further up the field, a small team of officers was conducting a fingertip search on their knees in a small area close to the bridge. Karen noticed a sheen of dampness across the muddy field. A second cordon had been set up around where Donna's body had been found. A white forensic tent remained in place, maintaining a sterile spot where crime scene investigators could continue their work undisturbed.

Karen paused and took a moment to survey the scene. She glanced back over her shoulder to the road and imagined the scene playing out in front of her. She closed her eyes and played back the images in her mind. *A lone woman being dragged whilst simultaneously being attacked through the overgrown bushes and into a muddy field. She's screaming, fighting for her life. The blows are raining down on her. She is helpless, powerless. She's pleading for her life. No! No. She's screaming, "Please help, help!"* Karen's eyes returned to the bridge. Somehow, she had managed to reach that point. Whether Donna had run away and only got that far, or whether her killer had dragged her to that point, Karen wasn't sure. Karen closed her eyes again. *The woman's head is caving in, the fragility of her skull cracking like an eggshell. Her body is riddled with pain. It's dark already, but it's getting darker by the second. The pain takes her, and she closes her eyes once more... forever.*

Karen took a deep breath and opened her eyes. She scanned the horizon, looking for any evidence of nearby buildings. There were none. *She really didn't have a chance.*

"There were two sets of footprints discovered in the mud, leading to this bridge," Zac pointed out. "Judging by the spacing between the footsteps, they appear to be too far spaced out for someone who was walking."

"So she was running? Running away..." Karen offered, filling in the blanks.

Zac nodded. "Though, there's evidence of long drag marks accompanied by one set of footprints, which suggests that the victim was dragged as she attempted to get away."

"She was definitely fighting for her life. But he clearly overpowered her."

Whilst they were talking, shouts rang out a short distance from them. Karen and Zac made their way over towards the stream, and the trees that lined both banks. At first the source of the shouting wasn't clear, until they weaved through the trees and down a small bank to the stream.

"What have you got?" Zac asked the PolSA team supervisor.

"We've discovered some remains, and what looks like a heart. We can't be certain it's human, but more than likely, considering the proximity to where the body was found."

If Karen had any doubt whether this brutal attack was connected to the other two cases, the discovery of the organ wiped it away. Resting on a shallow bank that dipped towards the water lay the grey remains of what appeared to be a heart. A few inches more to the right, and the organ would have landed in the water, and possibly washed away never to be found.

Zac requested crime scene investigators to photograph and catalogue the evidence and the scene before the search teams continued their work.

"Have you seen enough?" Zac asked as he watched the search teams spread out in a long line, and begin their work across a different part of the field.

Karen nodded, keen to visit the other crime scene, where the nurse was attacked.

THE LOCATION of where Danilo Reyes was killed was equally challenging. A long stretch of road that ran alongside the River Ouse, with a housing development setback off the road and hidden behind a wall of trees. Parkland surrounded the river and was popular amongst local dog walkers.

Zac pulled into a lay-by and crossed over the road towards a scene. They trudged through the overgrowth until they came to a small area that had only recently been cleared by specialist search teams after Danilo's body was discovered.

"This is where his body was found. As you can see it's closer to town, and would have been in earshot of local residents," Zac pointed out, jabbing a finger in the direction of where they had come from. Zac went on to describe Danilo's route home, and how he was moments away from being safe when he was brutally attacked.

"Is there much traffic down this road in the evenings?" Karen asked.

"It's sporadic. It's one of the routes into the housing estate across the road. With the street lights, it's relatively well-lit, but it would only take seconds for a pedestrian to be dragged from the pavement and into this overgrown area. After which point, no one would even know they're there."

Karen surveyed the scene. Dense bushes and brambles surrounded them. The trees were tall and mature, and in daylight, only speckled light snaked its way through the dense canopy. Had it have not been for the dog, his body could have remained here for weeks undiscovered. The closer she examined the scene, the more she realised how cunning the killer had been. He had chosen this location specifically. A dense overgrown area, a secluded stretch of road, with intermittent traffic, and the closest houses had their view shielded by a wall of trees that skirted the boundary of the estate. It was perfect.

"It's unlikely that the killer chose this location at random. The bastard knows the area. He either grew up here, or lived here, or worse… still lives here," Karen said, turning towards Zac. "Donna's murder has similarities. Isolated location, easy to dispose of a body, and not overlooked."

"You're suggesting that he chose these locations specifically, rather than them being randomised attacks?"

Karen shook her head. "Not specifically, as in these spots have a meaning of significance. To me it looks like he scoped the areas thoroughly before deciding where would be the best place to attack where he wouldn't be seen, nor be caught."

"He's from the local area?"

Karen shrugged a shoulder. "Quite possibly. He knew where my victim lived. He knew his routine. Doctor Kumar never went out at night and followed the same pattern day in and day out. *Our* killer knew that routine, and also knew that he wouldn't be able to attack Doctor Kumar on his morning walk, because it was too public. His only choice was to target Kumar in his house."

Zac rubbed his temples. "The local residents have been shocked and alarmed by the murder of this nurse. There's been a public outpouring of grief. His colleagues at the hospital were devastated. The press release on Donna has only heightened the anxiety amongst people living within the city." Zac bit his bottom lip. "If we had another victim, the city would be gripped with fear, and the publicity could drive the killer underground."

Zac's thoughts sat uncomfortably with both of them as they made their way back to the car.

29

Karen slid into one of the chairs in the main incident room as Zac gathered his team together. Officers planted themselves wherever they could to hear him. A few perched on the edge of desks, whilst others swivelled around in computer chairs. Karen scanned their faces. There was in excess of twenty officers and support staff, many of whom were still idly chatting, smiling amongst themselves, and ribbing one another.

An officer that Karen hadn't met dodged between his gathered colleagues and sat heavily on one of the desks. Its top creaked under his weight. He was a big lad in Karen's opinion, six-foot plus, pushing at least seventeen- or eighteen-stone, and judging by his facial features, loved his rugby. His broken nose skewed to one side, and the beginnings of a cauliflower ear were classic telltale signs. Karen wasn't surprised that he carried the battle scars. She had no doubt he would be a formidable opponent on the rugby pitch, and even a colleague would think twice about tackling him.

"Dan, if you break that desk, don't ask any of us to pick

wooden splinters out of your arse!" an officer shouted from the middle of the crowd.

A roar of laughter broke out amongst the team, as Dan swivelled on the desk and gave the officer a one-finger salute. "If I needed splinters picked out of my arse, I'd at least ask someone who was better looking than you," Dan looked around the team, "and judging by those gathered, that is everyone else in the room… If I wanted to listen to an arsehole I'd fart."

The laughter continued as the officers slung insults at each other.

"All right. That's enough, or I'll send you both to the naughty corner," Zac said as he interrupted them. It seemed to have the desired effect as the voices trailed off.

Karen sat to one side, watching Zac run the show. He was a complex character in her mind. Charismatic, authoritative, funny and attractive.

She took a moment to glance around the office again, still in awe at how clean, vibrant and modern it was. Glass walls partitioned many of the smaller offices, and even in the main incident room, it was separated from the hallway by glass panelling. She wondered how much had been spent on refurbishing the offices. Everything was spotless, right down to the mugs in the kitchen, and even clean loos. A small detail, but, welcomed. It was all a big contrast to London and refreshing in her eyes.

Zac began the briefing. Though details were bare, his team focused on identifying the white vehicle seen close to the scene of Donna Anderson's murder. They had started to revisit available footage from close to where Danilo was murdered in the hope that a white vehicle was seen. So far, the search hadn't thrown up any matches.

Cathy, a member of the forensic team, chipped in next, outlining how the team had been able to identify blue clothing fibres snagged on bramble bushes close to where Danilo was found. The composition was one hundred per cent polyester with a polyurethane membrane coating. Neither Danilo nor the dog walker who discovered his body were wearing any clothing that matched the fibres recovered.

"What kind of clothing are we looking for?" Zac asked.

Cathy pushed her glasses back up the bridge of her nose before continuing. "We're probably looking at a waterproof, water resistant jacket or trousers. Probably a jacket. Outdoor clothing retailers and brands tend to have jackets that come with a waxy or polyurethane coating. It basically makes them showerproof."

"Like Barbour jackets?"

Cathy nodded. "Certainly the lighter jackets that they do would fit the bill. Their heavier wax jackets tend to have much denser fibres with waxy layers, which make the jackets stiffer and more resilient to rain."

That was progress as far as Zac was concerned. It was highly likely that Danilo's murderer was wearing a blue jacket.

Belinda stepped in next. "According to her website, Donna Anderson was a solicitor who specialised in private practice, matrimonial and criminal cases. A search of her house confirmed no signs of a disturbance nor robbery. And considering she still had her phone, credit cards and purse with her, I think we can rule out robbery for sure."

A sea of heads nodded, as the officers listened intently. Several scribbled down notes as the meeting continued.

Zac turned towards Karen. "Karen, do you want to give the team a quick rundown of your case? I think it would be helpful for them to build a bigger picture of what we're dealing with," he said, raising his brows, which creased his forehead.

"Yep, sounds good to me." Karen turned and faced the team. All eyes were on her, and for a brief moment, she felt a rush of heat in her cheeks. "Doctor Anil Kumar was a retired psychiatric consultant. He had been working in private practice for the last couple of years of his career before retiring early to care for his wife, a dementia sufferer."

Karen passed around images of her crime scene and went on to explain the circumstances of the attack, and the parallels with the cases that Zac's team were dealing with in terms of the injuries, and the hearts being removed. She pointed out how Doctor Kumar's family were from York, and why she suspected that the answers lay in York rather than London.

"Is there a possibility that all three victims had worked together at one point in their careers?" an officer asked.

Karen raised a brow and offered a shrug. "That's certainly a possibility, and not one we had thought about yet," she added, casting a quick glance in Zac's direction, who grimaced.

Zac instructed his team to investigate the angle and report

back to him as he glanced at the time on his watch. "I've got to go into a briefing shortly, but the post-mortem on Donna Anderson is due to take place later, so Anita, can you attend on my behalf, and take Karen with you when she returns from visiting Doctor Kumar's family?" Zac asked, turning towards his DI, who nodded in reply. "Anita, can you also organise resources to build a full victimology on Donna Anderson?" Zac turned his back on the team and stared at the whiteboard. The smiling faces of Donna Anderson and Danilo Reyes stared back at him, evidence of happier times in their lives. "So what's the connection? Is there a connection? Or were they the victims of a random psycho?"

Karen rested her chin on the back of her hand as she leant on one armrest. "I'm wondering if it's a patient? That could tie in the nurse and psychiatric consultant angle, but it wouldn't explain Donna's murder." There had been many cases documented over the years where unstable patients with deep-rooted psychiatric problems had turned on those who were there to help them. She could think of several cases that spanned the length and breadth of the country.

Zac closed the briefing not long after before he headed to his meeting, leaving Karen with Tyler to visit Doctor Kumar's family.

30

Tyler took one of the job cars and drove the short twenty-minute journey to Wheldrake, south-east of the city centre. Karen couldn't help but admire that within minutes of leaving the city, they were driving through unspoiled landscapes, along narrow roads skirted with tall hedgerows, agricultural land, and large swathes of mature trees. She could have sworn that even the air smelt different up here.

Twenty minutes out of central London and she'd still hit Whitechapel, a melting pot of cultures, narrow streets lined with one hundred-year-old houses, and an infrastructure creaking at its seams. The smell of diesel fumes hung in the air, and a grittiness clung to the inside of her nose and dried out her throat. The discomfort only increased in London as the temperature got hotter, and the air got drier during the summer months. There would be days when she would struggle to breathe properly because of the pollution.

"Have you always been up here, Tyler?" Karen asked, as her eyes were drawn to the ploughed fields.

"Pretty much, boss. I've had chances to move around the country, but seriously, I'd miss all this..." he replied, waving his hand in front of him. "I've got family all over the place. Glasgow, Liverpool, Manchester, and Trinidad of course!" Tyler laughed; his booming voice filled the car.

"Is that where your family is from?"

"Oh, yeah. The whole gang. My mum, my dad, grandparents, cousins, uncles and aunties. You name it. I don't think any of them would ever leave. Big foodies, all of us. In fact, Trinidadians love their food. Have you ever tried any, boss?"

Karen pursed her lips together and shook her head. "Never. Nice?"

Tyler's eyes lit up. "Oh my God, boss. It's the best. If I ever come down to London, I'll take you for proper Trinidadian food."

"I'll look forward to that." Karen hadn't experienced much diversity in her palate. Every time the team had gone out for a celebration, it had only been a curry. And that was spicy enough for her. Karen returned her gaze outside. "It's beautiful here. Very relaxing."

"It is, boss. A much slower pace of life. Well... It was until these murders landed on our desk."

"How do you find working with the DCI?" Karen wasn't sure if Tyler would be honest or open for that matter considering both herself and Zac were senior officers to him, but she was taken aback by his openness.

"Zac's great. I've not worked for a boss like that. Well, even though he is my boss, he doesn't feel like it... If you know what I mean?" he replied, glancing across to Karen to see if she understood.

"Do you not address Zac as boss, or guv?"

"Sorry, boss. I know what you're saying, but Zac doesn't want us calling him the boss, or guv, or anything like that. He's really open and down-to-earth. Everyone is on first-name terms unless you are addressing the super."

Karen raised a brow, unsure whether she would be happy at not having a clean line of authority when addressing a higher rank. It wasn't something she was used to.

Tyler pulled up after weaving through a small estate, and they both stepped from the car. It was a relatively modern development of single-storey bungalows, a uniform dwarf brick wall around the perimeter of each garden, with matching driveways and small lawns.

Karen rang the doorbell and waited. A small thin Asian man answered the door and eyed them both with suspicion.

"Suresh Kumar?"

The man nodded. "And you are?"

Karen and Tyler held up their warrant cards. "I'm Detective Inspector Karen Heath from the Metropolitan Police in London, and this is my colleague Detective Constable Tyler Owen from York city police. It's about your brother. May we come in?"

The man's eyes fell before he nodded and stepped aside to allow them in. He led them through to the lounge and offered them a seat.

The first thing Karen noticed was how similar it was in layout to Doctor Kumar's house. The small alcove contained photographs, and above the fireplace, in a prominent position, hung a large picture of an Indian god, the same image she had seen in Doctor Kumar's house. A hint of Indian spices hung in the air, and the sound of pots being rattled came from the kitchen.

"Suresh, we're really sorry about your brother. I'm the senior investigating officer for your brother's case, and I specifically wanted to meet with you to find out more about him and his family."

Suresh offered the slightest of nods in appreciation. "What would you like to know?" he said, folding his arms across his chest.

"Can you tell me a bit about the work he was involved in before he retired?"

Suresh's face tightened for a minute before he looked up towards the ceiling, deep in thought. "My brother's job was very stressful. He dealt with lots of difficult people. People with problems in their minds. Many of them on tablets."

Karen sensed that Suresh found it difficult to describe his brother's work. Whether that was because he didn't understand it, or whether Anil Kumar didn't speak about it, she wasn't sure. But she nevertheless continued to probe him about Anil's work.

"Did he ever mention anything about being in trouble, or upsetting anyone?"

"Are you saying that he knew the person who killed him?"

"Not at all, Suresh. We're exploring all avenues and keeping an open mind."

"I'm not aware of anyone threatening him. But I do recall a

time not long ago before he retired where he was particularly occupied. Like there was something on his mind. I did ask him, but he didn't say. He seemed nervous. As I said, it was a very stressful job. His wife put a lot of pressure on him to do other jobs instead, because she was worried about him."

Karen nodded, whilst Tyler made notes.

"And did he think of changing careers?" she asked.

Suresh offered the smallest of smiles. "I don't think he had time to consider anything else. Aruna fell badly one day in the street and spent five weeks in hospital. She hit her head." Suresh placed his hand on the side of his head. "The doctors found a bleed on her brain, which they treated. But then afterwards she started to experience a lot of headaches, dizziness, and her health deteriorated. She was never the same again."

"Was that the beginning of her dementia?"

Suresh nodded. "He couldn't cope any more. And I'm too old to help. My wife has enough to do here with the children, and the grandchildren. Our son and daughter-in-law work full-time. We look after their two children. They are only four and seven years old." He looked over his shoulder towards pictures on a shelf.

Karen followed his eyes and noticed a few pictures of what appeared to be an extended family, with several young children sitting on the floor in front of the adults.

"But that's okay. It's how our culture works. My son still lives here. It's only natural that we look after our grandchildren."

"And how did Aruna's illness affect everyone?"

"Anil couldn't cope. There were certain things that he needed help with. That's why he moved to London so that Aruna could be near her sister, and they could rely on her help a bit more."

Karen asked a few more questions before leaving, curious about what Doctor Kumar had been nervous about.

THE FIRST THING Karen did after returning to the office was call Hinchcliff with an update. Though he pressed as to when she was returning, Karen sidetracked his question by telling him about their visit to Doctor Kumar's family, and promising that she would update him shortly. She hung up and called Jade whilst walking up and down the corridor outside the incident room.

"Hi, Karen. How's it going up there?"

"Slowly. But I'll tell you something, I'm very impressed with the setup up here. Swanky offices, a solid team, and beautiful surroundings. It's a complete contrast to us in London, a much quieter and slower pace of life."

"Hey, don't get too settled up there. You're needed back here," Jade teased.

Karen filled Jade in on her visit to Doctor Kumar's family, and asked her to look into Doctor Kumar's work in greater detail, including any case files of patients that they were able to get their hands on.

"Have we been able to progress our case in any way?" Karen asked.

"We're still looking. We've found no credible eyewitnesses, nor have we been able to trace the car."

"Press appeal results?"

"Again, nothing credible. We are still going through the enquiries and chasing up any of interest. It's surprising how many dead ends and wasted leads we've had. And to be honest, there's been a lot of enquiries from concerned residents. I've spoken to the duty inspector, and he's confirmed that they are increasing police presence in the area to reassure everyone."

"Well, that's good from a PR point of view. I'm pretty certain this wasn't a random killing, so I don't think residents have got anything to worry about, but the less we say the better," Karen replied. "Anything from forensics?"

"Nope, we're still waiting. But here's an interesting case dating back eighteen years. A boxer by the name of Victor Radich ripped out the heart of his training partner whilst he was still alive after becoming convinced that he was possessed by the devil. He also cut out his victim's tongue, and ripped off most of his face, in what the investigating team described as a scene from a horror movie."

Karen took in a sharp intake of breath as she listened to Jade.

"When police arrived, they found Victor standing over his training partner, with body parts strewn all around them, including an eyeball and the heart. When police interviewed him, he said he heard voices telling him that his training partner was possessed, and out to kill him."

"Blimey, that's savage. There's killing someone, and then

there is really killing someone!" Karen sighed, shocked at the level of brutality that humans could inflict.

"Victor was covered from head to foot in blood, and was pacing around the room, waving his arms in the air, attempting to chase away the devil. Officers had to taser him three times before they could get anywhere near him."

"Is Victor still inside?" Karen asked.

"No. He was released last year with four years left on his sentence and put under the care of a psychiatric unit as an outpatient. He's in Horbling."

"Shit. So not only did they release him early, but he is free to roam the streets?" Karen fumed, her pulse rising as her muscles stiffened. "Where is Horbling?"

"Midway between York and London, Karen."

"Jade, get local officers to attend and question him as a matter of urgency. Also search prison records for anyone else released within the last year who has committed a similar crime."

"Anything else, Karen?"

"No. Nothing else. I've got to shoot off now anyway. I'm attending the post-mortem on the latest victim. I'll update you as soon as I can. See you in a bit." Karen hung up before heading back onto the incident floor.

31

"You met the Terminator then?"

Karen glanced across at DI Anita Mani with a confused look across her face. "The Terminator?"

Anita slowed at traffic lights as she made her way to York Hospital. "The chief super, Laura. We call her the Terminator. Obviously not to her face, and only a select few in our team know about her affectionate nickname," Anita added, rolling her eyes.

"Go on, spill the beans," Karen prompted as she watched people cross in front of their car. Some hurried across, even though the green man still glowed.

"Well, behind that smiling exterior, and all the supportive words that she spews, Laura has a propensity for getting rid of people and having them shifted to different departments if she doesn't like them."

Karen raised a brow. "I've met loads like that. I think it comes with the territory, doesn't it?"

Anita shrugged. "I guess. Don't get me wrong. She's straight-talking, and supportive, but you don't want to piss her off. Like Marmite, you love her or hate her."

Karen wondered which camp Anita was in. She'd only spoken to Anita a few times, and so remained guarded. "You seem to have a pretty good team around you, and a great setup. How are you liking the job?"

Anita nodded, as a warm smile returned to her face. "They're a great bunch. I quite like the idea of us being able to consider ourselves friends both in and out of the job. You know yourself how hard it can be, with the stress, and long hours. If you didn't have a good bunch around you, the job would break you. I think Zac is brilliant. He's created a really good harmonious team, and yes, we do have moments when we get pissed off with each other, but we all know that when we walk out of the door at the end of each shift, we wipe the slate clean and start afresh."

Everything Karen had heard about Zac was nothing but complimentary. A great boss, a great friend, and perhaps even a great parent from the few hours she had spent over dinner with him and his daughter.

"Zac has been very supportive," Anita continued. "Ash, my husband, and I had a few problems with our daughter Samara when she was in sixth form. She was getting picked on, shit stuff being written about her on Snapchat and Facebook. The usual bullying bollocks. Bless her. Samara is petite and quiet. She has a heart of gold, and is very soft and gentle, and because of that, she was well liked by teachers."

Even though she had not met Samara, she already felt sorry for her.

"Anyway, Zac really stepped in when Ash and I were struggling to uplift Samara's spirits. He let me work from home, so I could be there for her. He even invited the three of us over to his house to spend a few evenings with him and Summer so we could all chill with a movie and pizza."

"Is Samara okay now?" Karen asked.

Anita batted the question away with her hand. "Oh God, yeah. She's nineteen now and at Exeter University studying sports science."

"Really? I didn't think you were that old?" Karen threw a hand over her mouth, realising her observation had come out the wrong way. "Shit, sorry. I didn't mean that you looked older or anything. Nor did I mean that you were a child bride or anything like that. I'm digging myself into a big pit here, so I'll shut up now."

Anita laughed. "Don't be silly. You mean I'm drop dead gorgeous for my age, and I don't look a day older than twenty-five."

Karen joined her in the laughter.

"I had an arranged marriage at nineteen and had Samara when I was twenty."

Many would have found that draconian, but having met many Asian families in London, Karen understood that arranged marriages were part of the culture and tradition. Anita went on to explain how she already knew Ash prior to getting engaged and had secretly fallen in love. So, when the topic of getting married came up in Anita's family, Ash and Anita manufactured the opportunity for both families to meet formally, and proposals to be made.

After arriving at the hospital, Karen followed Anita as they made their way through the main entrance. It was a long walkway with shops on either side, and an interesting domed roof that ran its full length. Seats had been arranged in horseshoe-shapes, whilst patients and visitors waited. A quick right, and they were by the mortuary. Once Anita and Karen were shown in, they were guided towards the main examination room. It didn't matter which mortuary she had visited during her career, they all felt the same. A corridor lined on both sides with fridges, a demarcation line separating the clean and dirty zones, as well as a section of fridges for those with infectious diseases, infants, or no next of kin.

The familiar smell of air freshener mixed with detergent, and disinfectant hung in the air as the officers went through to the examination room. Three steel tables greeted Karen, the central one occupied by Donna's body which was being expertly worked on by the pathologist. The sound of rock music blared around the cavernous room, and the figure of a red-headed woman nodded her head to the beat. Karen watched as the pathologist sang along, badly, with the chorus before she looked up to see her visitors.

"Hi, Isabella. I'd like to introduce you to Detective Inspector Karen Heath from the Metropolitan Police. She's joined us on this case because they've had a murder with the same M.O."

Isabella glanced up and held her bloodied gloved hands in front of her. "Metallica!"

Karen narrowed her eyes in confusion. "Sorry?"

Isabella jabbed a finger up towards the ceiling. "Metallica. You can't beat a bit of Metallica, 'Nothing Else Matters'."

The chorus belted out once again, as the words "nothing else matters" were repeated. It was only then Karen realised that Isabella was referring to the title of the song.

"Isabella Armitage, consultant pathologist here at this marvellous institution, mother of two dogs, urban warrior, terrible cook, and even worse air guitar rocker," she said, introducing herself.

Karen glanced over at Anita, who hid a smile behind her hand. Anita had said on their journey over that the pathologist was a gregarious character, and her colleague's assessment had been right. She had bright copper red hair pinned back in a ponytail. A tattooed sleeve covered her left arm, although from where she stood, Karen couldn't make out the intricacies of the design. But she could be certain of one thing — Isabella Armitage was the complete opposite of Wainwright.

"How are you finding York, Karen?" Isabella asked.

Karen stared wide-eyed as she took in the larger-than-life character conducting proceedings.

"It's been interesting, certainly not what I expected."

Isabella tipped her head back and roared with laughter, as if expecting her diplomatic response.

Karen returned her gaze to the cadaver and took a moment to cast her eyes over the body of Donna Anderson. Her chest had been opened and held in place with metal clamps, which gave Isabella space to work. She couldn't see much of Donna's face, the skin on her scalp had been delicately loosened, and reflected back over her face, exposing the remnants of her shattered skull. Donna's hands had been placed inside plastic bags to preserve vital evidence.

"What have you found out so far?" Anita asked as she moved up towards the head of the table for a closer look.

"Chocolate…! Lots of chocolate."

"Sorry?"

"Our victim had scoffed a lot of chocolate as her last meal," Isabella replied.

"Right, not sure that's the breakthrough we need. Anything else?" Anita pushed.

"Well, there's not a lot left of Donna's head to be honest," Isabella began. "I've seen more brain on a butchers table than what's left here. She experienced significant trauma with a blunt instrument, and a heavy one too. I'd say metal, as I've not found any wood splinters. A tyre lever, or a small length of scaffold pole would be enough to cause this. We removed remnants of the brain, but I would say that less than ten per cent remained."

"And her heart?"

"Yes, we've examined the remnants of the heart discovered close to the scene. I'm fairly certain that it belongs to the victim. Further tests will confirm that. Her cause of death was significant trauma to her head, and blood loss."

As Karen listened to Isabella's running commentary, she leant in and studied the bruising along Donna's arms, around her face, and her neck. She noticed other bruising to parts of her thighs and shins. "He really did a number on her, didn't he?"

Anita and Isabella stopped talking to examine further

injuries. "I'd say that many of these are defensive marks," Isabella added, pointing to the scratch marks along Donna's arms and the back of her hands. "She certainly put up a fight, despite her injuries."

"Until she couldn't fight any more…" Anita added.

The three of them paused for a minute, deep in reflection before Isabella added, "I've taken tissue samples, toxicology, and I'll be taking scrapings from beneath her fingernails. Hopefully, we might get something. I think due to the location where she was found, we may have lost vital evidence because of the wet and muddy ground."

Anita and Karen thanked Isabella for her time before leaving her to conclude the examination.

32

Like all his other targets, the killer had tracked this one on and off for a few weeks now. Keeping a safe distance, he had followed him through the streets, dipping into shop doorways, peering around street corners, and often walking on the opposite side of the road one hundred yards behind, but never losing sight of him.

Today was no different, and seeing the man filled him with a sense of anger and fury. It had taken every ounce of patience to not chase the man down and rip his throat out. Everything needed to be done in order, and one by one he had ticked off each victim from his mental notepad, leaving the best until last. This piece of shit had been unrelenting in bringing him down, and now the tables were turned. The hunter becoming the hunted.

There were plenty of people in the street, the morning rush hour well underway. The pavements were busy, and buses snaked around the streets.

He laughed. His victims did the same thing every day, so he

knew their routines better than they did. Their monotony made it so easy for him. He needed to keep a safe distance and lurk in the shadows. Today was no different as he tracked his victim across town. He watched as the man popped into a local shop close to where he lived to pick up a few bits. Today, it was a loaf of bread, a packet of B & H Lights, probably because he was trying to cut down his smoking on health grounds, and two pints of milk. If his victim was worried about dying of lung cancer, he was happy to speed up his journey to hell.

The man was scared. The killer had made sure of that. In the darkness of night, he'd broken into the man's garden, and moved items of garden furniture around. Nothing too obvious to the eye, but if you stopped to look at it, you'd realise that something was odd. A flowerpot moved from one side of the patio to the other. The garden chairs once folded and propped against the wall now sat on the floor. The padlock from the shed at the end of his garden broken and on the floor, though nothing was disturbed inside. He was sure his victim blamed foxes for the chairs, but the shed had left him worried and scared.

The funeral wreath delivered to his front door had terrified his victim more than anything else. The killer had watched from a distance as his intended victim had raced from his front door to the pavement, his eyes scanning up and down the road, his movements jittery and nervous. The killer had smiled as his victim had turned on the delivery driver, grabbing him by his jacket, and screaming obscenities at him whilst demanding to know who had sent it. Of course, he'd cleverly used false details and a stolen credit card to complete the purchase and terrorise the man.

These little subtle touches made his final victim edgy. He

knew he'd got to him when a police car had visited, with two plain-clothes officers spending an hour at the property before leaving.

A few weeks had passed before surveillance started again. In the interim, the killer had travelled up and down the country over hundreds of miles, being patient, and taking care of business whilst controlling the ball of fury that simmered deep inside him like a cauldron of fire ready to spew scalding venom each time he met one of his victims.

Following his intended target today had only reinforced his burning desire to see his plans through, as he started up the ignition and pulled away, his target put the key in his door and disappeared into his house.

It would soon be time to put this shitbag out of his misery as well.

33

Karen swiped in, picking up a bacon roll and a cup of tea from the canteen before making her way to her desk amongst Zac's team.

Karen's time in York had taken longer than anticipated. Hinchcliff was on her back, wanting continuous updates, and with little to offer him, the man grew more impatient as each day passed. She fed him as much as she was able to, but knew it wasn't enough to satisfy her boss. As she dressed for work this morning, doubts grew in her mind whether it had been a wasted journey. Teams from two forces were chasing an elusive killer who could be anywhere now. The leads were thin, the forensic evidence patchy at best, and there was a real possibility that both cases could be consigned to the unsolved list.

Karen had pushed that thought to the back of her mind as she'd left the hotel this morning. Zac hadn't been able to pick her up, so she'd grabbed a taxi and made a few calls on her journey in. There were no further updates on her sister. In a way, it was reassuring, but frustrating, nevertheless. She didn't want her sister stable and responding; she wanted her better, and back in a familiar environment.

Her impatience had grown as the taxi driver had edged through morning traffic at a speed that made her wonder whether she could walk faster. But one thing was becoming clearer, everything was slower than in London, and that included the traffic and pace of life.

As Karen fired up her computer, she took a moment to glance around the floor. There were a handful of officers in, with many still out following up every conceivable lead, witness and sighting. The incident board towards the far end of the room appeared to have little new information added overnight.

"How did you get on at the PM yesterday?" Zac asked as he came up behind her.

His sudden question broke her reverie. She glanced around to see Zac hovering inches from her. The overpowering scent of his aftershave invaded her space and tickled her nostrils. It wasn't a bad smell, she liked it, but there was too much of it.

"The victim was beaten savagely. There really wasn't much of the back of the head, and even less of her brain." Karen went on to explain the rest of the findings, and Isabella's conclusions.

Zac smiled. "Ah, you met Isabella. Interesting character…"

Karen nodded. "To say the least. But she knows her shit. I'm hoping that her full report throws us a lifeline."

"Agreed. In the meantime, the team has uncovered interesting information on Donna Anderson." As Karen swivelled in her chair, Zac perched on the end of her table.

"Donna was admitted to York Hospital thirteen months ago following a violent assault. We managed to obtain her medical records. She was attacked by an earlier client called Charles Dixon, a convicted armed robber."

The corner of Karen's lips dropped as she wondered where this was going, as Zac continued.

"She refused to press charges at the time. It later transpired that she had been in a clandestine relationship with Dixon after working with him as a client. My guess is that she was already in a relationship with him whilst he was her client."

"Possible motive…" Karen speculated.

Zac nodded in agreement. "Dixon is a violent man with a string of arrests and convictions. Records show she had contacted the police on three separate occasions after being intimidated with death threats by Dixon following their split. Again, she wanted the police to have a word with him but refused to press charges."

"Definitely worth giving him a tug then. He has a motive, revenge."

"That's what I thought, Karen. He's still in York, so how about we pay him a visit?"

"Pointless me firing up my computer," Karen said as she jumped up from her chair, not needing to be asked twice.

"When you said he lives in York, I didn't realise you meant two minutes down the road!" Karen said as she stepped from Zac's car.

Zac laughed. "Oh, didn't I mention that small fact?"

"No. The bloody heaters in the car didn't have time to warm up. I barely put the seatbelt on."

"Well, I didn't want you to get too comfortable and warm," Zac teased.

"Do you get a kick out of winding people up?" she added, raising a brow.

Zac glanced over his shoulder and nodded for her to follow. "Come on. I don't want you moaning that you're cold."

Karen mumbled something to herself as she caught up with Zac. The apartment block appeared untidy. Plastic crates, discarded mattresses and bed bases, broken cupboards, and tatty old children's bicycles lay scattered on the small grassy area to the front. The security lock to the communal door was broken. Zac used the sleeve of his coat to open the door and step into the hallway, followed by Karen, who scrunched her nose at the stale smell.

Zac paused in front of the door that looked as if it had been kicked in several times. Dirty boot marks and chipped paint confirmed his suspicions as he knocked. It felt like several minutes before the door opened, and a bald-headed man of African descent peered through the gap.

"Yeah, what you want?" he demanded, his voice gruff and menacing.

"Charles Dixon?"

"Who wants to know?"

"A word, please," Zac replied, as both he and Karen held up their warrant cards.

"Fuck sake man, can't you lot leave me alone?" he hissed as he tutted.

"It won't take long. The sooner you let us in, the quicker we can be out of your hair," Zac replied, smiling as he stared at the man's bald head.

Dixon rolled his eyes before opening the door further, and walking away into the lounge. He fell back onto the sofa, his hands interlocked and resting on his belly, his legs stretched out in front of him, and his head dropped to one side as he examined his visitors with a smile that showed a gold tooth.

Karen walked around the lounge, casting an eye over the unopened circulars stacked on the table, plus several mobile phones. The carpets were threadbare, and the room hadn't been aired in months. The smell of dampness lingered in the air. Empty pizza boxes sat on top of an already full bin, and a half-bottle of Glenmorangie took pride of place on an empty mantelpiece.

Zac stood directly in front of Dixon, a few feet separating them. He crossed his arms in defiance and stared at the man. "We're here about Donna Anderson…"

Before Zac could finish his sentence, Dixon pursed his lips in defiance, and shook his head. "I know nuttin' bro about da bitch. Me and her were over long time!" he said, his accent thickened with a Jamaican twang.

"She was beaten to death last Sunday, and when I mean beaten, like there was nothing left of her head. When was the last time you saw her?"

Karen stood back observing Dixon, whilst Zac asked the questions. She occasionally peered through the window at the street beyond in case any of Dixon's associates turned up.

Dixon shrugged. "And…?"

"When was the last time you saw her?" Zac pressed again.

"Who knows? One year ago. She's nuttin'."

"Do you own a car?"

"Nope. Never passed my test. Who needs a car, man, when my brethren take me wherever I want?"

"Any of your mates got a white car?"

"Nope."

"Where were you last Sunday evening?" Zac asked.

Dixon stared up towards the ceiling as if pretending to recall where he was. "Here, I was here."

"Can anyone vouch for you?"

Dixon let out a roar of laughter that antagonised Zac and made him clench his fists.

"Go upstairs to number six, speak to Asha. She was here with me, in my bed, doing 'tings. Want me to show you a picture on my phone, she's sucking me off?" he said defiantly. "You ras-clat!"

Dixon's Jamaican twang annoyed Zac. No matter how many times he heard those phrases, it still grated him.

"We understand Donna Anderson represented you both at court, and during your parole board meeting. Once released, she entered into a relationship with you. That was convenient? Are you sure you weren't in a relationship with her already before you went down?"

"You watch your mouth… officer," Dixon snarled.

"I'm watching it all right. Don't you worry about that. I wonder how much you manipulated her for your own purposes, and when you didn't need her any more, you did away with her. Perhaps she never got over you, and when she hassled you too much, you beat the shit out of her?"

Dixon laughed. "Get your arse out here, before I mash you up! And take that skanky 'ting with you unless she wants to hang around for a bit of action with my meat…" he said, rubbing his groin with a roar of laughter.

"Consider this a friendly visit, Dixon. The next time I come here, I'll be dragging your arse back to the station," Zac replied as they left.

"He was a charming chap. What a fucking prick," Karen said, getting back in the car. "I would happily have torn him a new arsehole with my baton."

Zac felt the same. Just before they'd left, they had visited Asha at number six, who confirmed she had been with Dixon on Sunday night.

"I can see the possibility of bad blood between Dixon and Donna Anderson. I can't see the connection between him and the doctor or the nurse," Karen said as she aired her thoughts.

Zac agreed as he reported back to the team, and instructed Belinda to dig up any dirt on Dixon, his contacts and associates, or people he had shared a cell with.

34

"Zac, we've had a bit of a result in the latest TV appeal," Tyler shouted as Zac and Karen returned to the team.

There was a noticeable buzz of energy in the room that had lifted everyone's spirits. Karen felt her heartbeat quicken at the news. Was this the breakthrough they needed? *I hope so.*

"What have we got?" Zac asked.

"We had an eyewitness come forward, who noticed a white car parked on the side of the road on Sunday night at around seven thirty p.m. The witness said the car had its hazard lights flashing."

"Anyone near the vehicle?"

Tyler shook his head. "She doesn't believe so. She was more worried about going around the vehicle because it was so dark. Here's the interesting point. She thinks it was a white Ford Focus but could only remember a partial index, EK18."

"I don't suppose she saw anyone inside?"

"Nope. She only had a quick glance as she drove past, but thought the car was empty, and perhaps it had run out of petrol. Considering there was a petrol station further up the road, she thought the driver might have set off on foot."

"Right, we need to double our efforts on reviewing CCTV footage from the petrol station."

"I've already done that. There was no tape of any pedestrians, or anyone asking for help because they had broken down. We've checked the CCTV footage and spoken to the forecourt attendant on duty that night."

Zac stuffed his hands in his pockets and paced over towards the whiteboard. He studied all the details. The pictures of the victims jumped out from the board and overwhelmed his senses. He grabbed a pen and added the partial index to the information about the white car. He wrote the words Ford Focus in brackets.

Tyler joined him. "I've done a search already; we haven't got much to go on. There were one point two million Ford Focus's registered in 2018, of which four hundred and fourteen thousand were white, and as far as we can tell, two hundred and eighteen of them are registered in the York area."

The scale of the task ahead of them wasn't lost on Zac as he crunched the numbers. It made sense to start with the two hundred plus vehicles in the York area before extending their search, but there was also the possibility that the vehicle wasn't from York at all.

"Okay, Tyler, that's great news. It's a start. Speak to the DVLA and start running the index against registered owners in the area." Zac turned towards Belinda. "Any news from the prison service?"

Belinda shrugged. "Sorry, Zac. We're still waiting for the information. I've asked them to speed it up and will chase again in a few hours if I haven't heard anything."

"I'll call Jade," Karen said, pulling out her phone.

"Hi, Karen, how's it going?" Jade said as she answered. "I thought you'd forgotten about us."

"It's been manic, Jade. We've been going around in circles, but we've had our first breakthrough," Karen replied before updating Jade on the partial index. "Any further updates with our team?"

"Forensics have been doing a further detailed search of Doctor Kumar's house. Let me grab the paperwork whilst I'm on the phone to you. But there's nothing in London to suggest that his murder is related to anything or any activity he was involved with down here."

"I kind of figured that might be the case, Jade. I'm convinced that the answers are in York, where he spent most of his life."

"Ah, here it is. They've picked up unknown fibres from one of the sofas. They've not been able to link them back to any items of clothing, rugs, or cushions within the Kumars' house. They are alien to the property."

"Could it be their son? Maybe he visited recently?"

"We've checked that angle, Karen. It doesn't link back to him either. There's also no hair or liquid evidence. I know it's not much, but it's another piece of evidence which may link back to the killer."

Karen blew out her cheeks. Either the killer was forensically aware, or had been bloody lucky, in her opinion.

"I had local officers visit Victor Radich. By all accounts he's a scary character, built like a brick shithouse, and very tetchy. One of the officers who visited him said that he had knuckles the size of walnuts from his boxing days. Apparently, he used to punch brick walls without any gloves or protection on to strengthen his hands during training."

"And what was their assessment?"

"He's been diagnosed as violent schizophrenic and is under a local psychiatric unit and being monitored regularly. He's been treated with medication, but because he's an outpatient, the unit can't be certain that he is taking it regularly."

"And if he doesn't?" Karen asked.

"Then he becomes unbalanced, displays violent tendencies, and is easily provoked."

Karen couldn't understand why such violent individuals were allowed to roam the streets. She knew that space in psychiatric units were hard to come by, and with the rise in mental health issues, and health trusts referring more patients for psychiatric evaluation, resources and space were tight. It meant, sadly, that individuals slipped through the net and went on to commit heinous crimes.

"Were the officers able to confirm his whereabouts when the three murders took place?"

"Radich lives in a secure outpatient residence which has an on-site support worker. As far as records go, he would have been at home for both of the York murders, but the support worker couldn't confirm that. Residents are free to come and go and are only encouraged to be home in the evenings."

"In Doctor Kumar's case, Radich could have got on a train and travelled down to London and picked any person at random to attack?" Karen suggested.

"Only why would he go to London? If he wanted to attack someone, he could have done it closer to home."

Karen agreed, but one thing stuck in her mind, Radich had psychiatric problems, and Doctor Kumar was a retired psychiatric consultant.

Karen thanked Jade and promised to speak to her later before she joined Zac and the team to update them on the London investigation.

Zac agreed with Karen's assessment that the answer to Doctor Kumar's murder was in York and not in London. "I've put in a request to get access to cell site data for Dixon, if nothing else, just to eliminate him from our enquiries. But he's such a jacked-up tosser, I'd love to get something on him."

35

Sausage and mash were just the ticket as Karen grabbed a seat and waited for Zac to bring over the food. They had been so busy this morning they'd missed lunch, and had only managed to get to the canteen right before it closed its lunchtime service.

As Karen looked around a few officers lingered, lazily finishing off their food, dragging out their break for as long as they could. Three other officers sat in a small huddle on the comfy chairs to the far end of the canteen, papers spread out around them, deep in discussion. Karen watched as two female officers discarded their styrene containers, and continued their giggly conversation, one wide-eyed as she listened with intrigue to the other's story.

She turned to stare out of the window to her left, and across the lawns surrounding the building. Though the trees were bare of leaves, and fought to get through another cold winter, she imagined how lush and green it would be in a few months' time when their dappled green canopies added natural depth and vibrancy.

"Penny for your thoughts?" Zac asked as he rested the tray on the table.

"No thoughts in particular. I was imagining how luscious and green it would look out there in a few months' time. I'm surrounded by a concrete jungle, choking fumes and traffic, and discarded litter on the streets."

"Don't be fooled. There are plenty of places in York like that. We are very fortunate to be surrounded by a nice setting. Here you go, get stuck in."

Karen was flagging. A combination of no food, and not enough water had made her feel lethargic.

"Does it feel odd being up here?" Zac asked, wiping his mouth with a tissue.

Karen pondered the question for a minute, unsure of the answer. "I guess it did to begin with. It's not my patch, and it's not my team. You feel like a visitor, but you also want to get stuck in… Does that make sense?"

Zac nodded. "Absolutely. But you've got stuck in, and you've gone down well with the team. No one has anything bad to say about you, at least not to your face."

Cheeky fucker. Karen tapped her chin. "You've got something on your chin."

Zac hastily wiped his chin with a tissue.

"No, the third one down!"

It took a moment to register before Zac rolled his eyes. *Touché.*

"Keep rolling your eyes, you might eventually find a brain."

"You're getting good at this," Zac replied, realising that Karen was feistier than he'd anticipated.

Karen wanted to probe deeper and find out more about Zac. "How do you manage to juggle home life when Summer is with you, with the pressures of work I mean?"

"I manage, but it's hard sometimes," Zac replied, staring down at his food.

"I'm sure it is. I guess you'd want to spend more time with her? I know you said you had an arrangement of joint custody, but does your ex-wife let you see her when you want to, or when it's your turn?"

Zac's eyes turned from his food to the window, and the view beyond. Karen sensed that he was lost in deep thought as he fixed his stare. He offered nothing more than a nod in return to begin with. "We had a difficult divorce, and we fought a lot. I wanted to protect Summer, but she found it hard to see her parents fight. My ex-wife was violent at times, and that affected me more than you can imagine. It's taken me a long time to deal with the emotional fall out. It was painful to say the least."

When she noticed the sadness etched on his face, Karen moved on to a different topic, accepting that his home life was a prickly subject.

"I'm sorry to hear that." Karen paused until his expression softened before changing the subject. "Well, you've definitely got a good team vibe going here, Zac. It's harmonious, it's cohesive, and strong."

"Is it not like that in London? I admit I've not worked down there, but I thought it wouldn't be too dissimilar."

Karen placed her knife and fork on the side of her plate and took a sip from her can of Coke. "It's more challenging. I think there's a lot more pressure on us because it's a bigger population. Fewer resources and money mean we have to work harder. It's more stressful as a result, and though we work well as a team, because everyone is so scattered, we don't really meet up as much as you and your team do. That clearly has a beneficial effect from what I've seen."

"Yep. They're a good bunch. There's a lot going on up here, and they're constantly reorganising, mainly for greater efficiency. It keeps us on our toes."

"Do you think you'll ever move to another force, Zac?"

"I doubt it. And if I did, not for a long time. Summer still needs me, and I still like it around here."

Karen opened her mouth to ask whether he was in another relationship, when a DC from Zac's team came over her shoulder and grabbed a seat beside them. DC Edward Hyde was an officer she had been introduced to but hadn't had any dealings with so far. He was well-spoken, having pursued a law degree at university before choosing a career in the police rather than a legal one upon graduation. Each time she had seen him, he was impeccably dressed, with a dark suit, conservative tie, and pristine white shirt. His hair, though short, was well manicured with a curly top.

"Zac, following enquiries with the hospital, it transpires that Dixon also ended up there himself. During the last tussle on record when Donna Anderson and he fought, he had her pinned to the wall by her throat. When he released her and came at her again, she grabbed a glass vase and struck it across his head."

Karen and Zac exchanged a glance of interest, which was piqued further when Edward laid down photographs taken by police at the hospital. The images showed significant scratches, cuts and bruising to the side of Dixon's face. The pictures of Donna Anderson were revealing. There were clear bruising impressions on her neck where Dixon's fingers had gripped her. She had a swollen lip and bruising beneath her left eye.

Edward continued, "The interesting point here was that Dixon became violent and aggressive in hospital. So much so that hospital security was called. Dixon swore down the place and fought to get near Donna Anderson. He threatened to slice her up, or as he put it, *shank her*. It resulted in the police being called when A&E became a battlefield. Chairs were thrown around, trolleys were being upturned, and Dixon threatened to cut anyone who came near him."

"He has motive for killing her then," Zac speculated as the case against Dixon grew.

"Yes, that only connects him to the murder of Donna Anderson, not the others," Karen challenged.

Edward shook his head. "Dixon also assaulted a nurse who tended to his wounds and restrained him. Dixon threatened to come back and kill him if he got in his way. Guess who it was?"

Zac and Karen looked at each other for a brief second, before turning towards Edward.

"Yep, you guessed it, Danilo Reyes."

36

Despite the loose but probable motive, it was the only one they had which was enough in Zac's eyes. They had a strong connection between the two murders, and a likely suspect, and that was grounds enough to bring Dixon in for a formal interview and carry out a search of his place.

As the team waited for a warrant to be issued, Zac used the time to organise the extra resources needed to execute the arrest. A nervous energy buzzed around the team which fuelled their desire to get a result.

As darkness fell, and with the team taking their positions close to Dixon's apartment, Zac seized a final opportunity to run through the objectives for the evening.

Several officers gathered around Zac as he flipped open his boot and retrieved his stab jacket. Belinda had lent Karen a spare one, and with final instructions given the team made their way to the apartment. Several uniformed officers led from the front, one of them carrying the big red enforcer, with Zac, Karen and Belinda in tow. A dog handler held back in case Dixon made a run for it. Zac assigned extra officers to the rear of the apartment block to seal off any exit route.

The team made their way through the communal door and paused when they reached Dixon's apartment. One officer rested his ear on the door and listened for signs of activity from within the apartment. He nodded and whispered that he could hear music and the sound of a male voice.

Tension bristled amongst the team as cautious glances were exchanged. Karen felt her heartbeat quicken and thunder in her chest. She took a few deep breaths to steady herself. This wasn't even her collar, and yet her nerves jangled.

Zac gave the thumbs up, and a second later, the officer wielding the big red enforcer swung it backwards and sent it crashing through the flimsy door which offered little resistance.

"Police! Stay where you are!" screamed the first officers racing through the broken doorway. Zac and his team waited as officers charged through doorways, the shout of "clear" coming as each room was checked.

"Don't move! Get down on your knees! Get down on your fucking knees now!" screamed an officer as the entry team converged on the lounge. A small skirmish ensued before an officer poked his head into the hallway and gave Zac the thumbs up.

A heavy smell of cannabis filled the hallway as Karen followed through behind Zac and Belinda. They found Dixon bare-chested on his front, his hands secured behind his back. His protestations were ignored as Zac instructed officers to begin their search.

The apartment was as Karen had remembered, but with dim lighting. A smoky hue hung in the air which stung her eyes. Several unfinished cannabis joints sat on a plate beside the sofa along with a bottle of Coke, and a fresh bottle of Glenmorangie.

"You certainly know how to live," Zac said as he read Dixon his rights.

"I've done nuttin' wrong, you bomboclaat!" Dixon protested.

Zac replied, "Yeah, yeah. If I had a quid for every arsehole like you who has said that to me, I'd be a bloody millionaire. Get this toerag out of here."

Dixon was unceremoniously hoisted to his feet, and dragged from the apartment, jostling with the officers in the narrow hallway until they'd had enough and dropped him to the floor. Four officers grabbed a limb each and lifted him out of the doorway and to an awaiting van.

KAREN YAWNED as she stood in the hallway outside the interview suite. The bright glare of the strip lights tortured her eyeballs as she rubbed the soreness from them. Though the arrest of this first suspect was good news for Zac and his team, frustration still gnawed at her innards that her case hadn't progressed any further.

"Are you okay to do this?" Zac asked, handing her a bottle of water.

"Yep. Sleep is for wimps. I won't lie, I'm shattered, but keen to hear what Dixon has to say."

"I could get Belinda to take your place? Dixon's brief has arrived, so we can finally start."

Karen waved away the suggestion, reassuring Zac that she was fine.

A search of Dixon's apartment had been encouraging. The discovery of a baseball bat, a machete, and several large kitchen knives were disturbing. A large quantity of cannabis, pre-packaged in small plastic bags, ready for distribution, was also discovered beneath a pile of dirty clothes in a cupboard. Zac had instructed officers to bag everything up for forensic analysis whilst continuing their search with the help of SOCO.

In the meantime, he wanted to keep the pressure up and interview Dixon.

Dixon sat in a white forensic suit and remained handcuffed. A uniformed officer stood behind him as a precaution. Dixon's brief was a small woman, and a duty solicitor from the circuit. The scowl on her face clearly let everyone know that she had drawn the short straw.

Zac introduced those present and repeated the caution for the benefit of their recorder before beginning the interview. No sooner had he started than the duty solicitor interrupted.

Her voice was thin, croaky and sharp. "My client has asked me to read out a statement to you," she began before organising her papers. "I, Charles Dixon, am not connected to the death of Donna Anderson. We were in a relationship which has since ended. Since that time, we have had no contact by phone or in person. I uphold my right to respond to each of your questions with no comment."

An uncomfortable silence ensued as the solicitor placed her

papers down, and folded her arms in readiness for the questioning.

Zac raised a brow in Karen's direction to suggest *this is going to be one of those interviews*.

"When was the last time you saw Donna Anderson?" Zac asked.

"No comment," Dixon replied as he narrowed his dark, menacing eyes, and drilled them with precision into Zac.

"You made threats to kill her when you were both admitted into hospital with injuries following an argument. Did you carry out those threats and kill her, beating her to death?"

"No comment."

"You also threatened to kill a nurse, Danilo Reyes. He was murdered nine weeks ago. Savagely beaten around the head with his heart removed. The same way that Donna met her fate as well. Did you have anything to do with either of those two murders?"

"No comment," Dixon snarled as his frustration simmered to the surface.

Zac showed Dixon photographic evidence taken by officers who attended the hospital. He pushed Dixon, and questioned him about the incident, asking again about whether he had then snapped, and attacked the pair of them sometime later. Dixon remained silent, offering little in the way of assistance.

"When we first visited you, I asked you about the scratches on your face and on the back of your hand," Zac probed, pointing to Dixon's face. "You claimed to have received them in a fight at your local pub. I put it to you, that you sustained those injuries after you brutally attacked Donna Anderson. From what I gather, she put up a brave fight, and I wonder if those scratches are the ones that Donna gave you as she fought for her life?"

For the first time in the interview, the duty solicitor spoke. "My client received those injuries following a fight in a pub. We are happy to provide you with the details of the location, and time. He will not be answering any further questions around the incident."

Zac's persistent questioning prompted the slightest reaction in Dixon as his eyelids flickered, and he clenched his teeth. Both Zac and Karen noticed the change in his demeanour, as the point was pursued further.

"I think this time Donna didn't buckle. She had the measure of you and fought back valiantly. Donna wasn't going to give in without a fight and made sure of that by scratching the shit out of your face. I like to say that it may have improved your looks, but miracles don't just happen."

Dixon slammed his fists on the table. "You pussy-o, leff mi a bloodclaat lone and guh suck yuh mada. Yo drag me here, you got nuttin' but waste my time blood. Shut yuh raasclaat mout! Get out of here!"

Karen didn't know whether to laugh or cry as the words tripped from Dixon's mouth. She'd picked up on a few phrases during her time in London, and nothing that Dixon said was complimentary.

Zac rested his elbows on the table and leant in towards Dixon. "I could eat a bowl of alphabet soup and shit out a smarter statement than whatever you just said."

Zac suspended the interview and sent Dixon back to the cells overnight whilst enquiries continued.

"WE DIDN'T GET much from him," Karen summed up as Zac drove her back to the hotel. On their journey, they talked about the interview, and the evidence so far. It was a tenuous link between Dixon and the victims, but it was possible. A lot rested on the forensic sweep of Dixon's apartment and his possessions. Whilst that was being undertaken overnight, Zac wanted Dixon to sweat in the cells.

"It's early days yet. It's like a battle of wits, and though the clock is ticking, we're still building an evidential case against him. We've got two victims, both of which Dixon threatened to kill, and we know that Dixon was in a relationship with Donna until she called it off. That clearly didn't go down too well with him."

Zac pulled up outside the main entrance to the hotel. "Thanks for your help today. It's been good."

Karen smiled and nodded. "No prob. I think you did most of the hard work." Karen glanced towards the hotel lobby and then back towards Zac. "Do you fancy a drink in the bar?"

Zac hesitated for a moment, adding to the awkward silence between them.

"I'd love to, but I need to get back for Summer. She's still with me. I'm really sorry. Can I take a rain check?"

"Of course. Sorry. I didn't think of that. It's already very late. You must be worried about her. You head back, and I'll see you tomorrow morning,"

Zac hovered as he watched Karen disappear through the doors and into the lobby. He enjoyed Karen's company. She injected a bit of fun and energy into his life, and they appeared to get on well. He smiled as Karen glanced over her shoulder and threw him a small wave before disappearing into the lift.

37

Saving the environment isn't gonna save you, the killer thought.

The end to his days and weeks of planning had finally arrived. Though his victim was conscientious, and doing his bit to save the planet, unbeknownst to him, it had left him exposed and vulnerable. He'd left the man to fester in his own anxiety all day before returning later. It was the ideal opportunity. Every Wednesday evening, he would drive to a recycling bank situated towards the rear of a large open-air car park and deposit his empty bottles. There were plenty of those, the number increasing over the last few weeks.

He'd achieved the goal of terrorising his intended victim and leaving him petrified of his own shadow. The man had turned to drink as a saviour, drowning out the fear, nervous chatter, and worry.

The killer followed a few cars behind, and when his target turned off he pulled back to give the man space. A few minutes later he pulled into the car park and alongside. The man's silhouette was caught in the headlights as the killer pulled up.

He, too, stepped out of the car and flipped open the boot, pretending to retrieve something. He came around the front and towards the bottle banks. His victim glanced over his shoulder, concerned at the new arrival, and hastily continued with his task of emptying his bag.

"Evening," the killer shouted as he moved towards the adjacent container, and threw in an empty milk bottle that he had picked up from someone's doorstep. The victim stared at the darkened figure, and offered nothing more than a courteous nod, keen to return to his car.

The man threw the empty carrier bags in the boot, and had just closed the lid, when a voice from behind startled him. A voice that sounded vaguely familiar.

"I thought you'd be more careful," the killer said.

The man spun on his heels. In the darkness and with a few overhead lights that lit up the car park, it was hard to make out the features of the stranger. He narrowed his eyes, searching for any characteristics that jumped out at him. "I'm sorry. Do I know you?"

"Oh, you know me all right. You know me very well. I said I'd come and find you," he replied, taking a few steps forward so his victim could get a closer look at him.

It took a few seconds before the man took a step back, the shock rocking his body. His eyes widened as his mouth fell open. His voice was paralysed with fear as his palms began to sweat. "I… I… What…?" He patted down his jacket, keen to find his phone, whilst also fumbling for the keys in his pocket. He turned and raced towards his car door, but a thundering pain shot through his back that sent him crashing to the ground. The cold of the concrete slab shocked the side of his face. Spasms raced through his body as his vision blurred, and everything went black.

The killer glanced around before looping his arms under the man's chest and dragging his body to the boot of his car. With the limp body safely stored beneath a blanket, the killer took one final check of the scene before driving off.

38

The sound of jangling bells rattled in her ears before everything fell silent. It rang again, and from somewhere deep within her subconscious, her body willed her to wake up. Her eyes flickered and opened, her mind confused. It wasn't her bedroom — not the one she was used to. It took a few seconds before she realised where she was.

Karen's hand lazily swung from beneath the duvet and reached for her phone from the table beside her. She blinked hard as her eyes focused. They suddenly sprang open when she saw that it was Zac calling.

She hit the green button and tried to talk, but her lips were dry and tight as was her mouth.

"Karen, don't tell me you're still asleep? I'm downstairs."

There was a frustration in Zac's voice that Karen picked up on quickly. "Shit. Sorry. My alarm didn't go off. Listen, I'll be down in five minutes," she shouted before hanging up.

Her head thumped as the events of last night flooded back. A nightcap had turned into a skinful. Her head pounded now as if her brain was too big for its skull, and with her mouth feeling like a camel's armpit, she stumbled around the room, grabbing whatever clothes she could find. She raced into the bathroom, looked in the mirror and gasped. She looked like shit, with heavy bags under her eyes, and frizzy hair as if she'd been plugged into the mains.

With a quick wash of her face, and a brush of her hair and teeth, Karen hopped across the bedroom, jumping into a pair of trousers before slinging on her blouse, and a jacket over the top. She raced down the corridor towards the elevators, dodging around the hotel maid wheeling her trolley, and a few shocked guests returning from breakfast. She hammered on the buttons for minutes before the lift doors opened and Karen was greeted by an elderly couple who offered warm smiles before they exchanged puzzled looks.

Though they looked harmless, Karen sensed an air of displeasure and shock behind the smiles. It was only when she turned towards the mirrored panels inside the elevator to check her hair that she realised her blouse was undone to her belly button, leaving her bra and buxom chest on parade. Karen hastily did up the buttons before rolling her eyes, and offered the couple an embarrassed smile.

Karen raced through the lobby and towards the car park, cursing as she went. Not only had she run out of time to call the hospital for an update on Jane, but her state of semi-dress had been the reason that the hotel maids and guests had shot her looks of surprise. In their eyes, it probably looked like she was doing a runner after a night of illicit sex, and rather than a walk of shame the next morning, it was a sprint for freedom.

Zac laughed as he looked Karen over. "Late night?"

She widened her droopy eyelids. "Just a bit. I had a few glasses of wine with some food, and then couldn't fall asleep. Sod's Law really."

They drove in silence for a bit, Karen's head spinning, and her stomach doing cartwheels. No shower, no coffee, and no breakfast. It couldn't have been a worse start to the day.

"Hey, I'm really sorry for blowing you out last night. If Summer wasn't with me, I would definitely have taken you up on that drink. Although judging by the look of you this morning, I would have been taking my life in my own hands, and who knows where I would have ended up."

"I'm not that bad. I had a few drinks, and because I didn't eat much, it went to my head," Karen replied. "Besides, was Summer okay when you got home?"

Zac nodded. "Yeah, she was fine. She had made herself food, and was upstairs in her room on the PlayStation with headphones on."

"Ah, kids are in their own world these days, but it's nice that she wants to spend time with you."

"She does. Summer always brings a smile to my face every time I see her. She keeps me grounded. I'll tell you what, she wouldn't stop talking about you after you left. 'Karen's lovely this, Karen's lovely that.' You've got your own fan club there."

Karen laughed. "She's got good taste."

No sooner had they arrived at the police station, then Karen made her way to the canteen whilst Zac headed to his office. Karen ordered two black coffees, and a bacon roll, devouring them as she made her way through the building.

Feeling more like she was ready to join the human race once again, Karen joined Zac as they discussed evidence related to Dixon as well as the outcome of his second interview.

"The search of Dixon's apartment uncovered incriminating evidence under his bed." Zac laid out a series of photographs taken by SOCO.

The team crowded around the pictures which showed a small handgun, balaclava, and gloves, alongside an orange Sainsbury's carrier bag.

"It will be interesting to see if any ballistics matches get thrown up," Belinda commented. "What's that?" she asked, pointing towards discolouration on the grip of the gun.

"SOCO believe it to be blood. They've taken samples," Zac said. "The interviewing officers questioned Dixon about the discoveries, and all he would say was that the balaclava and gloves were to keep him warm during winter. He refused to answer any questions about the firearm."

"At the moment we have no way of knowing whether a firearm was used in any of the three murders, but if it was, it would be one way of getting compliance from the victims…" Karen speculated.

Zac agreed and confirmed he had authorised the forensic analysis of all three items to be fast-tracked and compared against DNA from the three murders. "Have you got anything else?" he asked, looking around the team.

Tyler placed a few handouts on the desk in front of them.

"This is cell site data from two of his phones, and unfortunately they don't put him in the London area."

Karen tapped the sheets. "He may have more phones than that. He could pick up a burner phone and discard it whenever. That would be ideal for him to use whilst on the go, leaving both of these phones at his apartment, creating the impression that he was still in York."

Zac folded his arms. "We haven't got much to hold him on at the moment. I had officers speak to the Three Crowns in York, who confirmed that Dixon was ejected for smashing a bottle and threatening another customer after a fight broke out between them. For now, his alibi has credibility."

Karen sensed the frustration in Zac's voice. She knew they were treading on thin ice, and though he'd been in contact with both Donna and Danilo, the evidence of further involvement with them was thin on the ground.

Tyler turned their attention to a monitor close to them where he relayed the body cam footage taken from hospital security guards. The team fell silent as they watched Dixon throw insults and threats to both security and staff. The verbal volley turned sour as guards attempted to contain Dixon in his cubicle. Karen stared with interest as a fight broke out with Dixon throwing punches at anyone who came within striking distance. A female nurse, and Danilo both intervened, attempting to calm Dixon which infuriated him further. He struck the female nurse with a plastic box containing nitrile gloves before punching Danilo, who came to her defence. Karen was shocked by the level of violence and profanity being used.

Tyler froze the tape at the point when Dixon lunged at Danilo, screaming, "I'm going to fucking kill you."

The officers watched the footage roll on again as two burly security officers appeared and intervened.

Karen had seen fights like this before where one attacker could fend off three or four people, and still come out the other end. In her opinion, Dixon was high on drugs which often gave people in that situation almost superhuman strength where they also felt little pain. It was a further few minutes and the arrival of extra security staff before Dixon was finally subdued and pinned to the floor, his screams and threats echoing around the department.

"What was Dixon's reply when this clip was shown to him?" Karen asked.

Tyler shrugged a shoulder. "As you'd expect, he said it was idle threats. Heat of the moment kind of stuff. He said that Danilo had annoyed him and had no right to stop him. He added that Danilo was only a fucking nurse, not security, and should have minded his own business."

"What does your gut instinct tell you?" Karen asked, turning towards Zac.

Zac looked over his shoulder towards the whiteboard. "It tells me that Dixon is a violent man, and very clever. He has a lot of connections and judging by his propensity for violence wouldn't let people get away with it if they pissed him off. He's the closest thing we've got to a suspect, so we need to keep digging into his background."

39

Following the interviews with Dixon, the lack of progress frustrated the team. Karen felt their angst as she stared at the details pinned to the whiteboard. Dixon was the only credible suspect, but it still niggled Karen. He wasn't in the frame for her murder case in London, nor could she see any tangible connection between Dixon and Doctor Kumar. But the manner in which Doctor Kumar had been bludgeoned to death and his heart ripped out was the reason Karen hung onto the hope all three murders were connected. If the M.O.s hadn't been similar, she may have lent weight to Kumar's death being a random stranger killing.

Dixon didn't own a car either, but that didn't stop him from being mobile. It was plausible he relied on friends and acquaintances to move around, and she had everything crossed that Zac's team did a deep dive into Dixon's connections. With the amount of people driving around without any tax or insurance, Dixon may have nicked a car, and used it as his mode of transport. None of it made sense as Edward joined her with more information which he pinned to the board.

"Boss, officers discovered a pair of jeans and a black hoodie at Dixon's property. Both had mud on them. The jeans in particular had a lot of mud around the knees and hem."

Karen took a moment to examine the pictures of the exhibits. It was hard to tell from the images whether the mud was fresh or old, but Edward confirmed the jeans were rolled up, and when laid out, there was dampness in the mud, which suggested it was recent.

"Forensics are examining the jeans as we speak, and they're going to cross-reference them with soil samples taken from the site where Donna was discovered."

"That's good work, Edward."

"Call me Ed, boss. Edward always sounds a bit regal, and the team are forever taking the piss out of me. Apparently, I was born with a plum in my mouth, and I'm too posh for the job."

"Don't worry about them, Ed. They're jealous. You're smartly dressed, well-spoken, and you have a good eye for detail. Zac talks very highly of you. If you could see some of the DCs I've come in contact with, you'd be shocked as to how they got through selection. You are an asset, and you should be proud of your background."

Karen offered Ed a reassuring smile. She sensed an awkwardness, and something in his face reflected hurt from the repeated jibes. He would have to get used to it. Though the police considered themselves one big family, there would always be pockets of bullying, racism and sexism, much the same way in any large institution. The police had recently increased their drive to recruit graduates directly into becoming trainee detectives, creating hostility from many seasoned officers who believed fresh graduates needed time in frontline roles to build their awareness, experience and maturity.

Ed smiled sheepishly. "Thanks, boss. It means a lot. None of this is making sense, is it?" he added, nodding towards the whiteboard.

Karen shook her head. "Unfortunately, not at the moment. I'm still keen to find a link to my case back in London. You've got credible leads here, but they're not helping me."

"That's true, boss. I can understand the reason for Dixon attacking and killing Donna Anderson, but going back to kill a nurse just because they restrained him doesn't make sense?"

"Sometimes these things don't make sense. Seething revenge, or even a small trigger, can be enough to set someone on the path to taking another life. Any news on the search for a white Ford Focus?"

"Nothing yet, boss. We are still chasing. The search is still ongoing," Ed replied, as Tyler joined in with further news.

"Boss, Zac asked me to update you. The ongoing fingertip search of the area where Donna's body was found has led to the discovery of a few clothing fibres snagged in bushes close by. It's not a lot, but the remoteness of the location suggests the find may have some significance. Officers on the ground checked with the farmer, and other than him and his farm labourers, no one else has access to his land. There is no bridle path, or public footpaths, so it's only going to be illegal trespassers who venture onto his field."

"Yes, you're right," Karen replied. "It's not a lot, but every shred of evidence could be moving us in the right direction."

"Fingers crossed. The clothing fibres are going to be cross-referenced with the clothes seized from Dixon's flat. It might be nothing. It's common for couples to park up and disappear into the fields for a bit of al fresco you know what!" Tyler pointed out.

Karen narrowed her eyes as she turned to Tyler. "Even in January? All sorts of bits would be going blue…"

"That's if you can find those bits in the freezing cold, and even if you did, I'm not sure you'd want to hang around too long," Tyler speculated, as he rolled his brows.

40

With nothing more than circumstantial evidence and the results from forensics not back yet, Zac had no choice other than to release Dixon on bail pending further enquiries. It was a blow to the team and Karen. She watched Dixon as he barged through the front doors of the station, shooting off his mouth about police harassment and messing with the wrong man. Two uniformed officers had escorted him to the entrance and hung around as Dixon continued to goad them, offering them a one-finger salute before he stepped into a blue Mercedes A-Class, its windows wound down, and the sound of reggae music blaring from its sound system.

Karen bit her bottom lip and glared at Dixon as the car accelerated off at speed, the sound of the music fading, its rear fishtailing in defiance of the ten miles an hour speed sign.

Karen's phone vibrated in her back pocket. She pulled it out to see Jade's number and welcomed the sound of her familiar voice.

"Hi, Karen, how's it going?"

"Well, their prime suspect has just left the building, and told us all to fuck off, and that's being polite."

"That good, huh?" Jade laughed.

"Oh, definitely. Their suspect, Dixon, is definitely in the frame, but they haven't got enough on him at the moment. I've just watched his sorry arse walk out of here shouting the odds. We found a firearm in his apartment, but he denied all knowledge of it. Zac's team are waiting for forensics to confirm if his prints are on it as well and if what we believe to be blood splatters on the grip belong to either of their victims."

Karen made her way back through the station towards the team. "Tell me you've got good news? Please?" Karen asked with a sigh.

"Nothing positive here, unfortunately, Karen. Local officers spoke to Radich and drew a blank. They've looked into his background and can't find any connection to him and the three victims. He claims to have never been in York or London."

"Bollocks. Then again, I wasn't sure what to expect."

"Me neither. He's working in a prison organised place of employment where his movements are tracked whilst out on licence. We've checked his phone records for the last two months, but cell site data shows that he's not left the area recently."

"We really need to get a result here, Jade. The super is gonna roast my backside on the nearest barbecue if we don't get a result soon."

Karen hovered in the hallway outside MIT staring through the glass partition.

Jade continued to update Karen on what various members of the team were doing. "I've got a couple of officers going through Doctor Kumar's office in the spare room. There is a filing cabinet of case files dating back over twenty years, if not more. It's going to take a while but we're going through them now."

"Okay, Jade. I'm going to grab lunch, since it's getting late. Keep in touch," Karen said as she hung up.

KAREN WAS ABOUT to head out for a walk to stretch her legs, and find something to eat from a local supermarket, when Zac asked if she'd join him for a late pub lunch. Though busy, a break away from the office seemed like a good idea.

Zac drove to the nearest pub, one well known by local officers at the station. He grabbed the table in the corner and took Karen's order before disappearing off to the bar.

It gave Karen the opportunity to call the hospital for an update. Having waited a few moments for one of the nurses on Jane's ward to track down someone who could update her, she was finally put through to a doctor by the name of Amrit Singh. The news was positive. Doctor Singh said that Jane had responded well to treatment, and that she was comfortable and stable, though he warned she still had a long way to go. It was the news that Karen had wanted to hear, and she let out a sigh of relief as she hung up. The relief left her body feeling loose and limp. She hadn't realised until that point how much tension she was holding onto, a subconscious worry about her sister that had left her on edge, uptight, and constantly worried.

"Is everything okay?" Zac asked as he returned, and noticed her staring towards the ceiling whilst blowing out her cheeks.

Karen nodded. "Yes. My sister is in hospital at the moment, and it was touch and go whether she would pull through."

Zac's eyes widened. "Shit. Sorry to hear that. Are you sure you're not needed back in London?"

Karen batted away his suggestion. "No. She's in capable hands. I'm keeping in touch with them practically every day. If there was any change in her condition, and it worsened, I would be on the first train back to London, regardless."

"What's the matter with her, if you don't mind me asking?"

Karen didn't want to go into too much detail, and just highlighted that Jane had serious physical and health problems that needed round-the-clock care, and a slight downturn in her health had required a visit to the hospital. It wasn't something she was comfortable talking about, not at the moment. Up until this point she had tried to keep it as professional as possible, but had found herself being drawn to Zac's easy personality.

They both sipped on a bottle of beer until the food arrived. Two large sausage baguettes, a side of chips, and a plate of salad to share. The warm aroma of sausages fired off her hunger as she nibbled at the chips whilst they chatted. For a change it was nice to not talk about the case, and talk as two work colleagues.

"Are you sure your boss isn't going to give you grief for

staying up here too long? I thought you said he'd only given you a day or two?" Zac asked, wiping excess tomato sauce from his lips.

Karen rolled her eyes. "He had. He thought I'd be up here for a day or two, crack the case, open a bottle of champagne, and be back on the train in no time."

Zac laughed. "Isn't it funny how the powers that be expect bloody miracles from us?"

Karen agreed. "Well, if we lived in our offices twenty-four hours a day, seven days a week, we could probably crack these cases in half the time. I wonder if they realise we have a life outside of work…"

"Exactly. We do have a life outside of work, and that seems to diminish hour by hour, day by day, as we get stretched to the limits."

Karen took a swig from her beer. "I haven't got kids which I sometimes think is a blessing because I struggle to look after myself sometimes. How do you cope with being a parent and juggling your role as a DCI?"

Zac stared at his food for a few moments before clearing his throat.

"I won't lie — it's hard. Summer is with me every other week. I'd love to spend all my time with her and get home at a decent hour to enjoy evenings with her and go out at weekends. But our work is so unpredictable that I feel like I let her down all the time. I've probably been letting Summer down for most of her life."

Karen leant in and rested her elbows on the table. "You're probably being too hard on yourself. Yes, the job takes up much of our time, but I didn't see anything in Summer's behaviour that made me think that she was upset or angry at not spending quality time with you. You've got a great connection."

Zac shook his head defiantly. "No. It goes deeper than that. When she's with me, my attention should be on her. And it annoys me that sometimes my job gets in the way. But then again, if I didn't work my nuts off, I wouldn't be able to pay for all the things that her mum wants me to pay for."

Karen felt a sense of awkwardness creep into the conversation. "Oh, it's like that, is it?"

"Pretty much. Michelle enjoyed the good things in life and was forever spoiling our daughter. And now she expects me to do the same for Summer, but I want to keep her grounded." Zac's eyes moistened as his thoughts dragged him back to a time in his life when being married should have been fun and loving. Instead, he was reminded of the arguments, drunken fights, tears and bruises. Zac bit his lip, his eyes everywhere but on Karen until they eventually returned to her.

Karen leant in closer as he looked so deeply into her eyes, "Hey, it's me." Her breathing became softer, the pensive look melting into a smile as soft as the morning light. Her body squirmed just a little as her muscles relaxed. There was something about that gaze of his she'd never found in another man, as if in that moment their thoughts had made a bridge. "I understand. You don't have to say anything else."

"Thanks, I've just found it hard getting over it and moving on, so I'm sorry if I come across a bit moody and cold. It's not intentional," he replied as he cleared his throat and offered her a warm smile. He took a bite of his baguette before steering the conversation back towards her. "What about you? Other than your sister, do you have any other siblings, or family in London?"

"No, just me and my sister. Oh, and of course my mum and dad. And not forgetting Manky."

Zac furrowed his brow and stared at her in confusion. "Manky?"

"Yeah. Manky, my cat. He doesn't get a lot of my attention either, and the poor fur bag spends his days, and sometimes his nights just sleeping, waiting for me to return."

"We should be condemned as useless parents." Zac laughed.

"I think I'm already condemned from a previous life and came back as a copper."

"How are you going to feel returning to London after a few days up here?" Zac asked.

Karen leant back in her chair and thought hard about the question. It wasn't something she'd considered, and in the short space of time whilst in York had adjusted well and slipped into everyday life without questioning it. "That's a good question. I'm not sure. I've not thought about it. But I'm going to miss York and everyone. From what I've seen, the city is beautiful, its historic, and I have to say that your working environment is fantastic compared to the dives that I've worked at. And I'll tell you one other thing, the air smells fresher up here. There's none of the choking pollution that seems to suffocate your lungs in London."

Zac finished the rest of his food whilst he considered Karen's perspective. "You know, the funny thing is when other officers visit us in York, many of them arrive at the same conclusion. The place has a magnetic attraction," he said as his eyes widened, and he wiggled his fingers as if performing a magic trick.

"Well, from what I've seen, I'm not surprised."

Karen wasn't sure if it was the beer or the ease with which they had flowed through their conversation that left her feeling relaxed. She could easily have stayed in the pub and had another drink, enjoying Zac's company.

41

The temperature was cold enough to make his bones shiver. The chill of the metal floor, and even colder steel walls offered little comfort as he trembled in the darkness. His eyes searched the black canvas for any clues of his location. It was like a metal box, a steel room, that had become his prison. The clanking of the metal chain broke the stillness and silence each time he tried to move. Its clasp firmly wrapped around his wrist; the other end secured to the wall that afforded him little opportunity to move more than a few feet. At first, he'd tried to reach the other side in a desperate attempt to gauge the size of the room, but the chain was too short.

He was cold, bruised and scared. His body had used up all its reserves, and now his stomach roared, the burning heat within, telling him how hungry he was. He had used the corner closest as his toilet and become accustomed to the smell that filled the darkened space.

Will anyone find me here? Does anyone else know where I was? Why?

He asked himself these questions repeatedly, and though he didn't have answers, tried to reassure himself that he would get out of this safe and well. But the waves of panic and doubt kept coming. He remembered one particular occasion where a woman had been abducted and held captive in an abandoned garage. Despite an extensive police search for her, she was never discovered until it was too late. Three weeks later, her decomposing remains were found by a couple of kids.

Is that going to be my fate?

The sound of a rattle coming from the darkness shook his thoughts. At first, he thought it might have been the wind, but the noise grew.

Have I been found? Am I about to be saved?

Pulses of both excitement and fear raced through his body at the clanking sound of a padlock and steel bolts being opened. The door pulled back, its hinges creaking in the stillness of the night. The screech hurt his eardrums and caused his eyes to narrow. It was night-time, that was plain to see, as he could barely make out the silhouette of the door against the darkness.

A solid pure beam of light cut through the night and burnt the back of his eyes, forcing him to throw a hand over his face. The visitor stood in a darkened entrance, the beam from his torch lighting up the cavernous space.

The man blinked furiously, willing his eyes to adjust to the intrusion, desperate to see whether the visitor was a friend or foe.

The visitor made his way inside the room. He walked

towards his captive and unlocked the shackles, causing his prisoner to flinch.

"Please don't hurt me. Why are you doing this?" the man asked, his voice rough and croaky. He licked his swollen and cracked lips as his heart thundered in his chest.

"Shut the fuck up!" the visitor hissed.

The man shouted and screamed as he was grabbed around his collar and yanked to his feet before being dragged to a chair.

"Shout as much as you want. No one is going to hear you. And no one fucking cares," the visitor replied as he dumped the man in the chair, and yanked his arms back to secure him by his wrists.

The man was powerless to defend himself. Weak, hungry and dehydrated, his body offered little in the way of defence.

The visitor came around the front of the man, and stood just inches away, shining his torch in his captive's face.

The man closed his eyes and turned his face to shield himself from the powerful beam of white light that burnt his retinas.

The visitor grabbed a handful of the man's hair and yanked his face back around. "Look at me! Look… at… me!" he growled, his voice slow, quiet, and menacing.

"Please stop. I haven't done anything wrong. I can give you money. I can give you my bank account details. Take whatever you want. But please, don't hurt me."

The visitor laughed before placing the torch on the floor, its light continuing to offer silhouetted shadows in the darkened space.

The man didn't see the first punch coming. The impact sent shards of pain pulsating around the side of his head. Waves of nausea quickly followed. The flurry of punches continued. Again, his stomach lurched and gurgled. He raised his heavy eyelids only for them to fall shut. He raised them again, desperate to see his attacker, but a mixture of darkness, and a wetness that stung his eyes made it almost impossible as the barrage continued.

The visitor grunted and snarled as dull thuds met his fists. His victim offered nothing more than a heavy exhale of breath as his body surrendered.

"I've been waiting for this moment for a long time. I'm sure you thought it would never come to this, did you? You piece of shit." The breathless visitor huffed as he paused for a moment and stepped back.

"Please…" the man whispered, his voice barely audible. He spat the blood from his mouth. "Why are you doing this?"

"You'll find out soon enough." The visitor retrieved a small pocketknife from his jacket and unlocked the blade. The steel blade caught a flicker of light from the torch before the visitor jabbed its tip into the man.

The man screamed and thrust his head back, his body shaking violently in the chair, desperate to get free.

The visitor jabbed his victim a few more times in and around the legs and abdomen, nothing more than small puncture wounds that would slowly bleed out. Not life-threatening immediately, but if left unattended for long enough, would eventually lead to death.

The man cried, his racking sobs echoing in the metal container. His body convulsed and shook in the chair, rocking back and forth. His pleas for mercy, and to be set free, fell on deaf ears. He thrashed his head from side to side, fighting the overwhelming sense of pain. His face was battered and bruised, his lips split, his teeth broken. His swollen eyes were beginning to close up, and a fire raged across his body as the pain from his stab wounds intensified.

"You fucking piece of shit. You deserve everything coming to you. I knew this time would come, and I've been waiting for it for so long," the visitor ranted as he walked around the space, kicking empty boxes that had been stored near the entrance to the room. "I can't be certain that I'll be back in time, but let's see how long you last. I want your death to be long and slow, not like the others. You screwed me over. You left me hanging. Now it's your turn." The visitor picked up his torch and walked back towards the door, stepping out into the darkness. The sound of the heavy metal door closing, and the metallic thrust of a bolt and lock being secured, signalled the end.

Silence fell once again.

The visitor stood by the door for a few moments and checked his surroundings. Confident he was still alone; he walked the short distance back to his car before driving away.

HE'D CHOSEN this patch of abandoned ground for a reason. At night there was no foot traffic, and very rarely any vehicles. It was a perfect place and bought him time. He stepped from his car and went around to the boot before pulling out a jerrycan of petrol. He opened all the car doors, and liberally sprinkled petrol across the back seats and carpets before moving to the front of the vehicle and pouring more of the stuff across the front seats and dashboard. He poured the rest of the petrol over the bodywork before throwing the empty jerrycan back into the vehicle.

He lit a match and tossed it inside. The flash of flames and the whooshing sound caught him by surprise as a wave of heat pushed him back a few feet, almost toppling him over.

His face lit up in the golden orange glow. It was like he was at his own Bonfire Night as the flames lit up the night sky. The warm air circled him, the heat warming his core.

With a final nod, he turned away and disappeared into the darkness of the night.

42

"Morning," Karen said as she walked into Zac's office with her handbag draped over her shoulder, and a cup of Costa coffee in one hand.

"Morning to you, too," Zac replied. "You didn't have to get a cab this morning. I would have picked you up."

Karen sat in the chair opposite Zac and drained the last of her coffee before tossing the empty cup in the bin beside her. "I know. But I felt bad for keeping you waiting yesterday. So, I thought I would sort myself out this morning and make my own way. Besides, I had to organise my laundry with the hotel. I thought I had packed enough for a few days, but I've run out of clothes."

"At this rate you'll have to go shopping for more. I know women like changing their outfit several times a day," Zac teased.

"Jealousy is a disease. Get well soon!" Karen fired back.

"You're clearly upset that I have a better dress sense than you."

Zac rolled his eyes and disagreed with her before offering a warm smile. "Thanks for yesterday. It probably came as a bit of shock when I told you stuff about my past. I've not told many. Anita and Laura know. But that's about it."

Karen's face softened as she stared into his grey eyes that carried sadness and sensitivity. She felt her breath quicken and her heart hammer. There was an attractiveness to his vulnerability that she found endearing. "I'm glad you felt you could open up and tell me. It must have been a very difficult time for you. We can talk again if you need to. I'm a good listener, I promise."

"That would be nice. I might just take you up on it at some point."

Returning to business, Karen asked, "Any updates?"

Zac wiggled the mouse on his desk to wake up his computer screen. "Definitely. But still work in progress. Forensics were able to extract unknown fibres from the solicitor's clothing. There's no DNA identified yet other than hers, but they're continuing to run further analysis."

Karen suggested that it would be interesting to see if the fibres matched any of the clothing secured from Dixon's apartment.

Zac continued as he scanned the case file on the system. "Index plate search on EK18 still continues. Of the two hundred and fifty vehicles registered in the York area, nine are registered to car hire firms, eighteen are registered to cab firms, six have been scrapped as write-offs, and the rest are now privately owned."

"That's still a fair whack to work through?"

"It is, but we've already chalked off eighty-five of them. There are over a hundred owners that we still need to track down. But this is where it gets interesting. When the team contacted the car hire and cab firms, they accounted for all but one car. A white Ford Focus was rented out under false details and not returned."

The news excited Karen as she sat up in the chair, her mind joining the dots.

Zac noticed the shift in Karen's body language. "That's great for us. We've already dispatched officers to obtain CCTV from the car hire firm, as well as copies of the ID used to rent the vehicle."

Zac was about to continue, when Karen's phone rang. She grabbed her handbag, and reached in before fishing out her phone. It was Jade.

"Morning, Jade. Sorry, you're on my list of people to call this morning, but you beat me to it. I'm here with Zac in his office."

"Morning, Karen. I'm glad you're both there. We've uncovered new information that we believe is crucial to all three investigations, so the DCI will be interested in hearing what I've got to say."

"Okay, let me put you on loudspeaker. Zac is in the room with us. Go ahead," Karen instructed as she placed the phone on the table between herself and Zac.

"Right. First thing. Mason's team has conducted further investigations on the bloodied footprint found in Doctor Kumar's property. The print is consistent with a make of Adidas trainer. Its official name is the Adidas TRX vintage trainer. It was a size nine, and the reason they were able to identify the actual brand and style was because the sole has a very distinct hexagon-shaped tread that runs down the centre of it."

"That's great news, Jade," Karen added.

"It is." Jade continued by saying, "For the pattern identification, they made use of the National Footwear Reference Collection coding system. They've also been able to identify the pattern of wear and tear, including small areas of damage to the sole, and in their opinion, it will be unique to that particular item. If we can find the trainer, we should be able to cross-reference it with the information they have gathered. Although, they did say that the crime scene mark showed evidence of slight movement and slippage when the mark was made."

Karen grimaced. She knew what that meant. It was likely that the mark was made on the undersole whilst it was wet with blood, which would impose limits on the extent of the comparison.

Jade continued, the excitement rising in her voice, "And that's not the best news. We think we've found a connection. Whilst reviewing case files from Doctor Kumar's office, we found one particular individual of interest to us. Dennis Bailey."

Karen and Zac exchanged looks of curiosity. "Why is he of interest, Jade?" Karen asked.

"Dennis 'Hatchet' Bailey was sentenced to twenty-one years for killing an underworld boss and cutting out his heart. He escaped three months ago after only serving seven years."

Karen questioned how he was linked to all three murders as she grabbed a pen from Zac's desk, and a blank sheet of paper to make notes.

"Bailey was assessed by Doctor Kumar both before and during his trial. Defence solicitors claimed that Bailey was unstable and needed psychiatric help. That's when they brought in Doctor Kumar to do a full psychiatric assessment on him. He was being represented at the time by Donna Anderson, his solicitor."

"Don't tell me, the psychiatric evaluation suggested that Bailey was sane?" Karen speculated.

"Yep. Bailey wanted to be locked up in a psychiatric hospital. His associates tried to bribe Kumar, but Kumar wasn't having it. After he was sentenced, Bailey went mental and threatened to break Kumar's legs for letting him down."

"And Donna Anderson?"

Jade sighed. "She was Bailey's brief, and he wasn't happy with how she had handled his case. From what I can gather, having spoken to officials at the Crown Court, there were frequent slanging matches between Bailey and Donna Anderson."

Zac listened quietly but typed away on his computer, searching for further intel. His eyes widened as information jumped out from the screen.

Interrupting Jade, Zac said, "Bailey was being held at Full Sutton, just outside of York."

"Yes, sir," Jade added. "I'm sending over scanned copies of all the evidence, but the bad news is that Bailey absconded and slipped out of the country. He was last known to be in Spain."

"Costa del crime. Where else?" Karen tutted.

"I'm afraid so, Karen. He has links to associates out there. It would be easy for them to hide him. We are doing a follow-up as we speak and tracking down his associates in the UK, including his family. I think the first place you can try is his brother," Jade said.

"Where is he?" Karen asked.

"York."

43

As Karen stepped from Zac's car, its warmth soon left her bones as the crisp bite of a chilly winter's morning shocked her lungs. She was certain the temperature had fallen a few degrees further since leaving for work this morning. The street they were in was on the outskirts of a small industrial estate. A mixture of brown multistorey office blocks stood shoulder to shoulder with commercial and industrial warehouse units.

Every hundred yards or so, a few old and mature trees dotted the pavements. Gazing at the winter trees, Karen struggled to imagine them reclothed in their finery. With roots buried deep in the frozen earth as they slept, clusters of twigs, gnarled and twisted, moved in the gentle breeze.

Karen hurried alongside Zac as they crossed the road and made their way to an industrial unit. Karen pulled up the collar on her coat to trap in the remnants of heat that her body clung onto.

"Tommy's got form," Zac said. "Assault and possession of class A. According to the system, when Dennis did a runner, the team investigating his disappearance visited Tommy, but had walked away empty-handed."

"Uncooperative?"

"Yep. Claimed that the last time he saw his brother was when he visited him inside."

Karen looked up at the signage on the railings that surrounded the industrial unit. TB Haulage Services — national and international transportation services. *Convenient.*

As they walked into the yard, the familiar smell of engine oil, grease and diesel hit them. It reminded Karen of every garage she'd visited in her life. A thick, cloying smell that was both nauseating and appealing at the same time. Around the edges of the compound, an assortment of trailers and cabs sat parked up, and to the far end beneath a corrugated roof sat the stripped down remains of a Mercedes cab. Its front panel was lifted, with two men bent over, fiddling with the mechanics of the vehicle.

"Over here," Karen said with a nod as she turned to her left and made her way over to a Portakabin which had an "Office" sign above it.

As the officers stepped through the door, they were greeted by a wall of heat emanating from a gas-fired portable heater, its orange glow burning brightly. Either side of them were several well-worn chairs, their black metal legs scratched, revealing a shiny silver surface beneath them. The padded seats were worn and frayed in places. To the far end was a large veneer desk, stacked high with paperwork, folders, and a few boxes.

A man with a shaved head that Karen put in his mid-to-late forties sat behind the desk, leaning back in his office chair with his hands interlocked behind his head. He'd been around police officers for much of his life to know when two walked through his door. He rolled his eyes with displeasure.

"It's suddenly got very fucking chilly in here," the man growled.

Zac walked up to the man's desk and pulled out his warrant card. "Tommy Bailey?"

"You know who the fuck I am. Can't you lot leave me alone? What have I done wrong now? Left the toilet seat up?" Tommy sniggered as he curled up his lip.

"Detective Chief Inspector Walker, York police, and this is my colleague Detective Inspector Heath from the Metropolitan Police."

Tommy nodded. "I'm honoured. Two police forces come knocking on my door at the same time. This must be serious. I guess you are not in the business of having a container moved?"

Karen took a moment to look around the office. Several large cork boards were crammed with what appeared to be invoices and schedules. A large whiteboard hung on the wall behind Tommy with a long list of names down one side of it, and dates, times, and destinations written alongside them. She presumed it was a work schedule for the drivers Tommy employed.

"It's a courtesy call more than anything else," Zac said. "How's business these days?"

Tommy shrugged and raised a brow. "Pretty good. We have

a good order book with plenty of jobs to keep the boys happy for the next couple of months. Why, you looking to do a bit of moonlighting? The police not paying you enough?"

Zac ignored the jibe. "Had any unusual jobs recently?"

Tommy narrowed his eyes and studied Zac with suspicion. "What do you want? I'm a busy man."

"When did you last see your brother, Dennis?"

Tommy pursed his lips and shook his head. "No idea, maybe six months ago. Prison visit."

"And you've not seen him since?"

"Nope. Not since he did a runner. You would have checked the system before coming here. I've already had a visit from your lot after he did a bunk. And I told them then that I hadn't seen him. And that still stands."

Zac nodded and then stuffed his hands in his trouser pockets. "I find that odd really. You're right. I did check the system. According to our information, you were inseparable. We even know about the drone you flew over the prison walls with a mobile phone hanging off the bottom of it, so you could speak to your brother."

Tommy laughed. "So?"

Zac smiled back. "I find it strange that you went to such lengths to keep in touch with your brother, and then you haven't heard from him in the last three months."

"Everyone is looking for him, so he is hardly gonna be waltzing in through those gates, is he?"

"Have you run any jobs over to Spain in the last three months, or picked up any consignments to bring back here?" Zac asked.

Tommy stared towards the ceiling, pretending to track back through his memory. "Not that I can remember."

"Mind if we look at your journey logs?"

Tommy shook his head. "Yeah, I do. That's private business. You got a warrant?" His tone was cold and clipped as his steely, menacing eyes bore into Zac.

"You know I haven't got one. If I did, I'd be kicking down your fucking doors, and flooding this place with officers."

"Well, then I can't help you. It's none of your business. Sorry, but that's the way it is."

Zac ignored the man's objections and continued to push. "Where do you deliver to then?"

"Mainly the UK. Europe, in particular Spain, Portugal and Germany. Why?"

"No reason. Just curious. What kind of consignments do you take?"

Tommy took in a deep breath and let out a long sigh. "Detective Chief Inspector," Tommy stretched out each word for effect. "This is getting fucking tedious. As I said, if you wanna know more about my business, come back with a warrant. I'm a very busy man, and you're taking up a lot of my time. The door is over there. This is private property. I suggest you leave now, or I'll get some of the lads out there to escort you off *my* property."

Zac shot back a wry smile. "Don't worry. As I said, this is a courtesy call. If you hear from your brother, I suggest you tell him to present himself at the nearest police station."

Zac and Karen left, the sound of Tommy's laughter ringing in their ears.

44

As they drove back, Zac went to great lengths to explain how the visit could lead to Tommy panicking and slipping up.

The concern with Dennis Bailey only intensified once they returned to the office. The team had been working flat out to uncover any shred of information that would lead to Bailey's whereabouts as well as the connections between him and his victims.

As Zac and Karen made their way onto the floor, Anita beckoned them over. Several officers had gathered around her desk and were in the midst of exchanging information.

"Zac, we've looked into the details of the case that led to Bailey being imprisoned. There are elements of the case that bear a striking resemblance to the cases that we're dealing with."

Zac squeezed in between two officers, whilst Karen went around to the other side and stood beside DS Mark Burton.

The man threw her a look as he shifted uncomfortably on the spot.

Anita laid photographs on the table. "Dennis 'Hatchet' Bailey was charged with the murder of Calvin Dwight, a local crime boss. Apparently, Bailey went to great lengths to cover his tracks according to the evidence presented by prosecutors. He broke into Dwight's house and waited for Dwight to return before killing him. He used bleach to remove blood from his hands and covered the interior of his getaway car with blankets to avoid transferring any blood evidence."

Zac listened intently, nodding his approval at the cunning of the man.

Anita continued as she pointed to the charred remains in the pictures. "Bailey burnt Dwight's body, his own clothing, and removed his cigarette butts from the scene which would have contained his DNA. Here's the interesting thing," Anita added, as she laid out more photographs.

Zac studied the images of a crowbar and a Stanley knife.

"Bailey tried to throw evidence into a lake twenty miles away, including a crowbar and knife he had used to bludgeon Dwight and remove his heart. But the weapons got caught in weeds, and Bailey flipped out when they remained partially submerged. He couldn't go in and retrieve them for fear of being seen, and so fled the scene."

There was a ripple of murmured conversations amongst those gathered as the details sunk in.

"We are dealing with a ruthless killer here, and his M.O. matches the three crimes that we're investigating," Zac said.

"I think we need to be checking ports and airports for anyone who entered the country from Spain in the last eight weeks matching Bailey's description?" Karen offered. "I'm not sure we'll have any luck, but he may have sneaked back in?"

Zac agreed.

Anita laid out further still images. "These are from video clips taken from the car hire firm. We've analysed them, but the man is in disguise. We can't really make out much, other than he is a white male, of stocky build, and probably around five eight, or five nine in height."

Zac tapped the photographs. "He knows he's being watched. He doesn't lift his head once, and stares at the counter for most of the time that he's there. Clever sod. Check to see if facial recognition mapping can match any features from the stills with Bailey's mugshot."

Zac's team had successfully deployed Retrospective Facial Recognition in identifying unknown suspects from CCTV in an earlier investigation, and he was hopeful the system would help again.

"Sure. We can't be certain that it's Bailey, but the physical description carries a resemblance, and the employee that dealt with him agreed that he resembled Bailey's mugshot," Anita added.

"Do we know much about the address given on the paperwork?"

Anita nodded. "Yes, Zac. The address turns out to be a bed and breakfast. We've contacted the owner, and a person matching the description of Bailey has been renting a room, though he hasn't been there for the last three days, even though he's paid for a whole week. And he's been using the name of Charlie Walsh."

"Great. Anita, you carry on running things from here, whilst Karen, myself and Belinda will head over there now."

THE BED and breakfast was situated towards the north of York, in the Clifton area, and was a large double-fronted property spread out over three floors that sat on a corner of a residential street. Zac asked two officers to stay outside, monitoring the property for any movement, whilst a third officer accompanied them into the property.

Not knowing what they were walking into, Zac had called ahead and arranged for uniformed backup to go with them.

They were met by the owner, Sally Bickerstaff, who, though curious at the arrival of the police, carried a degree of apprehension and concern in her face as she furrowed her brow. She led them up to the third floor, to one of two bedrooms that had been converted in the attic.

"Have you seen much of your guest?" Zac asked as they marched up the stairs.

Sally shook her head. "To be honest, other than when he registered and paid, he's hardly been here. He's certainly not come down for breakfast, and he's been coming and going at all times of the night. Unfortunately, these stairs creak, so I'm aware of when my guests come and go. And up here, only this bedroom is being used, so I know it's Mr Walsh."

"And you're sure he hasn't been here for a few days?" Zac

asked as he stopped outside the bedroom door, and whipped on a pair of nitrile gloves, handing out spares to Belinda and Karen.

Sally nodded to confirm before using her master key to unlock the door and let the officers in. Zac asked her to wait outside whilst they entered.

A mustiness hung in the air, as if the windows hadn't been opened in a few weeks. Brown 1970s floral curtains were drawn across the window, casting a darkness across the room. Several towels had been used and discarded on the floor, and Zac noticed that the bin beside the bed overflowed with empty sandwich wrappers and takeaway containers.

Karen moved off to a different part of the bedroom and stuck her head around the bathroom door. The first thing she noticed was the absence of personal effects. There was no toothpaste, toothbrush, shower gel, or shaving kit. The bathroom had been used with the toilet seat up, but other than that, it appeared untouched. She glanced over the bath rim, and noticed an absence of dried shower gel, or dirty water scum. In fact, the surface of the bath looked spotless, as if it had just been cleaned. *Had he not taken a bath at all since he had been here? Or had he washed away evidence?*

Zac pulled open the drawers to the bedside cabinet and found them empty other than a Gideon Bible. Belinda did the same with the dressing table, arriving at the same result.

The officers paused for a minute and studied the room. Other than a few clothes heaped in a pile on a chair, there was nothing else. No personal effects, no case or bag.

Karen moved over towards the chair, and rummaged through the clothes before pulling out a pair of faded jeans with dark stains splattered across them. She held them up and showed them to the others. "Could be blood?"

Zac agreed before instructing the uniformed officer to bag them up for analysis.

Karen grabbed a dark hoodie from the pile and rifled through its pockets before finding a sheet of paper neatly folded up several times. She carefully unfolded it to reveal four addresses. One of them was instantly recognisable.

"Check this out. There are four addresses on here, and one of them belongs to Doctor Kumar," she said, passing the paper to Zac.

"Shit. And I know who the other addresses belong to. Donna Anderson, and Danilo Reyes."

"You know who the fourth address belongs to?" Karen asked.

Zac shook his head. "It doesn't ring a bell. Belinda, can you ring through and get someone to check it?" Zac asked as he got down on his knees to check under the bed.

Belinda stepped out of the room and put a call through before hurrying back agitated a few moments later. "Zac, it belongs to Donald Carter."

Zac looked at her blankly, trying to make the connection. "Who is he?"

"He's one of us!"

45

Uniformed officers were already outside the property by the time Karen and Zac screeched to a halt. With darkness having descended, the blue lights of the patrol car strobed off the surrounding properties. Curtains twitched, heads peered through gaps, and several front doors were ajar, the occupants of those houses congregating in their front gardens to see what the fuss was about.

Headlights from other support units came into view from both ends of the street, their beams lighting up the pavements and the trees that marked the edge of the road.

Zac had left Belinda back at the bed and breakfast to oversee the work of the forensic team who were on their way to conduct an inch-by-inch examination of the bedroom. Karen stepped from Zac's car and surveyed the scene. It was a normal, quiet residential street tucked away from the main road, and Karen imagined that during the day very few vehicles would travel down it. Most of the properties had driveways, which left the road fairly clear.

Karen stuffed her hands in the pockets of her coat and marched towards the front door, her hot breath coming out in smoky plumes against the cold night air.

Zac stopped by a uniformed officer who hovered by the front door. "Is anyone home?" he asked.

The officer shook his head. "Not that we can tell, sir. I've knocked on the door a few times and rang the doorbell."

"Had a look around the back?" Zac asked as he took a few steps back, and surveyed the front of the house, checking the upstairs windows for any signs of movement.

"Yep, it's clear there as well. It looks like all the lights are off, and we can't see any movement inside."

Karen walked up to the front bay window and cupped her hands around her eyes, peering inside. The house belonged to Donald Carter, a retired detective inspector from the Met. With the information they now had, there was a serious threat to life that neither Karen nor Zac could ignore.

Karen pulled herself away and joined Zac by the front door. "I think we need to get in there to have a look. He could be severely injured, or worse."

The officer standing with them interrupted Karen's thoughts. "We've checked with neighbours either side. Mr Carter hasn't been seen since Wednesday evening, when they saw his car reversing from the drive. They assumed he had perhaps gone away for a few days."

The news raised the seriousness of the situation. With it now being Friday evening, Donald Carter hadn't been seen in two days.

"Put the door in," Zac instructed as he stepped away.

The uniformed officer put in a call for any nearby officers with tactical entry equipment to attend. None of the officers on scene had the strength, nor equipment to break through a UPVC front door with a five-bolt locking system.

It was an anxious ten-minute wait before a silver Audi estate pulled up and two burly plain-clothes officers stepped from the vehicle and retrieved the big red enforcer from the rear of the car. It took them less than a minute to prise the door from its frame with several repeated blows. Zac thanked them for their time before they left.

Karen and Zac snapped on nitrile gloves before entering the scene. Karen flicked on the hallway light, and a set of recessed halogen lights that dotted the ceiling instantly illuminated the darkness. A blast of heat enveloped her. She touched the nearest radiator with the back of her hand. It was hot. That suggested that Carter probably hadn't gone away. However, it did worry her that if Carter's body was somewhere within the property, the heat would have accelerated its decomposition. She sniffed the air, not noticing the familiar smell of rotting flesh and decomposition.

Zac shouted out a few times, signalling the presence of police before sending the uniformed officer upstairs to check the bedrooms. Karen and Zac spread out through the ground floor, and whilst Zac took the lounge, Karen made her way through to the rear. It was a clean and tidy long galley kitchen. She wasn't sure what to expect. Perhaps dirty dishes that hadn't been cleared away. Or even perhaps a meal that was in the middle of being prepared before Carter had been interrupted. But everything appeared untouched. She opened a few of the kitchen cabinets above the work surfaces. The shelves were well stocked with food. The usual essentials that you'd find in most kitchens, up and down the country. Condiments, herbs and spices, tins of food, jars of coffee, and a biscuit barrel.

Before joining Zac in the lounge, Karen checked the back door for any signs of forced entry. The door was still locked with the key placed on the windowsill.

"Nothing in the kitchen," Karen offered as she stepped into the lounge and surveyed the room.

"Same here. Certainly well lived in, but no signs of disturbance, and no evidence of a hasty exit."

Karen poked her head back into the hallway to check something before returning to join Zac. "There's a small bundle of post behind the door, and the milk is still in date. I checked the fridge."

"We have to treat his disappearance as suspicious. His car is missing, so we need to put out an ANPR alert for any sightings of it," Zac said as he checked his surroundings once more before making his way outside. He was joined by the police officer who'd searched upstairs and confirmed no evidence of a disturbance or body.

"We need to find out what the connection is," Karen said as she stood in the front garden and watched the growing number of neighbours hovering in the street, whispering in quiet huddles as they exchanged their own theories. "We've got four people linked to those four addresses on the sheet of paper. Three are dead, and one is missing. Our priority has to be in locating Donald Carter."

Zac agreed as he pulled out his phone, requesting his team pull up all the history on the retired officer.

46

Karen had to settle for playing the waiting game, as Zac's team actively chased down the last known movements of Donald Carter late into the evening. Zac had dropped her off at the hotel, whilst he went home. A part of her had wanted to be invited back for dinner. She wasn't sure why but appreciated that he needed time alone with his daughter.

Perhaps she wanted to experience the cosy family environment again, with laughter and teasing. Karen had seen a different side to Zac as a warm and caring parent. Not to say that he wasn't warm and caring at work, because that part of his nature appeared to come out naturally in him. It was that sense of family that she missed.

Not long after getting back to the hotel, she'd called the hospital for an update, only to be told of no change. She so wished that Jane could be better than that. To be able to see her sister open her eyes, or even utter the odd word, would be amazing. Maybe then she wouldn't feel so alone. Of course, she had her parents, but that wasn't the same as sharing special moments with a brother, sister, or even a partner.

Karen didn't enjoy the idea of going back to her small hotel bedroom that had become her space. It was a lovely room, but it wasn't personal. It wasn't filled with her own knick-knacks. As she sat on the end of her bed, looking around her surroundings, unsure what to do, the sense of loneliness and isolation crept up on her.

I'm a forty-something single woman, sitting on my own in a hotel room, feeling sorry for myself.

Conflicting thoughts raced in and out of her mind, confusing her further.

Why is it any different from going back to my apartment, where I feel that sense of isolation and loneliness? Is this all I have to look forward to in life?

Karen needed to push away the melancholy and punched the mattress to relieve the angst that flowed through her veins. She turned and stared through the window at the darkened space beyond. The night sky was heavy, the clouds hung low, and dampness filled the air. The bright lights of the city sparkled like tiny jewels in black sand.

Something niggled her, and for ages she couldn't put her finger on it. She narrowed her eyes as events, conversations, and places flashed through her mind, colliding with one another. That was it — the visit with Tommy Bailey bothered her. Not only had he been uncooperative, but smug and arrogant too. Call it a copper's intuition, but there was something about Tommy Bailey that rubbed her the wrong way. He knew more than he had let on during that visit. With that burning ember of suspicion growing even brighter in her mind, Karen grabbed her coat and handbag, and raced off to follow her hunch.

Karen asked the cab to drop her off further down the road to avoid being seen. Most industrial estates at night were quiet, with businesses shut. Karen made the short distance on foot, sticking to the shadows, and stopping behind trees and parked vehicles whilst she scanned her surroundings.

As she neared TB Haulage Services, she was surprised to see the floodlights on, lighting up the yard. Its steel gates were open with activity beyond the railings. Karen ducked down behind a van and peered around from its front whilst watching cars and vans come and go over the next thirty minutes. She noticed the odd pallet truck pull out and take a wide swing into the road before disappearing into the darkness.

Perhaps it's a 24-hour business?

Karen inched forward, desperate to get a better vantage point. From her current position, she couldn't make out the silhouettes, nor the conversations. She needed to move closer, but there were no other vehicles parked on the road closer to the entrance.

Shit.

Opposite the main entrance of TB Haulage was a tree, and though it afforded her little in the way of concealment, it was better than nothing. Karen crept forward, placing one foot in front of the other slowly, pausing every few steps to check that she hadn't been spotted.

Karen crouched again. Her view afforded her a direct line of sight to the Portakabin, and Tommy's office. Over the next hour Tommy talked to his visitors, shaking hands with them before they drove off. Karen made a note of each index on her phone before taking a photograph. Without the flash on, the images were dark and grainy, but she could still make out the make, model and registration of each car.

Muscle fatigue set in. Karen was desperate to stand up to stretch her achy legs but doing so would give away her position. She groaned and gritted her teeth, fighting the build-up of lactic acid. She was about to retrace her steps, when a large set of headlights turned into the road towards her. They were big beams, far larger than a car. Karen felt her muscles tense as she held her breath. There was a real risk that the beams would catch her if she moved.

The roar of the engine got louder, and it soon became clear that it was a box van. She watched as it turned into the compound. It came to a stop beside the Portakabin, and she saw three dark shadowy figures exit. They walked towards Tommy Bailey, and one of them embraced him. A strong manly hug that continued far longer than Karen anticipated. *Is this Dennis Bailey?* she wondered.

The dark figure pulled away from the embrace and retrieved a carrier bag from the footwell of the van, before rejoining Tommy. He handed the bag over to Tommy, who in return passed over a dark holdall. It was too dark for Karen to make out what was being exchanged, and she cursed silently.

Is it drugs? Guns? Cash?

From somewhere in the surrounding area, a siren wailed. As the seconds ticked by, the noise grew louder. It was enough to spook the men, who raced back to the van. The vehicle swung around in the courtyard. Its wheels screeched on the tarmac before it raced through the gate and down the road. The engine screamed as the driver pushed the vehicle through each of its gears.

Karen couldn't move from her position. To do so would put her in more danger, and without backup and working on a hunch, it had the potential to blow up in her face. Her heart thundered in her chest.

Is one of the three men Dennis Bailey? Did I witness our main suspect get away?

Karen continued to watch from her position as Tommy ran back into the office.

The sirens were so close. Karen looked to her left, watching a police car race across the junction, and disappear off into the darkness, no doubt responding to another emergency close by.

Karen pulled up Zac's number and punched redial, only to be greeted by the message, "It has not been possible to connect your call. Please try later." Karen glanced down at her screen. No signal. "Bollocks."

47

Karen's eyes shot open, and her body twitched in shock as the noise startled her. Her eyes danced around in the darkness until her brain clicked into gear. It was her phone rattling on the table beneath the TV. She threw her legs out of bed whilst coming to her senses and saw the illuminated screen from her phone a few feet away from her.

She stumbled into the darkness and made a grab for it. Karen had been in such a deep sleep, that she blinked hard at the realisation of missing two calls from Zac. The time on the phone told her that it was still the middle of the night, and she'd only slept for three hours.

"Hello," Karen replied, her throat dry, her voice croaky.

"Karen, we've had a significant breakthrough, and I've just got off the phone from the overnight team in the forensic department. I know it's early, but I wanted to phone you straightaway."

"Oh, right. That's good."

"It's not good; it's bloody brilliant. They've had a DNA match for the scrapings taken from underneath Donna Anderson's fingernails. It's Dennis Bailey."

"Shit," was all Karen said as she ran a hand through her knotted hair and headed towards a light switch. The sudden burst of light made her squint, forcing a hand over her brow to shield her eyes from the glare.

"This is the breakthrough that we needed for our cases," Zac said jubilantly.

"It is," Karen replied as a sinking feeling washed over her. The events of a few hours ago played heavily on her mind. "Zac, I tried to call you last night, but I couldn't get a signal. Something bothered me when I got back to the hotel." Karen was careful with the words she chose, wary of the possible reaction. "When we visited Tommy's haulage business, something didn't sit right with me."

"What do you mean?" Zac interrupted.

"I wasn't sure to begin with. But something about his behaviour made me think he was hiding something. I couldn't put my finger on it, but it kept gnawing away at me. So… I decided to get a cab over there last night to have a bit of a snoop around."

"You did what?" Zac said, a hint of anger and concern tainting his words.

"I didn't go in the compound or anything. I hovered in the road. At that time of night, I thought the compound would be closed, but it was the only business that was still going, and there was a lot of activity. Cars coming and going."

"What do you expect, Karen? It's a fucking haulage business. Most haulage businesses run a twenty-four seven operation. Karen, not only were you taking a huge risk, but this isn't your patch. You're a visiting officer. Have you forgotten that?" Zac's words were clipped and cold.

Karen knew she had overstepped the mark. "I know. Which is why I didn't get involved. I went to observe. Hear me out," she pleaded in her defence. "When I was there, a box van pulled up, and three men got out. I couldn't see their faces. It was too dark. But one of them hugged Tommy for quite a while. Maybe it was Dennis? There was an exchange of bags too."

Zac remained silent, his heavy breathing the only sign that he was still on the line.

"I'm sorry, Zac. I'm sorry if you feel I overstepped the mark, but curiosity got the better of me."

"Karen, I don't think you realise that you are a visiting officer, and secondly whilst you're on our patch, I have a responsibility for your safety. If something had happened to you, they would have roasted my nuts on the nearest bonfire."

Karen tried to lighten the mood. "And there was me thinking you didn't care?"

Still silence.

"Zac? Can you hear me?"

The silence continued which worried Karen further.

"Of course, I can, Karen. And yes, I do care about you. As a fellow senior officer, and as a friend. I care about you a lot. The last thing I need is you gallivanting across the city like a maverick cop. Get dressed, and I'll meet you in the office within the hour."

The line went dead. Karen pulled the phone away and stared at the blank screen, wondering if her battery had died. Zac had hung up. Her body slumped. There was a coldness in his voice that she didn't like. His last few words were direct, with no offer of picking her up.

Karen tossed the phone on her bed and let out a deep sigh. *Fuck. When will I learn my lesson?* She called down to reception asking for a cab pickup in ten minutes. That gave her enough time to race around her room to find some clothes to throw on before washing her face and brushing her teeth.

48

It was three a.m. by the time Karen swiped into the building and made her way to where the team was based. The place seemed empty and cold, much in the same way that Zac had been with her less than an hour ago on the phone. Dread washed over her at the thought of seeing him face to face. She passed a few faces in the corridor, uniformed officers from the night shift taking a break before heading back out.

Karen was annoyed at herself for creating waves. It didn't matter where she was or what she did; she'd press the self-destruct button and do something completely out of character for someone in her position and end up chin deep in elephant shit.

There was a sense of urgency and excitement in the few team members on the night shift as Karen made her way into the office. They were all gathered around a large table poring over the latest evidence and information that had come in. Zac looked up from his conversation and offered her a polite smile, but there was no depth or warmth behind it. Karen knew he was too professional to single her out in front of his team. Karen dropped her bag and coat by her desk before joining them. There were several smaller conversations going on, but Karen couldn't tune into any of them other than picking up random words here and there.

"I didn't expect you in," Belinda said as she greeted Karen with a smile, and then promptly stifled a yawn. "I thought you'd be safely tucked up in bed."

"I was until Zac called me with the good news. It sounds like we've hit a breakthrough, and that's what I'm up here for. At last, it looks like I've got good news to share with my super later this morning."

Zac pinned Bailey's picture on the board behind him and wrote his name beneath it. "I know it's the middle of the night, but it couldn't wait until the morning for the day shift to start. This is our lead suspect now," Zac said, tapping Bailey's picture. "He has been forensically linked to the killing of Donna Anderson. As we know, her address was found at the B & B that we believe Bailey is renting. We now also believe that Bailey rented the Ford Focus using the very same details he used to rent a room at the B & B."

An officer asked, "Any updates on the facial recognition mapping request?"

Zac shook his head. "We'll need to chase it up this morning. We still have SOCO on site at the B & B doing a detailed forensic search of the bedroom, so let's hope they throw something up to confirm it's Bailey."

"What about Dixon?" the officer added.

Zac pondered the question for a moment. "I'm not comfortable about removing Dixon from our enquiries altogether, but without any DNA evidence linking him to any of the crime scenes, we have to shift our focus to Bailey."

There were suitable nods of agreement from the dozen or so officers gathered around the table. Several more members of the team had also arrived, swelling the numbers, having been called in by Zac.

Zac turned towards Karen and locked eyes with her. "Karen decided to do a bit of her own investigating a few hours ago and visited Tommy Bailey's haulage business to observe activities. Though she was only there as an observer, Karen may have seen Bailey meeting his brother momentarily before being spooked by the sound of approaching sirens. They were only in contact with each other for a few minutes, and visibility was poor, but it may have been our first sighting of him."

Karen felt her face flush as more than a dozen officers turned in her direction. She wasn't sure if Zac wanted her to say anything, so remained tight-lipped as she scanned the faces of those around her. Whether she was being paranoid or not, she wasn't sure, but she could have sworn that they carried that look of "why didn't you do anything?" etched on their features. It left her feeling decidedly uncomfortable as she returned her eyes to Zac.

Sensing the awkward pause, Belinda broke the silence to steer the conversation in a different direction. "We also now have a misper to deal with. We believe we've found the missing link with Donald Carter, the retired detective. His car was found abandoned by a bottle bank. Unfortunately, there's no CCTV covering the area, so as far as we know that was his last known location."

"What's the link?" Zac asked.

"Donald Carter was the lead SIO in bringing Bailey to justice. It was alleged at the time that Carter took a ten-k bung from Bailey to make evidence disappear, but Carter still screwed him over, and Bailey was charged and imprisoned."

The revelation set tongues wagging as they digested the news. "Bent copper," someone murmured.

"Well, that gives us a motive for Carter's disappearance," Zac added. "He's either been abducted by Bailey or he deliberately staged his own disappearance, knowing that Bailey was out."

"My hunch is with the former," Karen added.

Another officer chipped in. "Me too. I've been doing a bit of digging. Carter had contacted the local nick about concerns regarding his safety. He had a visit from officers, claiming that he was being stalked and intimidated. The final straw for him was when a funeral wreath had been delivered to his door."

"So, it's plausible Carter was abducted when he visited the bottle bank?" Zac speculated.

Belinda nodded in agreement. "It looks that way. There were no signs of a disturbance in and around his car, and with no witnesses, it's hard for us to determine what exactly happened there. But what we do know is that Bailey is now linked to all four victims," Belinda continued as she opened up her laptop and did a quick search. "Bailey escaped when he was on a visit to the hospital after falling down a flight of stairs in the prison. Whether that was deliberate, or intentional to get out of the prison, is uncertain. But somehow, he managed to evade the guards who'd accompanied him. A male nurse tried to restrain him and nearly succeeded."

"Danilo?" Zac asked.

"Yep. It all kicked off, and in the melee, Danilo was viciously assaulted. Bailey came at the nurse and tried to throttle him with his bare hands, but Danilo stabbed Bailey with his scissors in self-defence." Belinda scanned the information on the database. "Bailey went crazy and made threats to kill Danilo. Sadly, the prison guards bungled their attempts at restraining Bailey, and Bailey got away."

"Jesus." Karen sighed. "Bailey has gone after everyone involved in his case. And as it stands, Carter could be his last victim?"

Zac scribbled a few notes on the whiteboard behind him. "We need to build a timeline of Donald Carter's last known movements. Find out who he's spoken to, where he's been, as well as where he could be."

"And Bailey?" Belinda asked.

"We get onto the press team first thing in the morning and put out a public appeal for any sightings of Bailey. We need to flush him out."

49

Karen followed Zac back into his office the minute the meeting ended. The corridors were empty and adjoining offices were shrouded in darkness, their occupants a few hours away from clocking in for the day shift. She had been given the cold shoulder by him after he'd breezed past her without acknowledging her presence. She closed the door behind her and leant back against it with arms wrapped around her waist. Zac looked up at her but remained tight-lipped as he flicked on his table lamp that cast a glow to the walls and his desk.

"Zac, we need to clear the air. I know you're pissed with me, and I'm sorry," Karen offered. "I have a habit of getting myself into trouble. It's only because I'm like a dog with a bone. Once I have something in my sights, I don't stop until I get it. And yes, that sometimes means that I'm a little unorthodox, or push the boundaries too far."

Zac tipped back in his chair and threw his arms up in the air before standing and coming around to face her. "Karen, you're wrong for what you did. I run a really good ship here, and I trust my team. But they never do anything without running it past me first. And I like it that way, because if the shit hits the fan, I could be prepared for it, and I could back them up. I've got a good mind to send you back on the next train," Zac looked at his watch, "which is only a few hours away. This is my investigation *and* my patch."

Karen placed her hands over her face and groaned. "I'm sorry," she muttered, her words muffled behind her hands.

An uncomfortable silence hung in the air for a few moments, neither of them willing to speak. Karen was furious with herself. "Listen, I'll go if I'm getting in your way. I accept it's not the way you do things up here, but I can't help myself sometimes. Back in London I'm known for doing stupid things like this, and I piss off my bosses, but I get results. I don't like wasting time, and I push for answers… fast."

Zac inched in closer. The smell of perfume lingered between them. His eyes studied every detail of her face. Her dark brown fringe shrouded her brown eyes, as she peered at him. "Yeah, you are a prat, but you're a nice prat. I understand your intentions were good, and often coppers just don't trust their intuition enough. You did. I don't want you to go back. I've got used to having you here as part of the team, and we started this, so we need to finish it. Agreed?" Zac said, softening his tone.

Karen smiled.

Zac reached for her hand and held it tight. His eyes fixed on her. "I do care about you Karen, and the more I see of you, the happier I feel. Yes, you're a pain in the arse, but no one's perfect."

Karen playfully punched him with her free hand.

"Easy! That's assaulting a police officer."

Karen leant in towards Zac, their bodies just inches apart. Her heart raced as her breath came in short, sharp gasps. *This is madness*, she thought.

Zac closed the gap and kissed her softly on the cheek before drawing Karen's lips towards his.

They separated seconds later; their faces flushed with embarrassment at being caught up in the moment.

"Am I forgiven?" Karen whispered.

"Apologies accepted," Zac smiled. "Let's grab a coffee and get to work." He opened the door and waved Karen through regally with a bow.

Zac watched as Karen rustled up two mugs of coffee for them, moving from cupboard to cupboard as she grabbed the jar of coffee from one, mugs from another, and the milk from the fridge. She swivelled around and opened up another cupboard before reaching in to grab the biscuit barrel, and plonking it down in front of Zac.

"You know your way around here now, don't you?" Zac teased.

"Well, I don't want to be accused of being lazy, or worse, expecting lower ranks to run around after me."

Zac nodded approvingly as Karen handed him his mug. "I was thinking, considering we got into the office early today, if we are able to knock off at a decent hour, we could grab dinner at mine. And talk? Summer is going back to her mum's tomorrow, so it would be the last time that you'd probably see her, and I know she'd like to see you again. How about it?"

Karen cupped her mug in both hands and felt the warmth penetrate her fingers. "I'd love that, as long as it's not inconveniencing you. I'm getting bored with going back to a hotel, staring at four walls, and channel-hopping whilst I lie in bed," she replied.

"It's not inconveniencing us at all. I sometimes think that Summer gets bored of staring at my ugly mug."

"I can understand where she's coming from. Too bad you can't photoshop your face!" Karen said, holding back a laugh as her shoulders shook.

Zac shook his head. "You can go off people really quickly, you know."

"Oh, really? I'll bear that in mind," Karen said as she ushered Zac out of the kitchen.

50

"Not again. Why the fuck can't you lot leave me alone?" Tommy Bailey snarled as he ran a hand over his shaved head.

Karen and Zac both agreed that following Karen's observations the night before, it would be worth giving Tommy Bailey a tug, and seeing what he had to say for himself.

Karen stood to one end of his desk whilst Zac positioned himself at the other, forcing Tommy to flick his head from left to right as he viewed both officers with suspicion.

"It's a friendly visit, and a few questions," Zac volunteered as he stepped back and glanced at Karen.

"No, no, no. I answered all your questions last time. I've got nothing else to add. This is harassment. Just because I've got form, and my brother's gone AWOL, you think you can keep knocking on my door and piling on the pressure. Sound about right?" If he was expecting Zac to reply, he was taken by surprise when Karen began the questioning.

"Who were you meeting with last night?"

Tommy spun in his chair and clenched his teeth. "What? What the fuck you talking about?"

"It's a simple question," Karen replied. "You had a meeting with three people last night, and after they left, you returned to this office."

"You must be mistaken, luv. I think whoever told you that jumped to conclusions. I've had my team going in and out of here practically all day and night for the last few weeks. Our order book is rammed."

Karen persisted and revealed more. "A boxed black van registered to your business came here last night, and three occupants got out. One of which you hugged for quite a while. Who were they?"

Tommy narrowed his eyes. "You lot spying on me? What is it? You got some observation vehicle parked outside, watching the comings and goings here?"

Karen noticed a tension bristling in his voice, as Tommy spat out his words. If she thought he would be spooked by the revelation, she was sorely mistaken as Tommy went on the defensive.

"I have people coming and going here all the time. Customers, my boys, and deliveries. Of course, it's gonna be busy as we have vehicles going in and out of here day and night."

"I'm sure you do. But we could easily seize your van and have forensics pore all over it. And once they have, and found every single clothing fibre, strand of hair, fag butt, empty can and fingerprint, what's the chances of us finding evidence belonging to your brother?"

Tommy shrank back in his chair and curled his fingers into tight fists.

"I wouldn't if I was you," Zac said as he stepped in closer to Tommy.

"Have I hit a raw nerve?" Karen said sarcastically. "The last thing I'd want to do is upset you. I'd hate to see a grown man cry."

Tommy shifted uncomfortably in his chair, desperate to launch his body in Karen's direction. "It's out on deliveries in Manchester."

Karen nodded. "That's fine. We'll have our Manchester colleagues seize it. Let me ask you again. Have you seen your brother, Dennis, in the last few weeks? And let me remind you that withholding evidence and impeding a police investigation is a criminal offence."

"No," Tommy snapped.

Karen glanced over towards a small television screen sat on top of a cupboard behind Tommy. The screen was split in four, with a live view of CCTV cameras situated around the yard. "We'll need a copy of the CCTV footage from last night."

Tommy smirked. "Be my guest. You'll find nothing on there. It started a fresh thirty-day cycle this morning at eight a.m.," he said, glancing at the wall clock.

"Convenient."

"You said it, luv." Tommy laughed as he watched Zac move over towards one of the windows in the Portakabin, and stare across the yard.

"I'm popping out to make a call," Zac said, throwing Karen a sly nod as she continued the questioning.

"Do you own any other properties?"

"My house. That's it. Listen, I've answered all your questions. I've been cooperative. I now need to get on with my work. Unless you want to charge me with something, we're done here," he replied, jumping from his seat, and heading towards the door.

Karen followed him out, and noticed Zac wander over towards one corner of the yard where several empty shipping containers sat. They were big steel monstrosities, blue and at least twenty feet long.

"What's he doing?" Tommy hissed.

Karen shrugged a shoulder. "Nothing as far as I can tell. He's having a look around," she replied as Zac made his way back towards them.

"Thanks for your time, Tommy. We've seen enough. We'll be in touch," Zac said as he joined Karen.

"What did you make of that?" Karen asked as they made their way back towards Zac's car.

"First impressions... Tommy was evasive and definitely hiding something."

Karen agreed, feeling vindicated. There was more to it than Tommy let on. Whether he was directly harbouring Dennis, or had been involved in planning his escape, she was unsure. But her instinct told her that one of the three men that visited Tommy last night was indeed his brother, Dennis.

As Zac was about to drive off, Tyler called. "Tyler, hello mate. What have you got?"

"Morning, Zac. I thought I'd give you a bit of an update. We've got officers doing door to door and chasing down any possible sightings of Donald Carter. We're also checking local shops for any CCTV footage. We've footage of him from a few days ago popping into a local Tesco Metro, but we saw nothing suspicious on the tape."

"Okay, thanks. Anything else?"

"Yes, forensics found a pair of bloodied gloves tucked beneath the mattress in the B & B. They have been sent away for analysis, and they'll be cross-referenced against the DNA profile on Dennis Bailey that's held on the system."

"That's fantastic news. Keep me updated on that. Also, whilst I think of it, can you set up an ANPR alert on the black box van Karen saw last night. The index is on the system already. We need to track its location. Can you also speak to Anita and get a warrant arranged to search Tommy Bailey's house and property? It's time we gave him a proper shakedown."

"Onto it now, Zac," Tyler replied before hanging up.

51

The day had started so early for them that Karen was famished by late morning. Her energy sagged, and her mind felt tired. Zac's team were busy in a flurry of activity with many of his officers joining the door-to-door enquiries about Donald Carter. With a hastily prepared press appeal released a few hours ago, Karen knew it was a waiting game until Zac's team received calls about possible sightings and concerns from local residents. She felt sorry for junior officers who manned the phones. Many calls would prove fruitless with sightings of their suspect from York and beyond.

Nevertheless, it needed to be done, and it was a matter of sorting the time-wasters from those with credible information. It was always a numbers game, in Karen's opinion. They could expect anything from a few dozen calls to hundreds, and each one needed to be answered.

"I don't suppose you fancy a bite, do you?" Karen asked, poking her head around Zac's door. "I'm famished, and I'm starting to flag."

Zac checked the time on his phone, and his to-do list on his computer screen. "It's gone eleven. It feels like we've been here all day."

Karen shrugged. "We've already done an eight-hour shift. Come on. I'll shout you brunch."

Zac didn't need to be asked twice as his stomach rumbled, and ten minutes later they were in a café on the outskirts of town. They both ordered a full fry-up, with an extra round of toast, and two steaming mugs of coffee. The breakfast crowd had gone, and the lunchtime rush hadn't started, so the place was quiet.

Zac mopped the sauce from his beans and the yoke from his eggs with a piece of toast, and groaned in happiness, feeling fully satiated.

"I forgot to ask. How is your sister?"

"No change. I've been calling every day, and as far as I know, she's stable and I'm happy with that. As long as she's not getting any worse, then that's good news."

Zac nodded in agreement. "It must be hard when you're so far away. I bet you'd much rather be in London, where you can visit her every day."

"Definitely. And if she'd taken a turn for the worse, I would have been there by her bedside. It's a difficult trade-off, between being there for her, and still getting on with work."

"I'm sure. But if there's any change in her circumstances, you do know that you could head back straight away. Even if it's in the middle of the night, and there're no trains running. You'd only have to give me a shout, and I'd drive you to London."

Karen was taken aback by Zac's suggestion. It was so kind and thoughtful that to begin with she was lost for words and stared at him open-mouthed for what seemed an eternity.

"What?" he asked.

"Um… nothing. That's very sweet of you, thank you."

"I'd do that for anyone I cared about," Zac offered, placing his hand over hers on the table.

"I didn't expect to come up to York and end up meeting someone."

"Is that a bad thing?" Zac probed.

Karen shook her head. "No, not at all. To be honest I'm a bit shocked by what happened back in your office." Karen stuttered for a moment, before continuing, "But in a good way."

Zac's chest dropped as he let out a breath he'd been hanging onto. "Phew! I thought it was a 'Dear John' moment."

"Not at all. I loved it when you kissed me. It felt good. Naughty, but good. Not to mention it's a disciplinary matter if we'd got caught," she smiled coyly. "And you're right, we could do with talking later…? I'm in London and, well, you're here in York…"

"That's stating the obvious," he said with a chuckle.

Karen playfully punched him in the arm. "I'm being serious!"

Zac nodded. "I guess we do." His stomach twisted as thoughts rushed through his mind. Confusion, embarrassment, and anger flooded his senses as painful memories returned to haunt him. *How can I tell her about the reasons why I walked away from my marriage? What will she think? Does it make me less of a man? Can I ever open up fully again and feel normal?* Zac questioned what normal even meant these days. It felt like an eternity since he'd been in a relationship and he wondered if he could ever experience happiness again.

His words hung in the air between them for a moment as they sat in silence, sipping on their coffee, and exchanging the odd smile, neither of them knowing what to say next. The awkwardness was broken when Zac's phone rang, and it rattled across the table. He grabbed it to see Anita's name pops up on the screen.

"Anita, what's up?"

"Hi, Zac. We've received more information on Bailey. He's got a lengthy history with us, and has been arrested on several occasions for assault, but in all cases, he was released without charge."

Carter, Zac thought.

Anita continued by saying, "Bailey also made threats towards Carter after he was sentenced, citing, and I quote, 'This isn't over. Watch your back.'"

"It sounds like Bailey was expecting Carter to get him off the hook?"

"That's what I thought. But Carter had a clean sheet. A solid work record with no reprimands or disciplinaries against him. According to his records, he was as clean as a whistle, and very reliable."

"Maybe that's a reflection of his earlier career, and considering that Bailey was one of his last cases before retirement, he was more open to receiving a backhander?"

"Possibly," Anita replied before giving him an update on a few other things and hanging up.

Zac updated Karen on the call as she paid up and they left the café.

"I do believe that Tommy Bailey is aiding and abetting a prisoner on the run. He's too cagey for my liking," Karen said. "He also has the international connections, and transportation routes to ferry Dennis Bailey in and out of the country without being spotted."

"Well, I've got the team scanning CCTV footage in and around the B & B, as well as the haulage business. They've been out since the crack of dawn in both locations, securing copies of any recordings over the last few days. If Dennis Bailey has been in either location recently, we'll find it."

Karen excused herself and promised Zac that she would meet him back in the office, citing the need to get a few more clothes. She hadn't anticipated staying in York so long and was tired of using the hotel's laundry service. Karen already knew that Hinchcliff would go mad at her expenses bill.

As she made her way into town, Karen called Jade for an update.

"Karen! Flipping heck, talk about disappearing off the radar. Have you swapped allegiances or something? We do need updates down here as well, you know."

"I'm so sorry. It's been manic here, and you won't believe it, but I've been in the office since three a.m. this morning. I'm gubbed already" Karen went on to explain the balls up she made of stepping on Zac's toes, by doing her own surveillance.

"Karen, you're supposed to charm him, not piss him off."

Karen laughed. "Will you stop it? I'm trying to work with him, not get him into bed."

"I've checked his pictures online, and he's a good-looking fella. Are you sure you're not tempted? I've heard all about the naughty forties."

"Jade, you are terrible. Yes, he is a good-looking fella, and I've even been to his for dinner, and met his daughter…" Karen stopped herself as the vision of Zac kissing her crept into her thoughts.

Jade screamed and interrupted her in mid-sentence. "Wait, hold the front page! You've been back to his for dinner, and you've met his daughter. OMG! And you're saying there's nothing in it?"

"Hold on, hold on. Stop jumping to conclusions," Karen protested. "There was nothing in it. He was being nice. Okay… maybe just a sliver."

"Yeah, yeah. If you say it enough, you might start believing it. Don't tell me you didn't enjoy that little… sliver?"

Karen refused to accept Jade's piss-take, though she'd enjoyed Zac and Summer's company.

"So, are you back in his good books again?" Jade laughed.

"We're not teenagers," Karen said forcefully. "We had a disagreement, spoke about it, and put it to bed."

Karen shook her head, and regretted those last few words, as Jade's roar of laughter echoed down the line. Desperate to move the conversation on, Karen returned her focus back to the investigation, and updated Jade on where they were, and how Bailey was their main suspect. She spoke about the haulage business, the bed and breakfast, and the false details used to rent the Ford Focus. Karen promised a further update again shortly as she hung up.

Karen checked the time on her phone, needing to dash around a few shops to pick up her essentials. She'd never been one to mooch around the shops, but York had a different vibe to London. It was quaint, with a network of narrow cobblestone streets. A few of the visitor guides in her hotel room detailed the history surrounding the city. Marauding armies had laid claim to the city throughout its history, from the Romans, through to the Anglo-Saxons, and then the Vikings.

She'd seen York Minster several times, it's magnificent Gothic structure and medieval glass preserved in a hundred and twenty-eight windows, and its two hundred and seventy-five steps up a spiral staircase to the top of its tower. There was so much to see, and she promised herself that one day she would visit and explore everything that York had to offer. Karen had read that Harry Potter fans were drawn to The Shambles, a 14th century walking precinct with buildings on either side so close they seemed to lean into one another and block out much of the natural light. Fans had commented that it looked like Diagon Alley.

Twenty minutes later Karen was done and hailing a cab.

52

Karen's journey back to the station was a familiar one as she headed south from the city. The landmarks and streets flashed by as she gazed at the pedestrians walking by and people stopping at traffic lights waiting for a lull in vehicles. It was on one such occasion as a small huddle of people waited to cross that she took a double take. Just a brief glance, but enough to rattle warning bells inside her mind. She spun in her seat to look out of the back window, her eyes scanning the faces. Had she been right?

The hairs on the back of her neck prickled as her breath quickened.

"Turn around, quick, please turn around!" she shouted.

The driver looked in his rear-view mirror before casting a glance over his shoulder. "What? I can't just turn around."

Karen whipped out her warrant card and thrust it in his face. "Turn around... now!" she shouted, scanning the crowd again.

There. She spotted his face.

She was certain. Bailey!

The mugshots she had seen of him were clearly etched in her mind. Karen grabbed her phone from her handbag. She was thrown across to the other side of the seat as the cab swerved and did a sharp U-turn. Karen cursed under her breath and steadied herself whilst dialling Zac's number, and stared at the dozens of faces desperate to not lose sight of him.

"Slow down," Karen instructed, as her call connected. "Zac, I've seen him. I've bloody seen him crossing the road."

"Where are you?" Zac asked.

Karen glanced around, attempting to get her bearings. "Crown Court. No, Barbican. No, we are near the fire station. He is on foot. I'm in a cab."

"Get out and follow him but keep a distance whilst I dispatch officers to the scene. Don't forget he could be armed and extremely dangerous."

Karen had already thrown a tenner at the taxi driver as she bundled herself out of the cab, snatching her bags from the back seat. She gave Zac a running commentary and could hear him repeating her words on another line, as he directed officers on the ground.

"Karen, I've got plain-clothes officers on their way. I'm going to deploy them covertly so they can do a hard stop on him. I need you to keep your distance. The officers are armed."

"Okay. He's crossed the road again. That's the second time he has done that in the last few minutes. I think he's surveillance savvy, because he keeps glancing over his shoulder." Karen felt the frustration simmer deep within her. She desperately wanted to run over there and tackle Bailey, but without backup, or her cuffs or baton, she risked both her own safety and those of other pedestrians close by. She watched as Bailey paused for a moment, and lit up a cigarette. He glanced up and down the road before staring in her direction.

Karen spun around to look at anything apart from him and swore as she stared at a bright blue graphic inside the window of the Mecca bingo hall. *Bingo hall! For fuck's sake.* She hoped that the window would give her an opportunity to see a reflection of the street behind her, but she couldn't see what was happening through the garish blue sign which read, "Come On In — What Happens In Bingo Stays In Bingo". Desperate to not lose sight of Bailey, she shuffled along to a clear glass pane, and looked at the reflection of the opposite pavement. She could see Bailey walking away towards an alleyway. Karen felt her insides turn. If backup didn't arrive soon, they risked losing him in a warren of streets and alleyways. She needed to act fast. Karen turned on her heels and raced across the road, weaving in and out of the slow traffic to make up the ground between her and Bailey.

From over to her right, she saw a blue BMW X5 approach at speed, followed by a silver Audi A4. They stopped a short distance away, and six men exited. Karen flashed her warrant card at two of the officers who made their way towards her. The other four had spread out to blend in with the crowd.

One of the officers pulled on his police cap. "Boss, Sergeant Dave Andrews. You've got the suspect in sight?"

Karen nodded, and pointed out Bailey as the man darted in front of two women pushing a pram, his pace quickening.

Andrews spoke into his radio before racing off in pursuit of Bailey. Screams replaced the serenity and calm as terrified shoppers scattered in all directions, cowering in doorways of neighbouring shops. Andrews and his fellow officers charged at Bailey with two officers drawing their handguns and screaming, "Police! Get down on your knees!"

Bailey dropped his hands to his sides, his head twisting in every direction, looking for an escape route. His feet shuffled on the spot, willing him to run, but officers had surrounded him on the pavement, and hemmed him in. No sooner had they converged on Bailey, than two officers charged at him, bringing him down to the ground. Bailey refused to be taken without a fight, and started to punch out and kick, thrusting his head back and connecting with the nose of one of the officers pinning him down. The officer rolled to one side, clutching his bleeding nose as other officers piled in. Bailey was like a man possessed as he growled and swore. His body bucked as he kicked out. His elbow crashed into the face of another officer who refused to let go. He was finally subdued, as four officers lay across his body whilst Andrews applied the cuffs.

53

Karen and Zac sat opposite Bailey in an interview suite. Bailey's brief, Martin Harp, had arrived promptly, keen to begin the interview. He was a stocky man, thick-necked, wearing an ill-fitting suit. His brown hair was parted, and slightly greasy.

Zac conducted the formalities and made sure the small video camera hanging from the ceiling was operational and relaying a live feed back to his team huddled around a large TV screen.

Karen took a moment to study the elusive man. Several days of grey stubbly beard growth matched his closely cropped hair. His eyes were thin and penetrating, and his lips pinched tight. He epitomised the vague look that an e-fit profiler might have come up with where they swapped in the eyes, nose and mouth onto a random round face. He seemed unperturbed as he sat back in his chair with his arms folded across his chest. His shoulders and chest were broad and muscly, and the reason it had taken so many officers to contain him.

Bailey had been trouble from the minute he had been captured. Not only had it taken five officers to restrain him at the scene, but he'd attacked an officer after being booked into the custody suite. The alarm had rung out as a scuffle ensued with officers charging through the doors of the custody suite to help officers caught up in the fight.

Bailey bore the scars, scratches across his face and forehead, and the beginnings of a black eye. He had been checked by a police doctor and cleared fit for an interview. As a precaution, an officer stood on either side of him.

Zac shuffled his papers before looking up at Bailey who locked eyes with him. Bailey's unflinching eyes were cold and menacing, whilst his lids flickered in fury.

"Dennis Bailey, you've been arrested on suspicion of the murder of Danilo Reyes, Doctor Anil Kumar, and Donna Anderson. Are these names familiar to you?"

"They don't ring a bell."

Zac smiled. "Really? Doctor Anil Kumar was a psychiatric consultant who assessed you before your trial, and even though you claimed you were schizophrenic, his assessment disagreed with you. Donna Anderson was your brief at the time of your court case. Don't tell me your memory is that short?"

Bailey shrugged a shoulder and refused to reply.

Zac continued questioning, presenting his theories as to how the three victims were connected to Bailey. Despite repeated questioning, Bailey denied any knowledge of being involved in their deaths.

As a change of tact, Karen took over. "I've been investigating the murder of Doctor Anil Kumar in London, and a white Ford Focus that we believe you hired, was not only seen in Doctor Kumar's road on several occasions before his death, but also close to the scene where Donna Anderson was stopped and attacked in York. We have CCTV footage from the car hire firm. The results of facial recognition mapping suggest a ninety-one per cent match with key characteristics between your face, and the partial profile captured on the footage. Have you got anything to say about that?"

"What can I say? I have a familiar face," Bailey said with a smirk.

"What are the chances that once we've downloaded data from the mobile phone that we took off you that it will show you being in the same locations where all three victims were found?"

"I doubt you'll find anything; I lost my phone. This is a new one," Bailey replied, pointing to a clear evidence bag on the table that contained a mobile phone. "The chances are another geezer picked up my old one, and whoever did is your killer."

"Possibly, but I doubt it. I think you're too clever for that. You've tried hard to stay in the shadows. Your phone is probably one of a long line of burner phones you've used over the last few months since your escape," Karen suggested.

Zac grabbed a few photos from a brown Manila folder and slid them across the desk in Bailey's direction. "For the tape, I'm showing Dennis Bailey photos of a pair of blood-stained gloves found beneath the mattress at the B & B."

Bailey's eyes flickered as he glanced down at the images before returning his stare in Zac's direction.

"What are the chances that once these gloves are forensically examined we'll find your DNA as well as the DNA from at least one of the victims?" Zac smiled.

Bailey shifted uncomfortably in his chair, and glanced at his brief, who furrowed his brow. The man tapped his hand on the table to suggest that Bailey should refrain from answering questions.

"You might be forensically aware, Bailey," Zac continued, "but we have your gloves, your clothes, and your trainers. Each one of those items could link you to any one of these crimes. We recovered a footprint impression from Doctor Kumar's property, and we are now examining your trainers. The impression appears to be the same brand, style and size as the trainers you were wearing when we arrested you."

Bailey shrugged. "There are probably thousands of people wearing the same fucking trainers out there. That doesn't mean shit," he spewed.

"You're right," Zac replied. "They probably are. But every single pair of trainers creates a unique impression based on the wear and tear, the surfaces it has been on, and the gait of the person wearing them. It's like a unique fingerprint for each pair of trainers. So, Dennis Bailey, let me ask you again. Were you involved in the attack and murder of Danilo Reyes, Doctor Anil Kumar, and Donna Anderson?"

"No. And you're throwing shit at me hoping that something will stick. If you think you're gonna break me, you've picked the wrong person to mess with," Bailey hissed as his eyes darted between Zac and Karen.

Zac let the silence settle between them before he glanced over to Karen and gave her the smallest of nods to hit Bailey with their trump card.

Karen retrieved DNA analysis reports from the folder and handed copies to Bailey and his brief. "During the post-mortem of Donna Anderson, scrapings were taken beneath her nails and the debris collected was sent away for forensic analysis. What do you think it told us?"

Bailey stiffened, the muscles in his jaws flexing, as he glanced nervously at his brief who pored over the data before swallowing hard.

Karen nodded. "The penny's dropped, hasn't it? You'd be absolutely right in thinking that. Donna Anderson put up a fight, didn't she? As you battered the living daylights out of her, she fought back, scratching your face." Karen tapped the findings. "The scrapings from beneath her nails confirmed that skin particles recovered were a ninety-nine point nine per cent match for you. It is without a doubt that you savagely attacked, murdered and mutilated Donna Anderson. And once she was dead, you removed her heart and tossed it away. Your unique M.O. for everyone you've attacked."

Bailey wrapped his arms around his chest and bowed his head. "No comment," he murmured.

"We know that all three victims were connected to you, with Doctor Anil Kumar, and Donna Anderson directly linked to your case. Is that why you went after them?" Zac asked. "You wanted revenge because you felt they were responsible for putting you away and not fighting your corner?"

"No comment."

"Retired Detective Inspector Donald Carter was the only other person directly linked to your case because he was the SIO. He's gone missing. His car was found abandoned near a bottle bank. Were you involved in Donald Carter's disappearance?"

Bailey remained silent.

"Do you know of Donald Carter's whereabouts at the moment?"

Still nothing.

"Is Donald Carter still alive?"

Bailey raised his head ever so slightly, the corners of his mouth lifting in a chilling smile.

54

With the interview terminated, Karen dropped into her chair and tipped her head back before running her hands down her face. Her head pounded, and her body ached. She was shattered. It had gone seven p.m., and everyone was feeling the effects of the last few days.

"I thought you could do with this," Ed suggested as he put a mug of steaming coffee on Karen's desk.

"Aw, bless you. That's perfect. I don't suppose you have a drop of whiskey to put in it?" Karen asked with a wink.

"Not out here, but Zac has a bottle in his bottom drawer," he replied, thumbing towards Zac's office.

"Problem is I don't think a drop of the strong stuff would help. If anything, it would probably send me to sleep."

General updates circulated around the team as Zac pulled up a chair to discuss their next steps.

One officer commented that they had recovered CCTV

footage showing Donald Carter going into and leaving a local shop on Wednesday. There was nothing in his behaviour that suggested he was concerned, nor was there any evidence of him being followed. The officer confirmed that Donald Carter hadn't been seen since.

Zac turned towards Mark, his DS. "Mark, can you get through to the press team this evening, and see if we can put out a public appeal for any sightings on Carter. Just the usual stuff about how he hasn't been seen for the last few days, and we are concerned about his welfare and safety."

Mark made a few notes and swivelled in his chair to grab his phone to get the ball rolling.

Belinda chipped in next. "We've been building a full profile on Bailey and his movements. Even before his conviction, he had no fixed abode, and we couldn't find any property details in his name."

"Bank records?" Karen asked.

"Less than a thousand pounds in his account," Belinda confirmed. "My guess is that he has money hidden somewhere else, perhaps under various aliases. Or even being held by friends or family."

Karen stood up and went to the whiteboard where she examined Tommy Bailey's details. She tapped on his picture before turning to the team. "I'm convinced that Tommy Bailey is holding back and knows more than he's letting on. It looks like we've got Dennis pinned for three murders, but there's a strong risk we could be looking for a fourth body."

Zac joined her at the board. "Well, we're about to find out as the warrants have come through to raid his premises and home. I know we're all shattered, but I'd rather not wait until tomorrow, especially whilst we've got Dennis downstairs in the cells. We need to move on this fast, especially whilst Carter is unaccounted for."

ZAC SENT officers to execute a search at Tommy Bailey's house whilst Karen and Belinda joined him as they raided the haulage business.

They kept their approach silent as Zac led the way with two squad cars and a van full of uniformed officers following behind. The vehicles took a hard right and screeched into the compound, taking Tommy's employees by surprise. Officers jumped from their vehicles and scattered in all directions to secure everyone on site.

"I want everyone to stay where they are! We have a warrant to search this premises!" Zac shouted, so that everyone could hear.

Vehicles that were in the middle of manoeuvring around the compound stopped in their tracks, their drivers escorted from their cabs and rallied along one wall of the compound where they were searched, and their details taken.

At the commotion, Tommy Bailey tore through the door of the Portakabin, his face seething, spittle erupting from his mouth. "What the fuck is going on! Who the fuck do you think you are tearing in here like this?"

Zac waved the document. "Tommy Bailey, we have a warrant to search this premises."

"What for?" Tommy screamed as he snatched the paperwork from Zac's hand and ripped it to shreds. He marched towards Zac who held his ground. The two men stood nose to nose, neither wanting to back down.

Karen stepped in between them. "Tommy Bailey, calm down. We are searching for any evidence linking your brother to three murders as well as the disappearance of a retired police officer."

"You what? You can't fit him up with three murders." Tommy protested.

"I think he's done that for himself," Karen suggested. "We've identified DNA linking him directly to the murder of one victim, and it's only a matter of time before we link him to the others."

Tommy laughed. "You've got no jurisdiction up here, lady. The only clout you've got is in London. So fuck off!" he shouted.

Zac walked off towards the Portakabin, snapping on a pair of latex gloves. "My colleague might not have the jurisdiction in York, but I do. So wet your pants as much as you want, but this is going to happen with or without your cooperation."

Karen fought back a smile as she followed Tommy who raced off after Zac.

The Portakabin was warm and in marked contrast to the cold chill of the night. Karen, Zac and Belinda moved around the space, opening filing cabinets, pulling out folders, and sifting through any incriminating paperwork. Tommy's protestations bounced around the room as he flapped his arms. Two uniformed officers stood either side of him, making sure that he didn't impede the search nor make a run for it.

Karen opened a small cupboard behind the desk to find a safe with a digital keypad. "What do you keep in this?"

Tommy rolled his eyes. "Paperwork, spare keys for the vehicles, and that kind of stuff. Nothing important."

"I'll decide if it's important or not. Open it."

"I told you that there's nothing in there. Besides, I can't remember the combination. I keep getting it wrong. Too many tries, and I get locked out."

Karen sighed. "Stop fucking about. Open it now, or I'll get someone to come along and break it open. Your choice."

Tommy shook his head before punching in the code and releasing the door.

Karen peered inside. There was paperwork, and a small box of vehicle keys. But two carrier bags stuffed full of cash piqued her interest. Tommy shuffled uncomfortably on the spot as Karen glanced back at him.

As the officers started counting, the total soon racked up, and once finished, they were looking at sixty thousand pounds in cash spread across the table.

Karen's hunch had been right. The exchange she had seen was with one of these carrier bags, and it was almost certain that Tommy Bailey had received the money for safekeeping from his brother, something he denied when asked.

"We'll be confiscating these bags as potential evidence. If we find any DNA on them linked to Dennis Bailey, you'll be arrested for withholding information and harbouring a criminal on the run," Zac said firmly, ignoring Tommy's aggressive protests.

55

There was no chance of a rest day for Karen as her eyes flickered. With a missing person, every hour counted. Karen had left Zac's team working through the night and had gone back to grab a few hours' sleep before doing it all again today.

Her body willed her to stay beneath the covers in the warm cocoon she had created, but her mind jolted her back to reality. She scooped herself out of bed, aching and tired, and padded into the bathroom before leaning against the sink and taking a long, hard look at herself in the mirror. Karen groaned. "I look like shit."

Karen examined the bags under her eyes, and her sagging cheeks, prodding them with her fingers, knowing she'd hardly win any beauty contests with her pale face, crow lines, and messy hair.

After showering, putting on a bit of slap, and finding clothes that weren't creased, Karen took one last look in the mirror before meeting Zac who had waited patiently in the car park with the engine running.

Karen shot Zac a double take, but smiled, trying hard to hide her surprise. Zac didn't look much better than she had after waking, but the smell of freshly brewed coffee distracted her as the aroma wafted in her direction.

"Morning. You look nice," Zac said as he took her in and kissed her on the cheek. His eyes were warm and thoughtful.

It was the first time Zac had complimented her in that way, and she wasn't sure how to respond, other than make a joke of it. "You wouldn't have said that twenty minutes ago when I got out of bed. It's amazing what a load of cement and plaster can do to hide the cracks!"

Zac laughed, adding, "I'm sure that wasn't the case. Anyway, here's a coffee for you and a chocolate croissant. I figured you'd not get the chance to grab brekkie before we head in."

"You thought right," Karen replied, taking up the offer and enjoying the warm, gooey comfort of chocolate as they set off.

They discussed the events of the day before and their plan of action today as they made their way to the station. News had come in overnight from the forensic team that had sealed Bailey's fate.

BAILEY LOOKED DISHEVELLED and tired as he sat in the interview suite in joggers and a sweatshirt that the custody suite had found for him. He looked as miserable as his brief Martin Harp, whose scrunched-up face showed his displeasure at being called in on a Sunday morning.

"Before we start, Dennis, do you have anything to add following our interview yesterday?" Zac asked.

Bailey shook his head.

"Dennis has replied with a shake of the head," Zac added for the benefit of the tape.

"I'll ask you again, did you attack and murder Danilo Reyes, Doctor Anil Kumar, and Donna Anderson?"

"No." Bailey's answer was less than convincing.

Zac retrieved photographs and an analysis report from his folder before sliding them across the desk towards Bailey and his brief. "I'm showing Dennis pictures of a pair of bloodied gloves recovered from beneath the mattress in the B & B. Do you recognise these?"

"No comment."

"As you can see from the forensic analysis report, the gloves have been linked to all three murders, with DNA from all three victims on them. The inside of both gloves contained skin particles which were a forensic match to your DNA. That suggests that you wore these gloves when you viciously attacked and murdered all three victims. What do you say to that?"

Bailey refused to answer as he closed his eyes and hung his head, perhaps knowing that the net was finally closing around him.

Karen took over and continued to apply the pressure by presenting even more startling evidence. "I'm now showing the suspect photographs of his trainers. Are these your trainers?"

Bailey remained silent, so Karen continued.

"We had your trainers forensically examined, and fourteen features from the soles of these trainers matched the bloodied footprint recovered from Doctor Anil Kumar's home. Forensics concluded that it was a ninety-four per cent probability match that you were there, and the evidence from the gloves proves that." Karen let the information soak in, watching Bailey's shoulders drop as he sunk deeper into his chair.

Continuing, she presented more evidence. "You were quite clever, wiping and cleaning your trainers, but trace DNA evidence still remained in the creases and crevices of the footwear. That trace DNA evidence belonged to the nurse, doctor and solicitor." Karen retrieved another analysis report and slid the findings across the table. "The sides of the soles still carried faint traces of mud and blood stains. The chemical composition of the mud matched the crime scene where the solicitor was discovered."

Bailey shifted uncomfortably, licking his lips, and playing with his fingers as the evidence piled up.

"Give you credit, Bailey. You tried to cover your tracks, but you were sloppy," Karen said. "The clothes you wore came back clean, as did the pair of jeans we recovered from the B & B which had been thoroughly washed. But you made one big mistake, which in the end was another piece of evidence that has helped us to confirm that you murdered all three victims." Karen passed over one final piece of information. "You forgot to wash your socks. The very same pair of socks you'd been wearing at the time that you killed Donna Anderson. They contained forensic evidence, which meant we could prove that you were there when Donna Anderson was killed. A small, but crucial speck of blood."

Bailey reached over towards his brief and whispered something in his ear. Harp nodded before turning to the officers. "My client refuses to answer any further questions but admits to killing the three victims in revenge for putting him away."

56

Karen pressed the redial button and waited for the call to answer. She couldn't stand still and paced up and down the corridor. Karen had called Jade not long after Bailey had been arrested in town and updated her by text throughout the day.

"Jade, we got the bastard. Bailey admitted to killing all three victims!"

Jade's excitement bubbled over as she practically squealed on the other end. "That's bloody fantastic news. Absolutely brilliant. Well done to the team."

"We did our part in London. It's a shame that we didn't nick him on our patch. But forensics came through. He didn't have a leg to stand on. A pair of bloodied gloves that we found at the bed and breakfast linked him to all three crimes." Karen continued to fill Jade in on all the other evidence that they had gathered and presented to Bailey.

"How's DCI Romeo?" Jade teased.

"Zac is fine. He's really pleased with the result. Most of this was down to forensic evidence. It looks like we might be able to charge his brother with withholding information and harbouring a criminal on the run."

"Have you updated Hinchcliff?"

"Yep. He was practically screaming down the phone at me to begin with, but when I told him we'd nicked Bailey, he seemed to quieten down."

"So, you'll be heading back now?"

"Not yet, Jade. We've still got a missing fourth victim, the retired SIO. I'm going to help with that before returning. I've got to dash off now, because a briefing has started. I'll update you later," Karen said as she hung up and raced back into the room to catch what Zac was saying.

"The case isn't over yet. We need to find Donald Carter fast. Where are we on it?" Zac said as he addressed his team from the front of the room. Various officers were scattered around, notepads in hand, waiting on instructions.

Ed began first. "There've been no further sightings of him. We've gathered hours of CCTV footage from the area surrounding his house and the local shops. It's taken a while to go through them, but he's not appearing on anything. But we have found one piece of evidence. The white Ford Focus we've had in our sights was seen on three separate occasions in the days leading up to Carter's disappearance."

"The exact same vehicle?" Zac asked.

Ed nodded. "We've not had any ANPR alerts to show the vehicle is on the move, but the car hire firm has trackers on all its cars, and we've downloaded the data for that particular registration. Its location tallies with two of the crime scenes, one of those being in London," Ed said as he turned towards Karen.

That was good news as far as Karen was concerned. The sightings of a white vehicle near Doctor Kumar's house tied in with the data Ed offered.

Ed checked his paperwork before tapping the location into his computer and bringing up Google Maps. "The data confirms that the Ford Focus was last identified as being west of York, near Hessay. But it's a tiny village and out of the way."

Zac moved in to have a look at the images for himself. "Did Bailey have any connection to the area?"

"Not as far as we know."

"Okay, well let's check with the council to see if there've been any reports of abandoned vehicles in the area. It could even be stored in a barn, or a garage." Zac turned towards Mark. "Can you get a couple of bodies over there to start scouting the area for any possible hiding places?"

Mark nodded and pulled a face as he made a few notes.

Mark's reaction wasn't lost on Karen as she noticed his displeasure. She still hadn't figured him out. He was elusive, kept himself to himself, and very rarely took part in banter. She wondered if he even wanted to be here, because at times he often appeared uninterested in anything. And for a DS, that worried her. As a skipper, he should have been more hands-on with Tyler, Ed and Belinda.

Anita, who was on the phone and perched on a desk towards the back of the office, finished her call and joined the rest of the team. "Zac, earlier on the team were going through the paperwork recovered from the haulage business. We've looked at all the ownerships, assets, titles and deeds belonging to Tommy Bailey. Most of it is focused on his home, the yard, and the vehicles. But he's got a complicated network of companies tied into his name." Anita went over to the map and traced her finger across several locations. "He's got a small container facility over in Bridlington, and a warehouse in Tilbury. Both show him as being a joint director. He has the haulage business that we know about, and lastly he has a waste collection service in his name."

"Good work, Anita. Can we start making enquiries with all of those places? It might be nothing, but we need to eliminate all of these locations as potential places where Carter may have been taken."

"What's the chances of Carter still being alive?" Tyler asked. "For all we know, he could be dead like the others."

Zac nodded in agreement. "He could be out there lying dead in a ditch, in a pond or even the boot of the Focus. At the moment, we don't know if he's dead or alive."

57

A few hours passed whilst the team pulled apart the complicated network of businesses owned by Tommy Bailey. An enquiry with the council about abandoned vehicles had led to three being reported in the last few days. Two had been eliminated, but a third vehicle matching the details of the Ford Focus and its last known location confirmed that it had indeed been dumped in Hessay.

"When you said it was remote, you weren't kidding, were you?" Karen said as she stared out of the passenger window.

"Everywhere around here is remote," Zac remarked.

Karen was amazed at how a short fifteen-minute journey out of the city took them from the hustle and bustle to a serene landscape. Small A roads were lined with tall hedges that held back a patchwork of green agricultural land, isolated industrial units and small farmhouses that dotted the landscape. Even in the midst of winter, the peacefulness in her surroundings relaxed Karen. She knew from experience that travelling an hour in any direction in London would still leave you trapped in the sprawling metropolis, with congested streets, choking car fumes, and a melting pot of communities.

It was refreshing in her eyes. Everything seemed to happen in slow motion outside of London. People talked slower, moved slower, and the pace of life ambled on without a sense of urgency or stress.

Zac glanced across to Karen. "You're probably used to dealing with multiple homicides back in London. But up here, we get four or five a year in North Yorkshire, and in the last few years, most of those have gone without being charged or summoned. It's pushed my team out of its comfort zone."

"I can imagine it's a shock for you guys. London has the third highest homicide rate across England and Wales. We get about a hundred and fifty each year, but then we have a bigger population, so it probably balances itself out. Murders don't bother me as much as they should, but you become hardened to it," Karen reflected, as she watched the hedgerows whizz by.

The admission wasn't something that sat comfortably with her. Attending one homicide would be enough to shock most people, but when it became part of her everyday life, she'd learnt very quickly to separate her emotions from the job at hand. The only time it really affected her was when she had to deal with an infant death, but thankfully that was rare. It was the post-mortems that upset her the most. The delicate deconstruction of a body and the search for clues still turned her stomach to this day.

Zac pulled off when he saw the sign and followed the directions until they came to a small clearing on the edge of a field and the remains of a burnt-out car. There was not much left, outside its blackened metal frame. Springs remained where the seats once were, the dashboard nothing more than a congealed mess of dried plastic, and shattered remains of glass where the windows had blown out.

Karen peered into the car. "It's worth getting SOCO to attend to see if they can extract any evidence, but I doubt they'll find much. Burning the vehicle was the ideal way to remove anything that was combustible or degradable."

Zac snapped on a pair of nitrile gloves before lifting the boot lid. He held his breath not knowing what to expect. It was empty. Donald Carter was somewhere else.

They were back on the road minutes later and spent the next few hours acting on further information about Tommy's business interests. Tommy Bailey owned several rental properties in his girlfriend's name. Zac instructed the team to pass the details of those properties onto Mark who had organised officers to be in the local area whilst he and Karen picked off the last two rental properties.

The first rental was a small, terraced property that had seen better days. The small garden was unkempt, with several black plastic bags of rubbish piling up beside an already overflowing dustbin. The net curtains were dirty and in dire need of a wash. A small woman with bright red hair, pulled back into a ponytail, answered the door, with a young toddler hanging from her hip. She confirmed that Tommy Bailey was her landlord, but letting agents managed the property.

It was a dead end as far as Karen was concerned and so she thanked the renter for her time.

Zac took them on to the second property, a few streets away. Again, another terraced property, but unoccupied. Though the windows were boarded up, the front door was ajar a few inches. There were definite signs of a break-in, and someone dossing there when Karen found a dirty sleeping bag and pillow in the front room and empty food containers. The carpeted floor was littered with spilt drink and cigarette butts. Zac organised for SOCO to attend and take samples for any evidence that Carter had been held there.

Another dead end.

With the sun dipping low into the sky, and the chilly wind beginning to bite, Karen was hungry and tired. They had been on the go for hours and had turned up nothing. Zac pulled into a petrol station for them to stock up on food and take a quick loo break. Karen enjoyed the warmth of a hot coffee as she cradled it in her hands. She watched as a steady stream of drivers pulled in to fill up on petrol. One particular driver made her laugh as she watched the hapless woman park on the wrong side of the petrol pump. The woman tried to stretch the hose reel over her car to insert the nozzle into her petrol cap. She had completely misjudged the distance and fumed before returning the nozzle to the pump and repositioning her car, only to manoeuvre back and forward, and still move no closer to the pump.

Karen watched the spectacle continue for a few minutes as a queue of vehicles piled up behind her before the unfortunate driver threw her hands up in the air and jumped back into her car and drove off.

"We've only got one more place to visit," Zac said as he started the car and headed off to visit Tommy Bailey's waste collection service. By the time they arrived thirty minutes later, dusk was setting in, and the yard was floodlit. Several small flatbed vans arrived, and manoeuvred inside the yard whilst they dropped their load on a huge rubbish pile situated in one corner.

Zac parked his vehicle across the entrance to stop any further movement, much to the consternation of the drivers who hurled abuse in his direction until he pulled out his warrant card.

"Who's in charge?" Zac asked as he made his way towards a small huddle of men standing by a makeshift shed.

At first the men were reluctant to say anything, staring into their coffee mugs, until one man, in a puffer jacket, and a hi-vis vest stepped forward. "I'm the gaffer here. Wayne McCafferty, how can I help?" He was polite with an Irish gravelly voice, an unkempt beard, and long hair pulled into a ponytail.

"We understand this is a business owned by Tommy Bailey?"

"So it is. What's your business?"

"Tommy Bailey has been arrested in connection with harbouring a fugitive on the run. We are in the process of searching all his businesses for a missing person. And that's all you need to know."

McCafferty shook his head. "Don't you need a warrant or something to search this place?"

"We can do it that way, if you want. But it would make it so much easier if you gave us your cooperation and allowed us to have a quick look around?"

McCafferty nodded and waved them through. He watched them with suspicion as Karen and Zac split off in different directions.

Karen sensed a dozen pair of eyes watching her as she moved around the compound and neared a huge pile of rotting rubbish. It was definitely a male, testosterone driven environment, and she doubted that many women had set foot in the place. She glanced over to see Zac inspecting the vehicles, leaving her to scan the debris in front of her. There was building material, sinks, baths, offcuts of timber, broken plasterboard, and dozens of black bin liners full of rubbish. She estimated the pile to be sixty feet wide, and at least thirty feet high.

Zac joined her as she walked around the heap. The overpowering smell of rotting food waste, damp wood, and chemicals tickled her nostrils. She placed a hand over her nose as she scanned the heap. For all she knew, Carter could be in any one of those bags, but she doubted that Dennis Bailey would be that stupid to incriminate his brother. To the left of the pile was a small stack of fridges and fridge-freezers. A cold chill crept through her, not because of the outside temperature, but because the appliances reminded her of a case a few years back, where the headless remains of a victim had been found in a freezer discarded on a fly tip. She swallowed hard and opened a few doors to check inside.

Karen screamed when she heard scratching and saw a rat scurry over her feet and dive head first into the mountain of rubbish. A cacophony of laughter rang out behind her as the workmen collapsed in fits. Karen pursed her lips and gritted her teeth in anger. She glared at them before staring across to Zac, who smiled and shook his head. She silently mouthed, "piss off" in his direction before she too smiled, even though her heart hammered in her chest, and her temples throbbed.

It was Zac's turn to scream as he jumped back at the sight of more rats scurrying around between the different appliances.

"You're so brave and macho," Karen teased as Zac took a lambasting from the workmen.

"I'm not scared," Zac said defiantly. "They took me by surprise."

"Yeah, yeah. I believe you, but let's see what your team says when we get back. I can't wait to tell them."

"Don't you dare. You'll definitely be on a train back to London quicker than you can tie your shoelaces."

Zac and Karen were running out of options as they moved their search to the outbuildings. With darkness setting in, and no sightings or intelligence to suggest whether Donald Carter was alive or dead, Karen felt agitated.

"Have you found what you're looking for?" McCafferty asked.

Zac shook his head. "Unfortunately, not. We are in the middle of nowhere, surrounded by fields. We've searched every address connected to Tommy Bailey, and yet we still have a missing person. I think we're done here. There's nothing else to check. It's getting dark and cold, and I don't fancy hanging around here much longer," Zac replied, zipping up his coat against the damp mist.

"You've got the luck of the Irish." McCafferty laughed. "You've only started, officers."

Zac and Karen shot McCafferty a look of confusion.

"What do you mean?" Karen asked.

McCafferty laughed again. "You've only checked this yard. Tommy owns the field next door as well. We don't use it at the moment, unless Tommy decides to expand his business. There are only a few empty shipping containers towards the far end."

58

McCafferty led the way as they climbed over the metal gate leading to the field. Beams of light from their torches bounced across the ground and lit up the space in front of them. The mist crept in, greying out their brilliance but still affording them a hazy vision in the darkness. Karen's beam caught rabbits scurrying around in the long grass as they dashed for safety in the hedgerows.

Zac followed McCafferty's lead with Karen behind. In every direction, she was met with an inky blackness. Several of McCafferty's team followed, but when Karen glanced over her shoulder, they were no more than silhouettes, fluid black outlines that became clear as her eyes adjusted to the darkness.

McCafferty led the officers along the muddy path that ran along one side of the field closest to the road. It was dark, bumpy and heavy underfoot. Karen noticed deep tyre mark impressions, deeper than an average car which Karen thought were probably the tracks of a tractor, or other kind of heavy farm machinery.

"Have you seen anyone using this field recently?" Karen asked as the overgrown field slowed down their progress, the long grass wrapping around her knees.

McCafferty shouted back over his shoulder. "As I said, it's part of the business. We all have access to it, but we have no need to use it. I've not seen anyone on this land, but then again, I have no reason to come onto it."

It felt like they had been walking for ages, and Karen wondered how large the field was, and where they would end up, when McCafferty's beam landed on angular structures in the distance. It wasn't until they got nearer that Karen realised that there were four shipping containers stacked side by side in one corner of the field.

Three of the four containers were locked with hefty padlocks. The last container's doors were wide open. When Zac and Karen peered inside, there were signs of recent activity with remnants of a small fire, a bottle of whiskey, several Coke cans, and empty food wrappers.

Zac shone his torch on the ground in front of the other three and noticed the grass had been trampled recently in front of one particular container.

"Looks like there's been recent activity," Zac said as he examined the ground. From where he stood, the third container along appeared to have the most disturbance which raised his suspicions.

"It could be kids, or thieves. They're forever raiding these fields around here, looking to steal farm machinery, quad bikes, or red fuel," McCafferty added.

"Have you got any bolt croppers to open these locks?" Zac asked.

McCafferty nodded and sent one of his boys back to the yard. It was a nervous wait in the darkness, and even though it was only a few minutes, in Karen's mind it felt like an hour before the young lad returned and cut through the padlock. McCafferty and Zac grabbed a door each and pulled them back. The rusty hinges creaked as both men tugged hard, meeting more resistance than they had expected. The steel doors were heavy, but they slowly opened. Karen trained the light from her torch on the opening as it revealed a stack of boxes blocking the entrance.

"It's a bunch of bloody boxes!" Karen groaned as she moved closer. She was about to move away when something caught her attention. A slight whiff made her recoil before she stepped in again and took another sniff. Karen turned to Zac saying, "That smells like shit."

Karen dropped the torch on the floor and began to remove a few of the boxes. Zac did the same as McCafferty stood back offering them light from his torch. As a hole appeared in the boxes, Karen poked her head through and gasped before retreating and coughing violently, the acidic taste of bile scorching her throat. "We've got a body."

Zac tore away the boxes, tossing them to one side before he jumped through the space. Karen grabbed her torch and followed, throwing a hand over her nose and mouth.

There was a solitary chair in the middle of the container, and strapped to it was a man, his head bowed, his clothes in tatters and stained with blood. An overwhelming smell of human faeces and urine filled the space, causing Karen's stomach to retch. Zac crouched down and shone the light in the man's face.

"It's Carter!" Zac shouted as he searched for a pulse. "Donald Carter, can you hear me? It's the police. You're safe now."

For an anxious few moments, Karen watched Zac search the man's body, desperate to find signs of life as he reached for the man's neck, and then his wrist.

"He's breathing. It's very shallow, and he's got a pulse," Zac said in relief as he blew out his cheeks.

59

A round of applause raced around the room like a Mexican wave as Karen and Zac returned to the station. Anita and Ed shook Karen's hand first whilst the others gathered around Zac as he recalled the events and the discovery of Donald Carter.

"What a great result," Anita offered as a smile tugged at the corners of her mouth.

Karen nodded. "I think we got there in the nick of time, to be honest. Carter was bleeding out from several small puncture wounds. The paramedics who attended suggested that they were inflicted not with the intention of killing someone immediately, but if left unattended long enough, would lead to someone bleeding out, and death."

"So that was Bailey's intention?" Anita speculated. "Let Carter suffer a slow and painful death with his body perhaps not being found for weeks, if not months?"

"Or longer..." Karen added, wide-eyed. "We've got forensics over there at the moment, but as it stands, I think we have enough to charge Bailey with the abduction and unlawful imprisonment of Donald Carter."

A hushed silence fell around the room as Chief Superintendent Laura Kelly joined Zac and his team. The woman made her way to the front of the room with a beaming grin. She waited patiently for her audience to gather around her. With most of the team hovering in-between desks, and in small huddles, she glanced around the room, a sense of pride etched on her face as she grinned broadly.

"Anyone would think that she had done all the legwork," Anita whispered in Karen's ear.

"Don't they always?"

Anita rolled her eyes in agreement, knowing that most senior officers revelled in the glory and attention.

Laura cleared her throat and spoke through her smile as if it had been permanently tattooed to her face. "I wanted to take this opportunity to thank you all for your hard work. We've achieved a great result, and I know we've all worked tirelessly and sacrificed time with our families to get this result."

"You didn't, but we did…" Anita whispered again.

Karen had warmed to Anita. She was both funny and down-to-earth. Not one to be taken in by senior management bullshit, there was only one side to Anita and that was the one you always saw.

"I also want to take this opportunity to thank Karen for her assistance and expertise in bringing Dennis Bailey to justice," Laura added, starting another round of applause which spread around the room.

"No doubt you will be going down to the pub, and if you're quick enough, you'll be able to get a few rounds in before last orders. I assume the first round is on you, Zac?" Laura suggested, looking in Zac's direction.

With Laura putting Zac on the spot, he had no choice but to nod in agreement as he glanced across at Karen who hid her silent laugh behind a hand.

"Carry on," Laura said as she finished up her speech, allowing the team to break up into their own small groups and carry on their conversations.

Karen was about to head back to her desk when Laura came up to her and gently placed a hand around her elbow.

"Karen, can I have a word with you in the corridor?"

"Um... yes. Sure," Karen replied, her brow furrowed. She followed Laura out into the corridor, and away from the many conversations until they were surrounded by silence.

"Is everything okay, ma'am?"

Laura nodded as her smug smile returned. "I really wanted to take this opportunity to say thank you. Your experience in the Met, and no doubt dealing with more homicides than my whole team put together, has been invaluable to us. It added an extra layer of authority, reassurance, and command which I have no doubt led in part to getting the result."

Karen batted away the suggestion. "I didn't do much. Zac," she said, throwing a thumb over her shoulder, "led the charge, and he's got a good team behind him. You should be really proud of them, ma'am."

Laura looked beyond Karen, and through the glass partition

where some of the team were already logging off and throwing on their jackets. "They are a good team. We have a restructuring programme happening here in the coming months, and we could do with someone of your expertise up here. Zac and a few others from his team will be spearheading a new task force. And we have plans to create a stronger MIT." Laura let the news settle for a few moments before continuing, "You would be a strong candidate for interview, and you'd have my backing. It could be yours. As DCI, you'd have the opportunity to build a team around you, and cherry-pick the officers."

Karen's eyes flickered. She clasped her hands in front of her, both flattered and surprised by the offer. "Ma'am, that's very kind of you. And it's nice to know that you think I have the experience to lead such a team. But I'm not so sure... I guess what I'm trying to say is that I haven't been thinking about a move, or the next steps in my career. A lot has happened in recent months."

Laura threw up a hand and smiled. "I know. I took the opportunity to check you out. That's why a fresh start somewhere might be the ticket? I know it's a lot to take in, and probably the last thing you were expecting. But at least think about it. You could even bring officers with you. I'm sure the Met wouldn't miss one or two of them," Laura said, laughing. "As I said, have a think about it and let me know. Enjoy your evening."

Karen watched as Laura sauntered off, unsure how to take the offer.

ZAC and his team crowded towards one end of the bar of

the loud and rowdy pub. Karen stood with Zac, Belinda and Anita. It was a time to reflect and wind down. The days had been long and exhausting. They had put work before family life, and that was why so many officers struggled with personal relationships. Many of their partners and spouses were often let down at the last minute. Family dinners were put on hold, dinner dates were cancelled, and their social lives were anything but social.

Whilst Zac returned to the bar to order another round for them, it left Karen alone with Belinda and Anita.

"It's been really good working with you," Anita said.

"Yep, I agree with that one," Belinda interrupted as she raised her glass in Karen's direction.

Anita continued, "I know it's not on the scale of the Met, and we're like your country bumpkin cousins, but I hope you haven't found it too dull."

Karen laughed. "Being a copper is the same wherever you go. We still have a job to do. It's that sometimes the size of the teams, or the procedures might vary from region to region. But yes, it's been good working with you too. I'll miss you guys."

Anita hung around for another hour before checking her watch, and racing home to be with Ash. She gave Karen a hug before saying goodbye to the team and dashing off. Belinda disappeared into the crowd to catch up with the others, leaving Karen propped up against the bar with Zac in another of their awkward silences where neither of them knew what to say.

"I don't suppose you want to hang around for a bit? Maybe take a few days' leave? I could show you around, and besides, we didn't get the chance to talk again. It's going to be a bit strange not having you around," Zac eventually said.

Karen reflected for a moment, her eyes drifting off and fixing on nothing in particular. "Yeah, it's going to be a strange one. I'm looking forward to getting back to my team and my life. My poor cat has probably disowned me now, packed a suitcase, and moved to Spain. If I'm honest, I don't know what to say or do. Working up here has been great, and well, meeting you…" Karen's voice trailed off as she stared at Zac, searching his face for signs that he felt the same.

Karen felt torn. She had enjoyed her time in York, and the team had been fantastic, but everything was pulling her back to London. It was where she felt most comfortable, and it was her home.

"Perhaps, I can head back, close up my case and then take a few days off as annual leave. I've got a ton of days owing, and I'll need someone to show me around York? We could talk then? Maybe we need to see how we both feel. I'm in London, You're in York. It becomes complicated. Don't you think?"

Zac stared down at his drink, knowing that Karen made sense.

"Can you say goodbye to Summer for me? And apologise on my behalf for not being able to catch up with her."

Zac smiled. There was a warmth and sincerity in his face as they made idle chit-chat and talked about what Karen was looking forward to when she got back home. Several members of the team joined them over the next hour as the drinks flowed.

Karen listened to Ed recalling a story from his university days, and as the team roared with laughter, Karen's phone vibrated in her back pocket. Feeling light-headed, and with the alcohol taking effect, she clumsily fumbled for her phone, dropping it in the process. Leaning down, her head spun as she groped on the floor to pick it up, and then blinked hard to focus on the screen.

It was the hospital. She pressed the green button to connect the call, but the surrounding noise was deafening, and she could barely make out a word being said. She excused herself, and staggered out into the road, the fresh air hitting her face like a cold slap and jolting her senses as if she'd taken an ice bath.

Karen listened quietly.

Her voice trapped in her throat.

Her breath caught in her chest.

A tear squeezed from the corner of her eye before she hung up and went back inside.

60

Karen stood staring into the darkened pit. The vicar's words were soft and solemn, though none of them settled on Karen as she stared at her sister's coffin. Her parents, Anne and David, clung onto one another, her arm looped in his. Their age and fragility were clear as they stood silently, occasionally rocking back and forth.

A combination of a weakened heart and compromised immune system had stolen Jane from her family. Though she had responded well to medication following her recent illness, her heart had given up, and she'd slipped away peacefully without warning.

Karen's grief came in waves. At such random moments that it caught her off guard, replacing the feeling of normality with those familiar tears. Yet when those waves lessened, the good memories flooded in, allowing her brief moments to smile, and feel the warmth they offered.

A large throng of mourners gathered to pay their respects.

Karen allowed her gaze to drift amongst those congregated. She knew the vast majority, her team, family, Nurse Robyn Allen from the care home, and several other recognisable faces. A few colleagues Karen hadn't seen for a few years were there too. She noticed how many looked so different with a few extra pounds, saggy jowls, and weathered faces. It was the job. Long hours, poor diet, and mountains of stress which aged many of them.

Somewhere in amongst a sea of faces, Karen spotted Kevin Fenn, and offered him the smallest of smiles. She knew it wouldn't be long until he suffered the same anguish and pain.

But they were all there, united in paying their respects and saying their final goodbyes as the vicar finished, and the coffin was lowered. As the congregation melted away and made their way to the wake, several people gave Karen sympathetic nods, and warm embraces to express their condolences. Tears moistened her eyes, and a lump settled in her throat as she took a deep breath and held it for several seconds and then released it slowly, pulling her shoulders back to compose herself and push back the sobs that threatened to engulf her. The sadness was palpable, the mood sombre.

Karen dropped her gaze to the ground. She was finding it difficult to hold herself together and took lungfuls of air as she shivered.

Earlier, Jade had remained by her side for the whole service, stepping in to give Karen a hug when she needed one, and words of reassurance when doubts washed over her.

The vicar had taken a few moments to make sure Karen

and her parents were okay before delivering a beautiful service. He'd spoken about Jane's life in such an upbeat fashion and with such humour at times that you wouldn't have been mistaken for thinking that Jane had led a happy and active life.

During the service, Karen had drawn on all of her strength to deliver a heartfelt and loving eulogy. She'd recalled brief highlights of Jane's life, and a few pleasant memories as they were growing up as children. But there weren't as many as she had wanted there to be. Whilst Jane had been confined to bed, Karen's entertainment had come in the shape of her parents playing games with her, having water fights in the garden, and having movie and popcorn nights.

Those are all things I should have done with my sister, Karen had reflected.

There should have been laughter at the anecdotes.

There should have been birthdays, Christmases, and Easter bunny hunts where Karen fought with her sister over the best presents and the nicest chocolates.

But there weren't any.

Karen and her parents hadn't known what songs to choose for the funeral to begin with but settled for an upbeat version of "Somewhere Over the Rainbow" as Jane had arrived and picked "You Can Close Your Eyes" for the end of the service.

Staring at Jane's final resting place, the words flooded her mind once again as her airway constricted and the invisible band around her chest tightened.

Grief exploded through Karen as she started to weep.

THE CAR PARK was full by the time Karen got there. She'd chosen a small pub not far from the church. Though every cell of her being wanted to go back to her apartment and curl up in bed, duty called as she pulled her weary body into the pub. The place was busy with the usual lunchtime trade, but Karen had asked for a small section to be cordoned off so they could be afforded privacy.

Karen squeezed herself past guests, nodding to a few as she went in search of her parents only to find them with a few uncles and aunts. Satisfied that they were being looked after, Karen spotted Jade over the sea of recognisable heads, who waved a drink in her direction.

"Here you go. I thought you could do with this. How are you holding up?" Jade asked as she rubbed Karen's arm.

Karen gulped down the gin and tonic, in desperate need of something to relax her. "I was gagging for that. I feel exhausted."

"I think you did really well today. It's been so hard for you and your family. I only wish there was more I could do."

Karen smiled. "Just being here is more than enough. Thank you." Karen looked around. "I know most of the people here, but there are a fair few that are my parents' friends which I'm glad about. They've always known that this day would come, and that they'd lose Jane, but I still don't think they were prepared for the news when the call came."

Jade pursed her lips and stared at Karen's parents. "My heart goes out to them. I guess you can take comfort in knowing that at least your sister's at peace now. When are you coming back to work?"

Karen sighed. "In the next couple of days, once I've got my head straight. I need to go back over to the care home and pack away Jane's belongings before taking them to my parents' house. I also want to make sure that they are okay." The offer from Detective Chief Superintendent Laura Kelly sat heavily on her mind. She'd been flattered by the offer, but her heart was in London. They had pushed for an answer in recent days, and Zac had called that morning to say that he was thinking of her. They'd talked at length about her time in York, and Laura's offer. Zac had suggested that perhaps when she was in a better frame of mind, and ready for work, that a fresh start in a new place would be good for her.

She wanted to see Zac, and give them both the opportunity to see how they felt about one another now the case was over. The cocktail of a heavy workload, pressure for a result and limited time, hadn't given Karen time to just chill and relax around Zac. They'd agreed on the phone to keep in touch over the coming week, and once Karen had sorted out her sister's belongings, she would take a few days off to travel to York to see Zac, and see York through a different set of eyes. *Could it be a place where she could find love and happiness? Was York the next step in her career? Was now the chance to start afresh?*

There were so many loose ends, and with her mind swirling endlessly, it only left her more confused.

She hadn't mentioned Zac or the job offer to Jade because her emotions were in tatters, and whilst feeling like that she knew it would be hard to make a decision.

Karen excused herself from Jade's company for a moment, before she made her way outside and pulled out her phone. She brought up Laura's number and sent her a quick text.

Hi, ma'am, it's Karen here. Thank you so much for your kind offer. Unfortunately, I'm not in a position to give you an answer either way. With the death of my sister, and the fragility of my parents, I'm going to take a bit of time off to look after them, and to also deal with my grief. I hope you understand, and I promise I'll be in touch soon. Karen.

Karen dropped her phone back in her handbag, before taking in a deep breath, and heading back into the pub. She needed another drink.

SUBSCRIBE TO MY VIP GROUP

If you haven't already joined, then to say thank you for buying or downloading this book, I'd like to invite you to join my exclusive VIP group where new subscribers get some of my books for FREE. So, if you want to be notified of future releases and special offers ahead of the pack, sign up using the link below:

Subscribe to my VIP group

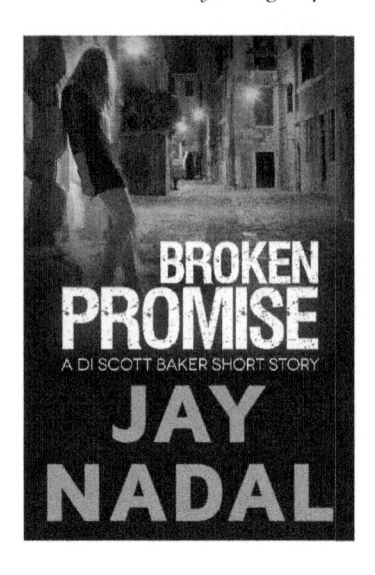

Type this link into your browser:
https://dl.bookfunnel.com/sjhhjs7ty4

CURRENT BOOK LIST

Current book list

Hop over to my website for a current list of books:

http://jaynadal.com/current-books/

ABOUT THE AUTHOR

I've always had a strong passion for whodunnits, crime series and books. The more I immersed myself in it, the stronger the fascination grew.

In my spare time you'll find me in the gym, reading books from authors in my genre or enjoying walks in the forest… It's amazing what you think of when you give yourself some space.

Oh, and I'm an avid people-watcher. I just love to watch the interaction between people, their mannerisms, their way of expressing their thoughts…Weird I know, but I could spend hours engrossed in it.

I hope you enjoy the stories that I craft for you.

Printed in Great Britain
by Amazon